CHRISTMAS WISH

AN INSURGENTS MC ROMANCE

CHIAH WILDER

I love hearing from my readers. You can email me at chiahwilder@gmail.com.

Make sure you sign up for my newsletter so you can keep up with my new releases, special sales, free short stories, and other treats only available to newsletter readers. When you sign up, you will receive a FREE hot and steamy novella. Sign up at: http://eepurl.com/bACCL1.

Visit me on facebook at facebook.com/AuthorChiahWilder

Insurgent MC Series:

Hawk's Property

Jax's Dilemma

Chas's Fervor

Axe's Fall

Banger's Ride

Jerry's Passion

Throttle's Seduction

Rock's Redemption

An Insurgent's Wedding

Outlaw Xmas

Wheelie's Challenge

Insurgents MC Romance Series: Insurgents Motorcycle Club Box Set (Books 1 – 4)

Insurgents MC Romance Series: Insurgents Motorcycle Club Box Set (Books 5 – 8)

Night Rebels MC Series:

STEEL

MUERTO

DIABLO

GOLDIE

PACO

SANGRE

ARMY

Steamy Contemporary Romance:

My Sexy Boss

CHAPTER ONE

EADLIGHTS ILLUMINATED THE fog like two glowing eyes.
Savannah Carlton nervously looked in her driver's side mirror and noticed another car fast approaching from behind. She took a deep breath, hunched up her shoulders, and leaned into the steering wheel. She quickly glanced down at the speedometer, which read forty-five miles an hour, then back to the side mirror as the car loomed closer.

Gripping the steering wheel tighter, Savannah's eyes darted to her son's reflection in the rear-view mirror, who was safely secured in his booster seat, and back again to the side mirrors. The other vehicle was rapidly approaching her SUV.

Savannah pressed down on the gas pedal, willing the SUV to move faster; unfortunately, the trailer in tow kept her car from gaining very much speed. Seconds later, the other car's high beams practically blinded her as they glared in all the mirrors. While Savannah readjusted them, sweat beaded along her hairline as a sense of uneasiness wove through her.

"What's wrong, Mommy?" Timmy asked.

"Nothing. It's just a little icy," she answered, her eyes still glued to the mirror.

The car fell back and Savannah glanced at Timmy and flashed him a quick smile. "We should be in Pinewood Springs soon, sweetie." Shifting her gaze back to the road, she estimated they were about forty miles away from the town. *I wish this jerk would just pass me. When we get to Pinewood Springs, I'll splurge and have us stay in a hotel.* Ever since Savannah took her son and ran away from her husband two weeks before, they'd been staying at campgrounds or wherever she could find a spot for the night. Her plan was to get as far away as possible from Bret and his controlling mother, so she kept driving west.

Once again, the headlights of the car grew brighter. Savannah let up on the gas pedal and slowed down, hoping the driver would pass her, but he didn't—instead, the vehicle slightly fell back. *What the hell?* A chill flowed through her in spite of the heat blasting from the vents. *I wonder if that car is following us.* She pressed her lips together in an attempt to calm down her chattering teeth. The image of a car parked in the far corner of the diner's parking lot flashed in her mind. A couple of hours before, she and Timmy had stopped at Chubby's Diner off the old highway to stretch their legs and get a bite to eat. As they ate, she'd noticed a car pulling into the parking lot without its headlights turned on. It looked like an Oldsmobile from the 1970s—big, vinyl top, and painted baby blue. The odd thing was that no one had gotten out of the car. It pulled into a space in the darkest corner of the lot and just stayed there. Even though it sounded silly, Savannah could *feel* the driver staring at them. It had unnerved her, and as hard as she tried to ignore the car, her eyes kept gravitating back to its direction.

When they'd finished their meal and walked back to their trailered SUV, she forced herself not to look at the parked vehicle. About fifteen minutes after she'd driven out of the parking lot, she noticed a car behind her. The vehicle had kept the same gap between their cars for more than an hour, but now things had changed. *Is it the same car from the diner?* Savannah couldn't be sure. The hazy darkness shrouded the car in anonymity, and she couldn't make out the make or model of the vehicle, so she wasn't sure if it was the creepy Oldsmobile from the diner.

Her paranoia kept whispering that the driver was a hired man with orders to drag her and Timmy back to Boston where Bret and Corinne would determine the appropriate punishment for Savannah's embarrassing behavior. *That's just crazy. How would anyone track me? I haven't left any type of paper trail.* Cleaning out her safety deposit box and selling a good portion of her jewelry had helped Savannah live a cash only life on the run. *Maybe the car following us has nothing to do with Bret. Maybe it's a serial killer. Oh God … no. Okay, Savannah, calm the hell down. Think of Timmy. Don't freak out.*

"Are we almost there, Mommy?"

"Just a little bit farther. Do you want a snack?"

"Uh-uh," Timmy said as he stared out the window.

Savannah looked in the mirror again and the car was still there. As the darkness swallowed up the road, fear crawled through her. Suddenly she spotted a small road to the right, and from the map, she knew there weren't any roads leading to other highways or back streets. *It must lead to a house.* Hope sprung up inside her. She accelerated a bit and the car behind followed suit.

"Hang on, Timmy."

Without braking, Savannah turned sharply and the trailer swayed madly as Timmy cried out. Struggling to maintain control, her hands clutched the steering wheel, holding so tightly her knuckles were white. Snowdrifts, pine trees, and evergreens whipped past, and a flash of panic tore through her as the SUV veered to the right. *Shit!* Tapping slowly on the brakes, Savannah used every bit of muscle power she had to keep the car steady and on the road.

Suddenly the car stopped, and Savannah rested her forehead on her hands and gulped in air for several seconds. She slowly lifted her head and turned to look at Timmy. The six-year-old had a huge grin on his freckled face.

"That was fun, Mommy. Do it again," he gushed.

Tears streamed down her cheeks as she laughed and shook her head. "One time is more than enough, sweetheart." Dread pushed down on her as she glanced in the mirror. Nothing but darkness.

"The car didn't turn," she said, relief sailing through her.

"What car?" Timmy asked, looking from side to side.

"The one behind us," Savannah said softly, but then apprehension crept in. *What if the driver double backs?* Inhaling and exhaling deeply, she took her foot off the brake and drove forward. She had to find a place for them to pull over for the night. As she drove forward, she saw a clearing on the right. Gritting her teeth, Savannah turned the car and it bumped and bounced over the terrain while Timmy squealed with delight. She pulled into a wild secluded spot nestled amid tall evergreens, and turned off the engine.

The snow had been falling faster and heavier, and the white powder quickly blanketed the entire area. Large flakes covered the trees, which glistened like diamonds in the night. A soft stillness descended around Savannah and Timmy as she carried him into the trailer.

"Do you want something to eat?" she asked, running her hand through his mop of dark hair.

Yawning, Timmy shook his head.

She kissed his cheek and pressed him tightly against her chest. "I love you so much," she murmured. Tears welled in her blue eyes, but she blinked them away. "Come brush your teeth, and I'll read you a bedtime story."

Timmy wiggled out of her arms and went over to the window and peeked out. "The snow is really coming down! Can we make a snowman tomorrow?"

Smiling, Savannah bobbed her head. "Sure, if it isn't still snowing. Now come over here and put your pjs on."

As Timmy changed, she pulled down the sofa cushions and made the bed. Timmy brushed his teeth quickly then jumped on the bed, laughing.

Savannah leaned over and pretended she was one of the monsters in the books he loved. Timmy roared in laughter as she bestowed kisses on his face, his neck, both arms, and his chest like she was eating him up. He threw his arms around her neck and kissed her cheek. "You're funny, Mommy."

"You're pretty goofy too," she replied as she pulled down the covers. "Climb in."

Timmy slid between the sheets and she wrapped the comforter snugly around him. "So you want me to finish the monster story from last night?"

"Uh-huh." Timmy stared at her with big brown eyes.

Savannah opened up one of the cupboards and took out the book, then she switched off all the lights except for the one over the bed. She had no idea how long the snowstorm would last, so using the lights sparingly helped to conserve energy. She was glad that she'd refilled the water tank at the last dump station. From the way the wind howled, it sounded like a strong storm was brewing.

Timmy fell asleep by the end of the fifth page, so Savannah quietly put the book away and then leaned down to kiss the top of his head. She went over to the small refrigerator and took out a cup of coffee, which she heated up in the microwave. She padded over to a short stool by the window and sat down, the mug of coffee nestled between her hands. Pushing up the blinds a bit, she stared out the window: The shrieking wind piled up snow in drifts, blinding the night with white ice-like dust. Clumps of large flakes hugged the trees as they loomed before her then vanished as the swirling snow swallowed them.

We should be in town instead of hidden on someone's property. Savannah took a sip of coffee, the dark liquid warming her as it slid down her throat. *Maybe the car wasn't following us. I probably just overreacted, but I wouldn't put anything past Bret or Corinne—especially Corinne.* Her mother-in-law was a piece of work. Corinne never accepted Savannah as part of the family, and she never thought Savannah was good enough for her son.

Savannah lightly massaged her right temple and pushed back all thoughts of Bret and Corinne. Her first goal was to settle somewhere far—maybe Alaska. She glanced over at Timmy and her heart swelled. There wasn't anything she wouldn't do for her precious son. Her eyes darted around the small trailer, and as she shook her head, blonde wisps of hair fell across her face. It was unbelievable; they'd gone from a 7000-square-foot house to a nineteen-square-foot trailer. *How am I ever going to get us through this?* She took another gulp of coffee. *You will. You're a survivor. You just need to take it day by day and forget about all the what ifs.*

Timmy moaned softly as he stirred in his sleep. Savannah closed the blinds and turned toward the bed. For a long time, she watched her sweet son sleep, knowing in her heart that she was doing the right thing. She wrapped her arms around herself to ward off the chill and walked over to the sink and set down her empty cup. Then she slipped between the sheets and burrowed under the comforter, letting all tension seep out of her as her eyelids fluttered closed.

CHAPTER TWO

I N HIS STRUGGLE to sit up, Ryder knocked over the empty whiskey bottle, and it rolled off the nightstand and landed on the hardwood floor with a thud. Pain shot through his skull, and he sank back down on the mattress and groaned.

"Fuck!" Ryder rubbed his sticky eyes and stared into the darkness. His German shepherd, Brutus, nudged his warm nose against Ryder's hand as he ran it over his soft fur.

Outside, the wind blustered, rattling against the windows and howling through the trees. Ryder gritted his teeth then tried to push up on his elbows as he ignored the stabs of pain circulating through his body. Sweat streamed down his face as he leaned against the headboard panting. After a few minutes, he switched on the table lamp beside the bed, and a soft golden glow illuminated the room. He gripped the aspirin bottle, shook out four tablets into the palm of his hand, and guzzled them down with a bottle of lukewarm water. Trickles of water slid down his chin, and he wiped them away with the back of his hand.

The house groaned against the wind, and Ryder darted his eyes to the window. White swirled about densely, erasing the world around him.

"They didn't predict this. Those sonsofbitches don't know shit about the weather," he said to Brutus, who jumped on the bed and sprawled beside him. "Make yourself comfortable." Ryder chuckled and ruffled the dog's black fur. He craned his neck to see the glowing red numbers of the digital clock face on the nightstand: 6:23 a.m. *There's no damn way I can get back to sleep now.* He reached over and grabbed his crutches then pulled himself up, groaning as the pain in his head ebbed and flowed. The empty bottle he kicked out of the way told him he'd killed the last of his Jack Daniels stash. How the hell he would get through the storm without any whiskey was something he didn't want to think about at that moment. The whiskey kept the memories locked away in the darkest corners of his mind.

Brutus ran over to the back door, his tail wagging as his black eyes darted from Ryder to the door then back to Ryder. The biker laughed and opened it, and a surge of frigid Arctic air slapped him in the face. "Shit, it's cold. Don't go too far," he said as Brutus bounced out of the house and disappeared into the whiteness.

As he placed six pieces of bacon in the cast-iron skillet, he heard Brutus barking in the distance. Looking out the window, all he could see was the blinding snow. *Probably came across some downed trees or something.* The bacon sizzled and its hickory scent filled the kitchen, mixing with the roasted aroma of brewing coffee. Just as Ryder took out three eggs, he heard the soft thud of Brutus's paws against the door. He smiled then hobbled over to open the door, and the dog, covered in white powder, came inside and shook himself vigorously. Water drops flew everywhere, and Ryder let out a hearty laugh as he grabbed a large green towel from a hook by the door and whistled for Brutus to come over. Seated on the chair, he covered the shepherd's body and thoroughly rubbed the towel over the wet fur.

"What were you barking at?" he asked. "Couldn't be a squirrel or a deer. They're huddled somewhere riding out the storm."

Satisfied that Brutus was dried off, Ryder pushed up from the chair and hung the towel back onto the hook then went back to cooking his breakfast.

He reclined against the back of the wooden chair and sipped his coffee as he looked down at the empty plate. The only sound in the kitchen was Brutus slurping from his water bowl. Ryder lived a quiet life except at night when he couldn't keep the memories away while he slept. When he'd first come back from Afghanistan, he'd moved into the Insurgents MC clubhouse. He'd been a member a long time ago, but had gone inactive when his dad suffered a stroke and he took over the family's plumbing business. After his dad had passed, they'd sold the business, and Ryder decided to join the Marines so he could go to college after his commitment period.

He scrubbed his hand over his unshaven face. He didn't want to go there; he didn't want to remember. Not since he was still fighting a hangover from his late night binge. Closing his eyes, he tilted his head back.

The noise at the clubhouse unnerved him, and he didn't feel like he belonged. Hawk told him he'd always be a brother of the Insurgents, but Ryder didn't feel like an Insurgent. As a matter of fact, he didn't feel like he belonged anywhere, so he bought several acres of land about forty miles from Pinewood Springs and hired a local builder to construct a home for him. That had been two years ago, and he'd never regretted his decision for one minute. His phone's ringtone sifted through his reveries, and he stared at it for a second then picked it up.

"What the hell are you doing up so damn early?" he asked Hawk.

The Insurgent's deep chuckle resonated through Ryder's earpiece, and the corner of his mouth curled slightly.

"Just making sure the fuckin' snow hasn't buried your sorry ass," Hawk replied.

"Still here. Are any of the stores open in town?"

"Probably not. They won't even begin plowing until the storm lessens. Throttle and Rags are on standby, but Throttle told me it'll probably be another day or so before he can get any plows out."

"Fuck," Ryder muttered under his breath.

"What'd you say?"

He cleared his throat. "You never answered my question as to why you're up so fucking early," Ryder said.

"Isa's sick. Cara was up with her all night, so I'm taking over and letting my old lady sleep."

"What's wrong with Isa?"

"She's got a fuckin' ear infection. The meds the doc gave should trigger in pretty soon. She's better than she was yesterday, but I feel for her … Do you need anything?"

Good ol' Hawk—always watching out for me. The outlaw biker had been the one who'd coaxed Ryder to attend the VA peer support group when he'd returned to Pinewood Springs.

"A bottle of Jack. I drank my last one last night, and I'm paying the price today."

"Bad night?"

In the background, Ryder heard the small whimpers of Hawk's daughter.

"Yeah," he answered.

"You wanna talk about it?"

The whimpers morphed into loud cries.

"Nah. Anyway, you got your hands full. Thanks for checking in. I'll call later and see how Isa's doing."

"Yeah, I gotta calm her down. Call if you need me."

Ryder put his phone down on the table and stared at the blank screen. If it hadn't been for Hawk and Tank, he wasn't sure if he would've made it through those dark days when he'd returned from a two-year stay at Brooke Army Medical Center in Houston. At first, Ryder preferred to deal with the demons clawing at his mind in his own way, but Hawk and Tank kept after him, so he finally relented just to shut the two guys up. Both Tank and Hawk had done tours in Afghanistan when they'd been in the armed forces, and they went with him to the first meeting. The group met a couple of times a month in one of the rooms at the town's community center. After a few meetings, Ryder had been hooked, and now he looked forward to going. He enjoyed the camaraderie and connecting with other men who understood and could relate to what he was going through. Tank had stopped going after six months, but Hawk usually attended at least one meeting a month.

Ryder picked up his phone and tapped in Tom's number then held his breath as he waited for the older man to pick up the phone. He was just about to cut off the call when a grouchy voice said, "Hello?"

"Hey, Tom. Ryder. Did I wake you?"

"What the hell do ya think?"

Ryder bit back a chuckle. "I didn't mean to, but I just wanted to come by and get a couple of bottles of whiskey before the storm gets worse."

"I jest got four left. When do ya wanna come git them?"

"I can be there in an hour. Does that work?"

"Yep. I'll be a waitin'."

Ryder stood up and put his dishes in the sink; he'd deal with the cleanup later that morning. He walked into the bedroom and leaned the crutches against the wall then grabbed the silicone liner and rolled it over the stump on his left leg. After he slipped on his prosthesis, he shed off his boxers, picked up the two large plastic bags he used to cover his artificial leg while showering, and made his way to the bathroom.

Less than two hours later, Ryder was behind the wheel of his Jeep Renegade and the three bottles of illegal moonshine whiskey were safely tucked underneath the rear driver's seat. Ice pellets bounced off the windshield as white flakes whirled all around obscuring everything within three feet of the jeep. He turned the vehicle onto the narrow road leading back to his cabin, and as he slowly drove along the snow-covered lane, Brutus went wild, barking and pushing his nose against the passenger window. Ryder looked at him and noticed the dog's eyes fixed on something he couldn't see.

When they'd left earlier to head to Tom's house, Ryder had taken the road behind the cabin, but he decided not to take that road back because the snowdrifts were worrisome. He didn't want to chance getting stuck in one of them.

"What's going on, boy?" He stopped the jeep and tried to see past the fog and swirling white powder, but he didn't have any luck. Brutus banged the side of his face against the window while he continued to bark and growl.

Ryder knew his dog didn't behave like this just for the hell of it. No ... something must be out there. A familiar stab in his gut told him that it wasn't just a lost deer or a squirrel. He switched off the motor and reached back to pick up his shotgun from the back seat.

"Let's see why the fuck you're making all this noise," Ryder said as he opened the car door. Brutus jumped out, woofing loudly, then disappeared into the blinding white. The wind raged, screaming through the trees and open spaces, bringing blasts of bone-chilling air.

"Fuck, it's cold," Ryder said aloud, his breath rising in white puffs of clouds. "Brutus! Where the fuck are you?" He wrapped the black wool scarf, which Addie—one of the old ladies—had knitted for him, tighter around his neck as he walked slowly to the right of the road. While cussing under his breath, he followed the sound of frantic barking.

The woofs became louder and Ryder narrowed his eyes against the blinding snow, then stopped when he walked through a cluster of trees. He saw an outline of something in the fog, but he wasn't sure what it was.

"Brutus!" The dog bounded over to him, his dark eyes sparkling and staring straight ahead. Ryder's gloved hand tightened its grip on the shotgun as he walked in closer with Brutus at his heels.

All of a sudden he saw it—a small travel trailer hitched to a brown SUV. Slivers of yellow light framed the ivory shades that covered the windows. *What the hell?* He just stared at the trailer for a few seconds, not really believing that someone had the gall to homestead on his property. The excuse of the storm wasn't something he was buying since it looked like the trailer was purposely hidden from the road. *Some goddamn asshole who thinks he can live rent-free on* my *land. Well ... fuck that.*

Brutus growled as he stared at the trailer, his body stiff and ready to protect. Ryder stretched his arm down and patted the dog on the head. "Down, boy. It looks like we got a squatter. I can handle this." Then he saw the shade move slightly; someone was looking at them, and it infuriated him.

"Get the hell out here!" Ryder shouted, but a gust of wind carried his words away. "Shit!" He walked over to the door and banged on it several times. Nothing. He put his ear next to the door and thought he could hear hushed talking coming from inside. He pounded on the door a few more times. Again nothing. Brutus started barking again, and Ryder jiggled the door handle a bit.

"I know you're in there. Open the fucking door or I'm gonna break it down!" he yelled into the door. At first, there was no reaction until he caught the shade by the side of the door move again. "Stop acting like a goddamn pussy. Man up and face me." Again nothing. "Fuck this! I'm coming in." He took a few steps backwards then lifted the butt of the shotgun and was poised to slam it into the door when it flew open.

Ryder stumbled back and stared. *Fuck. I wasn't expecting* that. Brutus rushed over and started to climb the steps when the woman cried out and closed the door. Ryder stood there staring at the cream-colored fiberglass. *Did I imagine that? Am I seeing a mirage like I sometimes had in the Afghan desert? Can you see a mirage in a snowstorm? What the hell is wrong with me? That chick sure as fuck wasn't an optical illusion.* He pounded on the door again and it cracked open a bit.

"Please keep your dog away from us." Anxiety laced her voice.

Us? She's got a man with her and he's letting her deal with me? What a fucking pussy. Ryder tugged on Brutus's collar. "Stay," he said sternly, and the dog froze in place, but his eyes stayed fixed on the woman.

"He won't hurt you," Ryder said, gesturing to Brutus. He watched her open the door and the glow from the inside light shimmered around her like the sun. He pressed his lips together and his eyes widened when she came into full view. She was gorgeous with her golden hair draped down softly past her shoulders, curling along the ends. The woman looked at him through apprehensive eyes that were the color of a perfect spring sky and were as deep as a blue columbine along the banks of a mountain stream.

Ryder lowered the shotgun and let his gaze roam over her body from the beautifully full breasts that made his dick twitch to the low-rise jeans emphasizing her small waist, and then finally resting on the rounded hips that he could imagine gripping while he pulled her on top of him.

He sucked in a breath and slowly brought his eyes back up to her face. She wasn't drop dead gorgeous, but beautiful in the girl-next-door kind of way with luminous skin free of makeup, long lashes framing almond-shaped brows, a short pert nose, and a mouth shaped with a luscious cupid's bow. *Damn.* He wanted to reach out and touch those lips, full and glossy pink, even in the fading light.

"Mommy, it's cold." A little boy's face peered out from behind the woman's shapely legs.

The voice snapped Ryder back to the moment, and he walked up to the two short steps, ignoring the strain of fear etched on her face. "What the hell are you doing on my property?" he asked.

Her eyes focused on the shotgun in his hand then slowly moved to his gaze. "It's only temporary … until the storm passes." Ryder put a foot on the step and the woman stumbled back into the camper. "I'm sorry. I didn't think anyone would find us before we left." She wrung her hands while she kept walking backward. "Please, don't hurt us," she said as her gaze looked downward.

"I'm not gonna hurt you. It's fucking cold out here." When he pulled himself up the stairs, he noticed the familiar look of surprise masking her face. He'd seen it more times than he could count since he'd lost his leg, and the sting of discomfort never went away. "Come on, Brutus," he said.

"Not the dog. I don't want it in here," she said, raising her eyes to meet his.

"You're the one trespassing, so you don't get to call the shots," he snarled. Brutus padded up the stairs, and the woman rushed over to the table. Ryder slammed the door behind him and looked around the place. The small boy now sat in the corner against one of the cushions around the table. His mop of dark hair and shining brown eyes reminded Ryder of Colt, but he'd be damned if he was going to think about him at that moment. Ryder shook his head and made the memories of a long-lost son scatter into the dark shadows of his mind.

"Can I pet your dog?" the boy asked in a small voice.

The woman slid in behind the table and scooted over to him then placed a protective arm around his shoulders. "Timmy, you shouldn't ask that," she said softly, her gaze darting between Ryder and Brutus.

"Why the fuck not?" Ryder knitted his brows as he walked up to the table and plopped down on the seat. "His name is Brutus and you can pet him in a minute. He's got to see that I'm cool with you both."

"He's a police dog, right?" The boy's gaze stayed on the dog.

"A German shepherd. The badges use that breed a lot." Ryder was keenly aware that the woman watched him. He turned to her. "What're you looking at?" Redness crept into her cheeks and he thought she looked even prettier when rattled.

"Uh … nothing. I mean … I was listening to what you were saying to Timmy."

Ryder grunted and pointed a thumb at the small boy. "I know his name now. What's yours?"

"Savannah," she said softly, but she didn't ask his.

He tipped his head. "Ryder." He snapped his fingers and pointed to the floor and Brutus immediately laid down. "So you got caught in the storm?"

Savannah nodded then lightly thrummed her fingers on the table. The noise drove him fucking crazy. "Stop that," he ordered, glaring at her. "There's no need to be nervous. I'm not gonna hurt you or your boy. I just wanted to know who was homesteading on my land."

"We weren't homesteading. I have every intention of leaving as soon as possible. I don't think the storm will last too much longer, do you?" Savannah's gaze met his and she smiled weakly.

"How the hell should I know?" Her face fell and Ryder almost reached out and tucked her hand into his. *I don't need to be feeling sorry for this chick or her boy.* He pushed himself up and Brutus rose. "When the storm clears, I want you the hell off my land." Ignoring the stunned look on her face, he put the shotgun under his arm and walked out.

As he lumbered away, he glanced back and saw Savannah watching him. When he locked his gaze on hers, she quickly dropped the shade.

Good. He trudged over to the jeep and let Brutus jump in before he slid onto the seat. As he drove to the cabin, he imagined how silky Savannah's hair would feel wrapped around his fingers. He shifted in his seat as her image filled his mind. During most of the time he'd been in the trailer, her arms were folded across her chest like a shield, but when he got up to leave, she dropped her guard, and his gaze fell on her rounded breasts. Very impressive. There was no doubt about it—he was a tit man. A fine ass, shapely legs, and nice rounded hips got his blood pumping, but a decent rack made his dick jump to attention every time. To him, a work of art was a pair of natural breasts that filled his hands just right.

"It's really coming down," he muttered under his breath as he increased the speed of the windshield wipers. *I bet her nipples are pink just like her lips.* Damn … he wanted to slide into her warm bed and feel those naked curves, snug and yielding against his flesh. "Fuck!"

Brutus whined and put his head down on his paws.

"It's cool, boy. I'm just pissed 'cause I'm getting hard thinking about that sexy woman." *I'm gonna have to get over to the clubhouse once the storm passes and spend some time with Brandi.* She was the club girl he liked the best because when they were together, she acted like she *really* wanted to be with him rather than it was just a mercy fuck.

The cabin drew near, and Ryder hit the remote and watched the garage door slide up before driving in. When he opened the back door, the heat from inside washed over him, and he walked into the kitchen and set down the three bottles of whiskey on the counter. He was glad he'd bought the booze since he was positive he was going to need it to get through the night. The unwanted tenant and her boy stirred up a whole lot of feelings and memories he didn't want to deal with.

Grabbing one of the bottles and a glass, he went into the family room and started a fire. He sat down on the couch and turned on the television in a desperate attempt to find a channel which would confirm that the storm would be over by the following day. But none of the stations did that—another day or two until it was over.

Ryder snapped off the television and stared at the flames curling and dancing over the logs. It seemed to him that the pretty woman and her son were running away from something. An abusive husband? *Maybe, but there's no damn way she's living in that small ass trailer with her boy just for the hell of it.* Long-buried emotions passed through the darkness of his heart, and he realized that something about her pulled him in, and he wanted to help and protect her. *And the boy ... fuck ... I'm not even going to go there.* Ryder couldn't. He needed the safety of the wall he'd built around his emotions. His self-imposed limits of not letting anyone get too close protected him from losing more than he already had.

His forehead creased in a scowl. *The sooner they get the fuck off my property, the better.*

Ryder picked up the remote and turned on the television again then poured the whiskey into the tumbler and brought it to his lips.

CHAPTER THREE

SAVANNAH PULLED UP the shade on the window and looked out at the frenzied snowfall and tugged the cardigan tighter around her. The fine lines across her forehead deepened as she estimated how much water and energy they'd used up so far. If the storm continued longer than another day, she feared that she'd have to ask Ryder for help.

"I hope it doesn't come to that," she muttered under her breath as she stared into the darkness.

"Why did the man with the dog tell us to leave?" Timmy asked.

Savannah pulled down the shade and turned around. "I guess he's mad that we're on his property."

"How can we go with all the snow?" Timmy scooped up a large amount of macaroni and cheese on his spoon.

"Not such a big bite, sweetie." Savannah went over to the table and slid in beside him. "We're going to have to wait until the snow stops."

"His dog was big. He was too." Timmy giggled and turned the spoon upside down then put a smaller amount on it.

"Yeah."

While Savannah watched Timmy eat his dinner, the image of Ryder floated in her mind. He was so different from Bret or any of the men in their social circle. Bret was a pretty boy who had soft features, and he was always clean shaven and impeccably dressed. She would describe Ryder as imperfectly masculine and ruggedly handsome. When he'd come into the trailer, she noticed his tousled dark chocolate-brown hair and his impossibly dark eyes that stared at her intensely. Unlike Bret's soft features, Ryder's were rough around the edges and a bit weathered, probably from being outdoors too much. He had a strong nose, a defined jawline, and a smattering of dark stubble. He had eyebrows which sloped downwards in a serious expression, and the fine lines around his mouth framed full lips ripe for the kissing. *Whoa ... that came out of nowhere.* Savannah twirled a strand of hair between her fingers as Bret's vexed face flashed in her mind. Bret hated that nervous habit of hers and always called her out on it, but he wasn't here now, and a thread of satisfaction wove through her as she pulled lightly on the blonde tendril. *There's no way I should be thinking about Ryder in that way ... or any way.*

"Are you gonna eat, Mommy?" Timmy's voice snapped her back to the moment.

"I'm not so hungry. Was your mac n' cheese good?" She ran her hand through his thick mane, laughing as his eyes sparkled while he nodded emphatically.

"Can I play Super Mario Brothers?"

Savannah hesitated as she pictured the battery running down with all the electricity they'd been using, and if that happened the heat wouldn't kick on. The sprinkling of freckles across her son's cheeks and his large dark eyes pleading with her, tugged at her heart strings. She hated that they were living like vagabonds, especially with Christmas only a few weeks away. *We should be at home decorating the tree instead of stuck in a snowstorm in a trailer on someone else's property.*

"Please, Mommy."

Savannah drew Timmy to her and hugged him fiercely against her then kissed the top of his head. "I love you so much, sweetie." Her throat tightened with emotions, and she blinked several times and swallowed.

Timmy tilted his head back and looked into her eyes. "So can I?"

The lump in her throat wouldn't allow her to answer so she nodded at him.

"Yippee! Thanks, Mommy." Timmy scrambled away from the table and dashed to the cupboard, flinging it open. With the play system secure in his hands, he shuffled over to the table and nestled back into the cushions, his gaze fixed on the screen.

An ache filled her heart as she watched his small fingers working the controls and the deep concentration etched on his face. *How could Bret not love his son?* She sighed and leaned back against the banquette. They'd been married for six years before she'd received the best news in her life—she was pregnant. She'd made a special dinner, lit all the candles in the dining and living rooms, and set a beautiful table, but when she'd delivered the news, Bret blew out the candles and threw the dishes on the marble floor along with their dinner. *He wanted me to have an abortion. I never thought he'd ask—no, tell me—to do something like that.* Of course she'd refused, and he wiped his hands of her and Timmy from that day forward. The wonderful sex life they shared stopped, and he barely touched her at all.

When Timmy was around two and three years old, he cried for his father's attention, but Bret would turn a deaf ear and leave the room, or go out with his friends until Timmy stopped trying altogether.

"I'm inside the volcano!" Timmy's excitement broke into her reminiscing.

"That's great, sweetie. What are you trying to do?"

Shaking his head, Timmy glanced over at her for less than a second then looked back at the screen, his hands moving furiously. "I've got to get Princess Peach. She's not safe yet."

"I know you can do it." As Savannah looked over her son's shoulder as the cartoonish characters ran, jumped, and rolled over brightly colored graphics, her mind drifted back to Ryder. *I wonder what he's doing right now. Probably sitting in front of a cozy fire with his dog … and wife maybe? I'm sure he's married.* She guessed him to be around thirty-five years old, and she couldn't imagine a man so ruggedly sexy as he was living all alone in a cabin in the middle of nowhere. *What is he doing here? What's his story? Ugh! Stop thinking about him.* Savannah shook her head as if to scatter all thoughts, and slipped off the cushion.

"I'm going to call Grandma," she said to Timmy, who didn't answer. Smiling, she went into the kitchen and leaned against the counter.

The space between her and Timmy was rather close, yet she hoped he wouldn't hear too much of her conversation. Since he was so engaged in the game, she didn't think he'd be paying any attention to her phone call.

Savannah dreaded making the call and answering a slew of questions. Inhaling deeply, she tapped in her parents' phone number.

"Hello?" her mother said.

"Hi, Mom."

"Savannah! Thank God." Tears filled her mother's voice. "Where are you? We've been worried sick about you."

"I know and I'm sorry. I should've called sooner. Timmy and I are okay."

"I've been calling you nonstop for days."

"I left my phone behind. I'm calling you on a new one."

"Bret's worried sick about you and Timmy."

Oh, yeah ... right. He's probably playing the victimized husband to the hilt.

"What happened? Bret told us he had no idea, but I know something must've happened for you to disappear like this."

"Bret's been cheating on me," she said in a soft voice, her gaze glued on Timmy.

"All this drama for *that?*" Her mother laughed dryly. "I don't mean it's right, it's just that all wealthy men do it. It's pretty much a stereotype. You can't break up a good marriage over that. Talk to him. Bret loves you very much."

Savannah gripped the counter with her hand as she tried to keep her anger in check. "Bret only loves one person—himself. He'd have you believe he's the doting father and loving husband, but he's none of those things. He's a selfish, self-centered, spoiled prick."

Her mother sighed. "Most men are selfish. It takes a strong and savvy woman to keep a man still interested in her after years of marriage. You two are just going through a rough spot."

"I've suspected he's been cheating on me ever since I was pregnant with Timmy." *The minute I started to show, everything changed. It was like Bret couldn't deal with my changing body because he held a picture-perfect image of the woman he was sexually attracted to. My trim waist expanding, wearing maternity clothes, and blossoming a bit wasn't what he wanted.*

"Many men can't handle their wives being pregnant. It's more common than you think."

"Mom, he actually told me that I was rejecting him by wearing maternity clothes. Did Dad ever say that to you during your four pregnancies?"

"No," her mother whispered.

Savannah wanted to tell her mother that shortly after that, Bret stopped touching her, claiming that he couldn't get into it. When she'd suggested they didn't have to have sex but could just cuddle or kiss or hold hands while watching a movie, he didn't answer. After that, he started going out more and stayed out later.

"Are you still there?"

"Yes," she answered softly.

"I don't know why men cheat. I've been lucky that your father never did."

"Dad is a man of integrity and honor. I can't imagine him ever hurting you like that. Anyway, he loves you and you love him."

"But Bret does love you. A lot of men need variety when it comes to … well, you know what I'm talking about. It doesn't mean anything to them. It's not the same for a man as it is for a woman. We're more emotional and we get attached easily. Are you sure you're not too focused on Timmy?"

Streaks of anger blazed through her. "What does that mean? Timmy's my son."

"I know, and I don't mean to make you angry. Sometimes, we forget our husbands when we have children. I had to remind myself over and over to spend time with your father without you kids."

"I admit that in the post-birth chaos of sleepless nights, sex became an expendable option for me, but afterward, I tried to make time for

Bret and me. He complained that I still had some weight to lose and that I wasn't as—" Savannah stopped before she said "tight." It felt weird to talk to her mother about something like that even though Bret made it a big issue … *and his reason to withhold sex or any intimacy with her. We lived like roommates, and I just accepted it because I threw myself into being a mother. My marriage was so fucked up.*

"What were you going to say?" her mother asked, bringing Savannah out of her musings.

"Uh … attractive. Bret didn't find me attractive anymore after Timmy was born."

"That's silly. You're a beautiful woman. I've noticed a lot of men look at you when we go out."

"Maybe, but the only man I've ever wanted to look at me was my husband, and he isn't interested at all."

"He doesn't act like he's not interested. He's been worried sick over your disappearance, and he misses Timmy."

I think I'm going to be sick. "I have to go, Mom. I'll call again. Tell Dad I said hi. I just wanted you to know that we're okay."

"Wait. When are you coming back?"

"I'm not sure. I need time to think."

"Please believe me when I tell you that Bret wants you back. Remember how hard life was for our family when you were young? It still is, except for the help you give us now. Your dad's income as a butcher and mine as a school cook made for real tough times back in the day when all four of you were young, but I had your dad to lean on. If you don't go back, you'll be a single mother, and it won't be easy."

"I did just fine before I married Bret. I'd gladly forgo my Coach purses, Cartier jewelry, and Manolo Blahnik shoes to have a loving marriage. I'll do fine, Mom."

"I wouldn't be too hasty. Just take a few days and think about it."

"There's nothing to think about." She walked to the refrigerator and took out a bottle of orange juice and poured some in a glass. "I'm tired of living in a loveless marriage and watching him ignore his son. I'm done. It's that simple."

"Are you still pleasing him? It sounds like maybe he's mad because you don't want to have ... you know ... *sex* with him," her mother said in a hushed voice.

Clenching her hand in a fist, she bit back the words she wanted to say. "It's hard to have sex with a husband who doesn't want it anymore ... at least with me." She heard her mother cluck her tongue.

"You two should go to counseling. Many marriages have survived an affair. Remember Linda and Sean Doyle? She found out he was having an affair, and it almost broke up their marriage. Linda told me that it was a long road and a lot of work, but eventually, she trusted Sean again. That was ten years ago, and Linda tells me their marriage is better than ever. I'm just saying for you to think good and hard about throwing twelve years away. There is life after an affair."

"You sound like a promo for a Dr. Phil show." She took another gulp of juice. "How's Dad?"

"Worried sick. He'll be glad when he hears that you and Timmy are okay. He's still at work, on the late shift tonight. I honestly can't believe the store decided to keep the butcher department open until ten o'clock. Now getting back to your situation—"

"I have to go. I promise to call soon."

"Will you be back for Christmas?"

Christmas was just three weeks away, and Savannah hoped that they'd be in California or Oregon by then, but it would depend on the weather. One thing she was certain of was that she wouldn't be home for the holidays.

"I don't think so," she whispered.

"Not home for Christmas? But we've always had Christmas Eve or Christmas day together."

"I know, but this year is different. I really have to go, Mom. I'll talk to you soon. Tell Dad I said hi. Love you."

Savannah took a deep breath and pushed away from the counter, then she slipped the phone into her pocket and walked over to the banquette to sit down. Timmy's attention was fixed on the game, and she leaned back on the cushion and blinked rapidly. Her mother didn't know the whole story. No one did. She couldn't tell anyone—not her sister, Jill, her cousin, Mari, or her best friend, Lacey. The scars of Bret's emotional cruelty were hidden deep inside, clawing at her as she repeatedly fought to keep them buried. The love she'd once had for her husband died slowly with each reproach and rebuff of affection, and with every act of deliberate callousness until all that was left was coldness around her heart.

Thinking back on the day that she'd decided to leave, her skin crawled at the memory of one of the most humiliating moments of her life.

"I just got three more coins," Timmy said, saving her from replaying that dreadful day in her mind.

"That's great, sweetie. You have ten more minutes, then it's bedtime. We'll snuggle under the covers and continue with the story from last night."

"The monster one, right?" Timmy asked, his eyes glued to the screen.

"That's right." Savannah moved the shade over a bit and looked out the window. The falling snow didn't seem as frenzied as it had a few hours before, and she could actually see some of the trees in the distance. *Maybe the storm is moving out and we can head out soon. The last thing I want is Ryder coming back and throwing us off his property. We'll stay a few days in Pinewood Springs and then head out. God, I can't wait to soak in a bathtub.* She let go of the shade and closed her eyes. *All I want is to start a new life with Timmy, but Corinne won't let me do that.* When her soon-to-be ex-mother-in-law had found out that Savannah had seen a divorce attorney, she made it perfectly clear that she would fight for custody of Timmy. Considering that the Carltons were one of the richest families in Massachusetts, Corinne had been appalled that Bret had chosen a woman from Quincy—a working-class neighborhood—to be his wife. Wayne, Bret's father, hadn't been too thrilled either, but he'd accepted

Savannah and was decent to her. Corinne never did, and she took every opportunity to demean and belittle her. If Bret were around when she did it, he'd just give Savannah that what-can-I-do look and shrug his shoulders, but if Wayne were in earshot, he'd call Corinne on it every time and that would shut her vicious mouth.

There's no damn way I'm letting Corinne dictate what's best for Timmy. If she had it her way, he'd have a nanny and be enrolled in Grayson Boys Academy Boarding School. Her stomach twisted as she recalled the bitter argument she had with Corinne over sending Timmy to a boarding school when he turned nine. Hot streaks of anger shot through her as she remembered how unsupportive Bret had been, choosing to sit in the leather wingback chair and stare down at his phone. All he'd said after his mother left the room was that he'd gone to Grayson and it wasn't bad at all. Savannah had wanted to throttle him.

Her heart pounded and every one of her muscles tensed up. *I need to calm down. I'm getting all worked up again. I'll never let Corinne have Timmy. We'll flee to Australia and just disappear before I agree to that.*

"Is it ten minutes yet, Mommy?" Timmy's eyes were bleary.

"Yes. Put the Nintendo away and you can play it another time. It's good to give your eyes a rest."

Timmy shuffled over to the cupboard and put the game system back on one of the shelves. He went into the bathroom to get ready for bed as Savannah lowered the table and folded the cushions over to make the bed.

Soon, Timmy was tucked in under the covers, looking up at her as his eyes shone under the overhead reading light she'd switched on before turning out all other illumination. Running down the battery worried her, and she decided they'd have to start paying more attention to their electricity usage.

Savannah opened the picture book, and Timmy snuggled closer to her.

"The scratching grew louder as Kenny crept down the hall. He stopped in front of the coat closet," she read aloud.

"I bet the monster's in there," Timmy said.

"Maybe," she whispered. "His hand shook as he reached for the knob to open the closet door." Timmy gasped and Savannah smiled, then she continued reading the bedtime story.

CHAPTER FOUR

RYDER PUT DOWN the coping saw and grabbed his cell phone. As the jangling continued, he hit the button again before he realized it was the landline phone that interrupted his woodworking. He pushed up off the chair then brought the receiver to his ear.

"Hello?"

"Dude, I couldn't get through on your cell. Is everything okay?" Hawk asked.

"Yeah. The reception's been spotty since the snowstorm hit. I'm just finishing up a train set I've been working on. Does Braxton have one?"

"The question is, what the fuck doesn't my son have? Between Cara and her parents, I'm gonna have to get a big-ass shed for his and Isa's toys."

"Oh … and you don't spoil him?" Ryder cradled the phone in the crick of his neck. He went back over to the worktable and picked up the unfinished locomotive. Soon, the sound of sandpaper on wood filled the room.

"You fuckin' got me. I guess I want my kids to have everything I didn't, which is a helluva lot." Hawk chuckled. "Braxton would love one of those fire trucks you make. Remember, you made one for Harley a few months ago? Braxton's still talking about it."

"So is Banger." The two men laughed. "I can make one for Braxton. I can bring it to the Toys for Tots event. I've made a shitload of toys for the kids. I'll just include the train set. I'm almost done with it."

Toys for Tots was the Insurgents' annual Christmas charity to collect toys and distribute them to abused, sick, and underprivileged children. A lot of money was raised at the event, which took place a week before

Christmas. Since Ryder had come back to Pinewood Springs three years before, he was active in the charity. It gave his woodworking hobby purpose, and he loved helping out the kids.

"That'd be great. Are you buried in pretty deep?"

"Yep. I doubt my four wheeler could get through the drifts. When I last looked out the window, the snow had died down some."

"It's that way in town too. The brothers at the clubhouse can't get out, but they're closer to you than to town. Throttle said that he'll probably get the plows out tomorrow or the day after. He wants you to know he and Rags will come out your way and dig you out."

"Appreciate it. I'll have to give him a call. For now, I'm good. I bought some whiskey from Tom."

Hawk's hearty laugh rang through the phone line. "How's that fuckin' old moonshiner doing? I haven't seen him around much."

"He's slowing down. Since Martha died, he's not the same. He misses the hell outta her."

"It's gotta be tough—they were married for forty years. I can't even imagine what it's like for him. Hell, if Cara goes before me, I'll be fucked up for sure."

"Yeah … I feel for him, but his whiskey still has that kick that'll land you on your ass if you don't respect it."

"Speaking from experience?" Hawk chuckled.

"Too much experience." Ryder looked at Brutus, who sat at his feet looking up at him. "I gotta take Brutus out. Thanks for checking up on me, bro."

"Yeah. Later."

Ryder put the phone back in its cradle and ruffled the top of Brutus's head. "You wanna go outside?" Brutus barked and wagged his tail then dashed toward the front door. Ryder pulled on his boots and slipped his arm inside a jacket then closed the door behind him.

Cold slapped his naked face, squeezing tears from his eyes. *It's fucking freezing out here.* He immediately thought about the woman and her son in their small camper. *I wonder if they got enough heat. Why the fuck are they living in that damn thing?* Breath rolled from him in short frosted puffs. Treading slowly through deep, soft snow as the thin rays of light filtered through the ice-laden tree branches, he whistled for Brutus, who bounded out from behind the evergreens and ran over to him.

"It's too damn cold out here. Come on." Ryder plodded over to the garage and opened the door. Brutus barked and ran in circles as Ryder took off one glove and fished in the pocket of his parka for his car keys. When he opened the jeep's back door, the dog jumped in, then Ryder cranked up the heat and backed out.

The tires skidded on ice-slick snow as beams from the headlights danced on clusters of frosted firs lining the road. "Dammit," he muttered as he gripped the steering wheel. The snow began falling again—harder and faster. It erased the car's icy tracks on the road, and the trees that loomed in the distance vanished, swallowed up in white. The jeep's wipers now moved frantically over the windshield as Ryder drove toward the trailer.

Brutus's barks echoed eerily in the muted stillness as Ryder closed the car door. A thick quilt of snow surrounded the camper, and Ryder saw that there wasn't as much light coming from the small windows as there was the day before. He pushed on, cursing under his breath at the pain shooting through his residual limb. He'd been too damn lazy to put the liner sleeve over it when he'd gotten up that morning, never thinking he'd be plodding through two feet of snow. While stopping to rub his upper thigh, the cold air seared his lungs as the rest of him sweated beneath the parka. Savannah was peering out the window and he motioned for her to open the door. She stayed at the window for a few seconds, making him think he'd have to break down the damn door, but then she disappeared, and a faint sliver of light fell on the white ground as she stood in the doorway.

Ignoring the pain, Ryder gritted his teeth and walked toward her with Brutus by his side. With a fuzzy blanket wrapped around her, she stood aside as he pushed himself up into the trailer. After a few seconds, his eyes adjusted to the dim lighting and spotted Timmy sitting at the table with what looked like a puzzle in front of him. The boy wore a jacket and had a blanket wrapped around his thin shoulders. He saw Savannah looking at him from the corner of his eye and craned his neck to meet her gaze. After a short pause, she cleared her throat and looked away as a slight pinkish flush swept across her cheeks.

"Why are you here? You can't possibly think we can leave in this blizzard," she said softly.

"I came by to check up on you and the boy."

Timmy looked over and smiled, and Ryder's lips twitched when he noticed the boy's missing front tooth.

"Can I pet your Bluto now? He knows I'm okay," Timmy said.

"His name's *Brutus*, and if it's all right with your mom, you can come over here and pet him."

Timmy's eyes shone as he looked at Savannah. "Can I, Mommy? Please?"

She wrung her hands over and over as if she were washing them, and then nodded. "Just wait and let Ryder tell you when it's okay to pet his dog."

She remembered my name, and she keeps sneaking peeks at me. Maybe she's lonely for some male company.

Timmy padded over and Ryder could feel Brutus stiffen by his side. He hit the button in his prosthesis and his knee pushed out, making it easy for him to kneel down. The chaffing still hurt like hell, but he could deal with it. He put his arm around the German shepherd and leaned close to his ear. "Steady, boy." Brutus relaxed and Ryder waved Timmy to come closer.

The boy looked at his mom as apprehension began to line his face. "Are you going to pet him too, Mommy?"

"Uh … I wasn't planning on it." Savannah darted her eyes between the dog, Ryder, and Timmy.

"I think you should show your boy it's okay," Ryder said in a low voice.

She lifted her chin and stared at him coolly. "I don't need any suggestions from you on what I should do with my son."

I hit a nerve, and she's not as meek as I thought. "Whatever." He reached out his hand, and Timmy placed his small one into it. Before he could encourage him to come closer, Savannah knelt down next to him, and a clean scent with a hint of floral hugged him. *She smells damn good … and sexy.* He glanced sideways at her, but she kept her focus on her son.

"Do you wanna pet Brutus?" he asked her.

"Okay," she answered, but her tone said it was the last thing she wanted to do. She gasped when he grabbed her hand and guided it over to the dog's damp fur. As cold as her hand was, the skin was soft and silky, which made him wonder if her whole body was just as satiny.

It's just some chick's hand. Focus, man. Without thinking, he squeezed her hand then ran his thumb over its softness.

"Aren't I supposed to be petting the dog?" she asked.

He immediately loosened his grip. "Of course, but your hand is so damn cold that I was trying to warm it up so Brutus wouldn't freak out." Her quizzical look confirmed what he already knew—a piss-poor excuse for his pathetic actions. *There's no question about it—the first chance I get, I'm going to hook up with Brandi.* Before she could say anything, he put her hand on Brutus's back then let go of it.

"Is he soft, Mommy?"

"Yes, he is, but he's a little wet too."

Ryder drew the boy closer, and soon his small hand stroked the black fur. "He likes it," Timmy whispered.

"Once you both get to know each other better, you can rub his belly—he *loves* that." Timmy's eyes widened, and he heard Savannah make a sound like *tsk-tsk.* He turned to her and looked deep into her eyes. "What's your problem?"

Scraping a hand through her hair, Savannah looked away. "Nothing. It's just that we'll be leaving once the storm dies down. I don't like people promising things they can't deliver." She stood up and wrapped the blanket tighter around her.

Just hit another nerve. Someone broke a promise to you, didn't they, darlin'? "The storm will be around for a couple more days at least, and then it'll take time until the less traveled roads are cleared."

"In any event, we won't be here long." She rubbed the back of her neck.

"I think he likes me, Mommy," Timmy said, his face flushed.

Savannah's smile held all the love a mother has for her child, and it warmed Ryder to the core. He pushed up then pulled Brutus back.

"He does like you. That's enough for now because Brutus isn't used to many kids."

Nodding his head, Timmy drew his hand away and took a few steps backward.

"Go finish your puzzle, sweetie," Savannah said, and the young boy walked back to the table and slid onto the cushioned seat.

"It's in the single digits outside, and it's gonna be below zero tonight."

"Thanks for the weather update," Savannah said.

Ryder narrowed his dark eyes. "It's already too cold in here, and you fucking know it."

"What's your point?" She lifted up her chin.

"You two are gonna get sick if you stay in this cold. I can see your battery is running down because you don't have very many lights on."

"I appreciate all your observations, but none of this is your business. We'll be just fine." Savannah leaned against the counter.

"You're either fucking nuts or foolishly stubborn, but either way, you're putting yourself and your boy in danger."

"I'm neither. We can manage on our own."

"Bullshit. You want your son to be cold, not to have lights? What the hell are you thinking, woman?"

"What am I supposed to do about it?" she asked, frowning. "We're stuck. I'm doing the best I can." Her voice quivered, and she turned away quickly.

Fuck. "I didn't come here to judge you or make you feel bad," he said, his voice softening.

"You could have fooled me," she said.

"I came here to make sure you and your son were doing okay, and quite frankly, you're not. It's gonna get colder and snowier before the storm moves out. I got some room at my cabin where you can stay. I've also got a generator so there're no worries about downed power lines." Savannah's forehead wrinkled as she tugged on her bottom lip. Ryder shrugged. "It's up to you." He saw her gaze fix on Timmy.

"Is your wife okay with having strangers in the home?"

He jerked his head back. "I don't answer to anyone. Anyway, I don't have a wife—it's just me and Brutus."

"Well … you're not a psycho, are you?" She pulled back slightly.

"No … are you?"

"I've got issues but nothing psychotic."

"We've *all* got issues. So are you taking me up on my offer?"

Savannah tilted her head from side to side as if weighing the pros and cons of the situation. Ryder watched her without saying another word. If she declined his offer, he'd leave and check on them again the following day. From the chill in the air, he didn't think the heat would last more than twenty-four hours.

"I can't believe I'm actually agreeing to this," she said between nervous giggles.

"Look at it this way," he said as he put his gloves on, "sometimes life makes you trust your gut. What's it saying to you?"

"That it's okay. You know, even if you don't want to admit it, there's a streak of kindness in you." A bright smile curved her lips.

A faint spark flickered deep down inside him. "Don't get all fucking mushy. I don't want anyone to die on my property—that's all." He grasped the knob and pushed open the door. "I'll wait in the jeep." Ignoring her small gasp, he inhaled the cold air, satisfied that whatever shit he'd felt a few minutes before had been extinguished.

Ryder shut the door and made his way through the snow.

CHAPTER FIVE

"**W**HAT THE HELL am I doing? I don't even know this man," Savannah muttered under her breath as she threw their clothes into the suitcase. This was by far the craziest thing she'd ever done in her life, and doubt began to settle into every inch of her body.

"Where are we going?" Timmy stammered, his teeth chattering.

"Oh … sweetie," she said as she gathered him in her arms, cocooning him in the blanket. "Ryder has asked us to stay at his house until the snow stops. It's too cold in here and tonight is going to be worse."

Timmy tilted his head back and looked up at her. "Is Bluto going to be there too?"

Savannah tweaked his nose. "Yes." *I know it'll be all right. I see compassion behind his anger.* "Help me pack so we don't keep him waiting."

Soon, Savannah and Timmy were bumping against each other as they sat in the back of Ryder's jeep. The blasting heat inside the vehicle curled around them, banishing Timmy's chattering teeth and her body's shivers.

"Let me get the suitcase," Ryder said after they pulled into the garage. "The door's open, so just go in."

"I can bring in the suit—" His glare pierced her like a dart, and she slipped out of the car, holding Timmy's hand then walked away.

The first thing she noticed when she walked into the mud room was how pristine it was. Sitting on the bench, she pulled off her boots, then Timmy's, before hanging their coats on the large hooks.

Brutus rushed in then sat on his haunches, his gaze fixed at the doorway. Ryder came in and put the suitcase on the floor, then he grabbed a big green towel and wiped the dog down before taking off his boots and jacket. Savannah's attention was captured by the way the well-defined muscles in his upper arm bunched and flexed beneath the slim fitted material of his flannel shirt. The sight made her feel hot and bothered in a way she hadn't experienced in a very long time. Angry that it did, she turned away, not wanting Ryder to see her heated reaction to him.

Without saying a word to either of them, Ryder picked up the suitcase and walked out of the mudroom.

Timmy's face looked like the blood had been drained out of it, and Savannah folded her arms around him and kissed his head. "It's going to be okay, sweetie."

"I think he's mad at us."

"No, he isn't. He's probably just not used to a lot of people in his house." She ran her fingers over his soft cheeks. "Remember that he's the one who invited us."

"I know. Will he let me play my Mario game?"

"I can ask him."

"What are you still doing in the mudroom?" Ryder's gruff voice made them both jump. "Get in here." He stood there staring at her.

"Let's go," she whispered to Timmy. The intensity of Ryder's stare unnerved her.

The kitchen was spotless, and Savannah began to wonder if he had a girlfriend or a cleaning person who helped him out. The woodwork on the cabinets and crown molding was amazing.

"Do you want something to drink?" he asked.

"I'm good, thanks. What do you want, honey?"

"Do you have any orange juice? We finished ours this morning."

Ryder lifted his chin up and took out a carton then poured the juice into a tall glass. "Here you go," he said, sliding the glass over to Timmy.

"Thank you," the boy replied.

Ryder grunted. "If you want more, it's in the fridge." He settled his penetrating stare back on Savannah. "Feel like this is your place. If you want food or something to drink, don't ask me. If you do, it's gonna get real annoying."

"Okay. I'll remember that." She wanted to grab Timmy's arm and pull him out of the room, but he was barely finished with his juice. There was something about Ryder's brooding eyes that pulled her in, and she sensed he'd been deeply hurt and wondered if that was what intrigued her about him.

"I'll show you your rooms." Ryder picked up the suitcase and walked out of the kitchen.

"Do you want some, Mommy?" Timmy propped his elbows on the counter and leaned forward. "It's too much," he whispered.

Savannah smiled and picked up the glass, downing the contents in one large swallow. "Now let's see our new home for a few days." She rinsed the glass and put it in the dishwasher then grasped her son's hand.

When they turned down a hallway, Ryder stood in the doorway of a room tapping his foot.

"Timmy had to finish his juice," she said softly. He jutted his chin and went into the room.

"This is your room," he said to Timmy.

"Are those real arrows?" Timmy asked pointing at a framed collage of arrowheads.

"Yep." Ryder went over to the window and opened the shutters then took the display off the wall. "Come over here and you can see them up close."

As Timmy and Ryder talked about the Native American artifacts, Savannah glanced around, marveling at the exquisite craftsmanship and cozy feel of the room. Several beautiful quilts and afghans were either displayed on the walls, thrown over two plush chairs, or folded and stacked on top of a large chest at the foot of the bed. *I wonder if he's ever been married. I can't see him going into a store and buying these. Someone made them for him.*

"I'll show you your room." His gruff voice interrupted her thoughts, and she looked over at him and nodded.

Timmy was still fascinated by the arrowheads, so Savannah quietly followed Ryder to the room next door. A large four-poster bed with a stunning quilt spread over it was the first thing she noticed when she entered the bedroom. An overstuffed chair next to the window looked like the perfect place to curl up with a good book, and a well-crafted rocking chair sat in a corner on the opposite side.

"You have such a beautiful home. I love all the details in the woodwork." She walked over to the bed and ran her hand over the quilt. "This is exquisite. I always wished I could quilt, or even sew."

"Yeah."

"Did you buy it in Pinewood Springs?"

"No."

Savannah put her fingers against her lips and watched him open the curtains and then put the suitcase on top of the mattress.

"There's nothing in the closet, and you can use the first three drawers of the dresser." His dark brown eyes burned into hers.

"Thanks," she mumbled, unable to break contact.

Ryder's stare washed over her, head to toe … dripping slowly, and the heat of his gaze burned holes right through her, sending shockwaves straight to her core. Savannah could feel her face flushing but couldn't turn away; she just stood there rooted, feeling magnetically drawn toward him. A sexually charged silence sizzled between the two as desire sparked inside her.

"Your room's big, Mommy." Timmy's voice snapped her out of whatever was happening between her and Ryder, and she was grateful for it.

Dragging her eyes away from his penetrating ones, she ran her fingers through Timmy's thick hair and looked down at him. "It is large. Why don't we unpack your things and get settled in."

Timmy darted over to the suitcase and she followed hesitantly behind him. Ryder hadn't moved an inch nor had he averted his eyes away from her. Savannah unzipped the case, trying to focus on what she was doing rather than on the simmering desire crackling between them.

"Where are we gonna put everything?" Timmy asked.

"Uh … in the closet and drawers, I guess." Ryder's scent tangled around her, making her dizzy. *Stop it! Don't you dare go there.* She cleared her throat, threw back her shoulders, then began taking the clothes out of the bag.

"I'll leave you two. Let me know if you need anything," he said, fastening his hand lightly on her shoulder, his thumb sliding over the nape of her neck.

Savannah gasped, then warmth rushed through her from the twinkle in his eyes and the twitch of his lips. "Okay, and … thanks again," she said softly.

With that, he was gone and she instantly missed his presence. How crazy was that? Savannah barely knew him, yet his effect on her floored her. When she looked into his ardent, burning eyes, all of her insecurities and loneliness faded away in that moment. She'd never had such a magnetic attraction to any man in her life.

"Bluto is looking at us." Timmy's voice brought her out of her reverie, and she looked up and saw the German shepherd standing in the doorway.

"He's just checking us out," she said as she gathered her son's clothes in her arms and walked toward the door. "And his name is *Brutus* with an *r* and a *u-s.* Can you say it?"

By the time they were done practicing, the dog had laid down and put his face on top of his paws, his eyes never wavering from them.

"I'm sure we drove Brutus crazy." Savannah laughed.

"Can I pet him?" Timmy started to saunter over to him.

She reached for his arm and held him back. "I don't feel comfortable with you doing that without Ryder."

"Can you tell him to come here so I can pet Brutus?"

Ryder unnerved her with his quiet strength and intense stare; it was like he could see deep into her heart and mind and soul. He stirred up feelings—and desires—inside her that scared and titillated her. If he could manage all that in just a couple of days, there was no telling what maelstrom he'd create in her if they were to hook up. *Really? We're leaving in a few days. I can't get involved with him. What am I saying? I don't even know that he'd want to get involved. I have to get a grip here and stop acting like a schoolgirl with a fucking crush.*

"Are you gonna call him? I don't think the dog wants to move."

Savannah shook her head and approached the canine. "Brutus, can you let us out? Be a good boy." She snapped her fingers, waving her hand toward the hallway. "Go on now." The dog just looked at her, his chin still poised on his paws.

"He isn't listening," Timmy said.

"Shit," she muttered under her breath before crossing her arms in front of her chest. She pinched her lips together and stared at the German shepherd. "Please get up, Brutus. I have to put Timmy's clothes in his room." Nothing. The dog laid there like a sack of potatoes.

"Come on, Brutus." Ryder's husky baritone was sensuous and commanding. The dog pushed up and his nails clacked on the hardwood floor as he padded toward his owner.

Savannah's whole body tensed, expecting Ryder to walk through the doorway at any moment, but he didn't. Timmy poked his head out the door, looking down the hallway. Upset at letting herself be flustered by Ryder, she pressed the stack of clothes against her and walked with her chin held high over to Timmy's room.

A DUSTY PINK glow lit the edges of the clouds as darkness slowly crept in. The cabin was quiet; Timmy was napping and Savannah wasn't sure where Ryder and his dog were. She stepped into the hallway and noticed two more rooms—one door was closed, the other was ajar. Deciding to check out her surroundings, she padded over to the half-opened door and paused when she saw Ryder sitting on the edge of the bed in his boxers massaging his thigh, although it wasn't a full thigh. She pressed her fingers over her parted lips and scanned the room, her gaze landing on an artificial leg next to the nightstand. Brutus lay on the floor near the bed, and his ears perked up when he saw her. She slinked away quickly not wanting Ryder to know that she'd invaded his privacy. With a sick feeling in her stomach, she went into the living room and sank down on the couch. *I can't believe I violated his space like that.* Savannah stared at the dancing flames in the fireplace. She'd noticed he had trouble with stairs when he'd come into the trailer, but she just figured that he had joint pain or something. *I wonder if he lost his leg in a motorcycle accident.* She'd seen a Harley in his garage that morning. She knew of two people who'd had bad accidents while riding. One of her childhood friends' brother had lost a leg in a motorcycle crash when he was nineteen. *I wonder what Ryder's story is. Maybe the anger and bitterness that emanates from him are because he lost his leg.* She pulled up her legs and tucked them under her butt and let her mind drift.

"You need anything?" Savannah jumped at the sound of Ryder's voice. A low chuckle rumbled from him. "Didn't mean to scare you."

Shaking her head, she smiled. "It's fine. I must've dozed off. The fire is so warm and toasty." *Don't you dare look at his leg.*

"Yeah. It's hard to believe that it's twenty below outside. I'm gonna have a shot of whiskey. You want one?"

"No thanks." A grimace passed over his face, and his jaw tightened as he turned away and headed into the kitchen. *He's in pain. I bet if we weren't here, he wouldn't be wearing his prosthesis.* The guilt was like gasoline in her gut, tightening her chest and forming a thickness in her throat. She lowered her gaze when he came back into the room with a bottle in one hand and a glass in the other.

Ryder shoved aside several motorcycle magazines before putting the whiskey and tumbler down on the end table; he gripped the arm of the couch then plopped down, an audible curse resounding around the room. Savannah looked up and saw the sheen of perspiration on his face. After swallowing several times, she folded her arms and breathed deeply.

"Your home is beautiful. What kind of wood are the floors?" she asked.

"The floors and ceilings are made of reclaimed barn wood." Ryder brought the glass to his lips and took a sip then jerked his head toward the fireplace. "All the stone is local. Same with the one I have in the master." He shifted a few times as if trying to get comfortable.

"Everything's so well crafted. It's just stunning." Savannah's heart tugged each time Ryder massaged his upper left leg.

"Where're you from?" he asked, his look catching hers.

"Boston ... well, really south of Boston. Quincy. What about you?" That crazy connection between them was starting up again.

"I'm from here." He leaned back against the cushion and the gray T-shirt he wore outlined his finely toned chest. His muscular arms were covered in tattoos, and a strong desire to have them curled around her made her blush.

"You like what you see?" Ryder took another sip.

Without looking in a mirror, Savannah knew her face was flaming red; she could feel the heat under her skin. "Caught in the act." She laughed trying to brush it off. "I wish I had the discipline to work out more," she said, hoping that would end the discussion.

"Why ... you look damn good as you are." Ryder's gaze dropped to her breasts and lingered there.

Savannah instinctively crossed her arms, watching him, and feather-like lines crinkled around his eyes when he laughed before looking away. He poured more of the amber liquid into the glass and took a healthy drink. She watched him intently; she liked the curved bow of his mouth, the way his hair fell across his forehead, and how rough and warm his hand was when he'd touched her earlier.

"Are you sure you don't want one?" Ryder tipped the glass to her before throwing it back.

"I'm sure. I was going to check out the fridge and cupboards to see what I can make for dinner." She held her hand up, silencing him. "It's the least I can do to repay your kindness."

Ryder's gaze drifted to her mouth making her burn. *I can't believe how my body reacts to him.* "Go check it out." He rubbed his pant leg again while grinding his teeth.

Taking a deep breath, she slowly exhaled, hoping she wasn't making a mistake. "You don't have to sit there in pain. I accidentally—*no reason to say I was snooping*—saw you in your room earlier. You don't have to wear your prosthesis just because we're around. I want you to be comfortable in your own home."

For a pause that seemed like an eternity, Ryder's face darkened and he stared at the fire, a frown deepening into a scowl.

Shit. I shouldn't have said anything, but I know he's in pain. "I'm sorry," she whispered then started to get up.

"It's fine."

She relaxed and sank further into the cushion. "Was it a motorcycle accident? I noticed your killer bike in the garage. My dad's a Harley man."

"No, it wasn't." He kept staring at the curling flames.

"Do you want to talk about it?" She held her breath.

"No."

"Okay."

The fire crackled, tree branches scratched against the window with each gust of wind, and a long silence stretched between them. Savannah furtively glanced over at Ryder and noticed that his face was grave … pensive. The urge to thread her fingers through his thick dark hair then cradle his head against her chest started to overwhelm her, and she struggled to breathe normally. *Would he cringe at my touch? What if—*

He turned to look at her, and she felt the need to break the silence.

"Do you have any ground meat?"

He tipped his head, a lock of dark hair falling over his forehead. How she longed to sweep it away and press her palm against the rough stubble of his cheek. His intoxicating scent wisped around in the air, reminding her of the exotic spices she'd bought in the marketplace in Marrakech several years before.

"Do you like meatloaf?" Savannah stood up; she had to get out of there before she did something which would embarrass them both.

Another tip of his head.

"I'll let you know when dinner's ready." She spun around and scampered into the kitchen.

Ryder had a fully stocked pantry, refrigerator, and freezer, and it impressed the hell out of her. From the boxes of pasta from Italy to the flavored olive oils, she concluded that he must love to cook. *Or maybe he has a girlfriend who does.* The thought that Ryder might have a girlfriend shouldn't have bothered her, but it did. Her heart tripped then stumbled a little. Which meant … what? *What's going on with me?* She stared out the window at the blowing snow and wondered when the storm would end so she and Timmy could leave. For the sake of her pride, she hoped it'd be soon.

"It smells good, Mommy."

Savannah turned around and saw her son walking toward her, rubbing his eyes. She wet her hands and patted down the cowlick that always cropped up whenever he slept.

"Did you have a good nap?" she asked.

"Uh-huh."

"Do you want a banana? Dinner won't be ready for a while. I'm making your favorite—mashed potatoes." A goofy grin spread over his face and she laughed and embraced him. "I love you so much," she whispered as she bent down and kissed the top of his head.

"Me too. Where's my banana?"

Laughing, she unpeeled a small one and cut it in half. She lent a hand while Timmy tried to climb up on the stool.

"Ryder's making the best train," Timmy said while chewing.

"Don't eat with your mouth open, sweetie. A train …?"

"Yeah. He's got this room where he makes stuff. He's got a whole town too. Do you wanna come see?"

"Okay, but after you're done eating—and don't rush."

Before she could finish cutting up the carrots, Timmy scrambled down from the stool and tugged the hem of her sweater top.

"I'm done," he said.

She shook her head as she placed the carrots in water then let Timmy lead the way. He took her to a room on the opposite end of the hall from both of theirs. When they approached the opened door, Timmy slowed down and glanced up at her, pointing at the room.

"He's in there," he whispered, his brown eyes wide.

Savannah placed her hand on his shoulder and ambled to the doorway. The first thing she noticed was a large floor to ceiling glass cabinet filled with Iron Butterfly memorabilia. On the perpendicular wall was a large firearm collection of various sizes and designs showcased either in framed displays, iron racks, or hanging freestyle. An apprehensive shiver slid up her spine as she counted twenty-two guns. *I wonder if they're loaded. I'll have to talk to Ryder about that.* A steady scraping sound diverted her attention from the weapons to a worktable against the back wall stacked with drills, hammers, glue guns, saws, and blocks of wood.

Ryder sat on a low stool with his back to them, running sandpaper over what looked like a miniature church. In front of him were paintbrushes, small bottles of craft paint, and several train cars. Brutus lay at his feet until, suddenly, his ears perked up and a dull, thumping noise resonated as he wagged his tail with his black eyes fixed on them. Ryder looked over his shoulder then stopped what he was doing and spun around.

"Dinner already?" His gaze swept over her quickly then focused on her face.

Savannah cleared her throat. "No. Timmy said that you're making a train set, and he wanted me to check it out. Sorry if we're invading your space."

Ryder clucked his tongue, his gaze never leaving hers. "You wanna see what I'm making, Timmy?" The young boy's eyes shone as a big smile spread across his face. "Come on over here. Your mom can come too if she's interested."

Timmy rushed over as Savannah sauntered, happy that Ryder wasn't perturbed. "Timmy loves trains," she said.

"Go ahead and touch them. I'm gonna start painting them tomorrow."

"Do they run on the track?" the boy asked.

"Yep. I've got a kickass motor in the locomotive, lights … the whole nine yards. Do you got a train set?"

Timmy bobbed his head up and down. "Back home. My daddy got me one, but it doesn't work so good, does it, Mommy?"

She sank her fingers in her son's hair. "No. The cars were made of steel and were too heavy or something for the track. It kept tipping over."

"That sucks. Did your dad exchange it?"

Timmy hung his head down. "No. He didn't have time. He never has time." He stared at the caboose. "Can I see that one?"

"Sure." Ryder picked it up and placed it in the boy's small hand.

"It's really smooth. Did you make it?"

"Yeah. I made all of this. I like doing it. It helps to keep me from thinking about … never mind."

What are you keeping buried deep inside you? Savannah ran her finger-tips over the smooth wood on the train car that her son had shared with her.

"Are you making it for you to play with?" Timmy asked.

"Nah. Making it for this charity the bikers run every year at Christmas for kids who don't get any presents."

Timmy took the caboose from his mom and put it back on the table. "Don't their mommies and daddies love them?"

Savannah's heart ached as she thought of how cold and indifferent Bret was to their son.

"Not all moms and dads give a shit about their kids. It sucks, but that's the way it is. Sometimes, the parents love them but don't have enough money to give them any toys."

Timmy lifted his head and looked up at Savannah. "Am I getting any presents this Christmas?"

She dipped her chin down as her skin prickled up the back of her neck and across her chin. "Of course you are."

"But no one knows where we are."

Savannah was keenly aware of Ryder's piercing gaze, and she pretended to be unaffected by giving a nonchalant shrug while her insides were twisting. "Santa does."

Timmy's eyes brightened. "Oh ... yeah."

Ryder hadn't moved a muscle, and his quiet assessment of her, or at least that's what she thought he was doing, bothered the hell out of her. He had no right to judge her. He didn't know the whole story—no one did. She'd make sure Timmy had a great Christmas, and it'd be a hell of a lot better than the ones he had with an indifferent father who couldn't give a shit about his son.

"You okay?" Ryder's deep voice snapped her to the present. She nodded. "You sure? 'Cause your face is all red and you look real upset." His low husky voice made her senses reel.

"I'm fine," she said curtly, dismissing him. She lightly squeezed Timmy's shoulder. "I'm going to go back and finish dinner."

Timmy's face fell.

"I need a helper. You can stay here if your mom's cool with that."

Before Timmy could ask her, Savannah smiled. "That's fine. Just be careful, and don't pick up any of the saws or drills, honey."

In her hurried rush to get the hell out of there, she almost tripped and landed on her butt. *That's all I need to make me feel even more foolish than I already do around* him. Her emotions ping-ponged in her chest. Why did his intense stare pull her in and make her want to cling to him? And why the hell did the thought of doing so freak her out?

"Just let me know if you need *anything*." Ryder's soft, hoarse tone made her head spin.

Savannah paused and looked over her shoulder at him. Riveted, he gazed at her face, then slowly moved over her body.

Her pulse pounded and she looked away.

"Anything at all," he said in a low voice.

Without looking back, Savannah stepped through the door and made her way to the kitchen.

CHAPTER SIX

"I DON'T KNOW where she is, Mother. Asking me over and over isn't going to change that." Bret pinched the bridge of his nose before glancing over at the twenty-year-old's naked body stretched across the bed.

"Have you heard anything at all from her?" His mother's high-pitched voice grated on his nerves.

"No." The young woman spread her legs wide showing off her young, pink pussy. "I have to go, Mother. I have a meeting I'm already late for."

"Have you hired the investigation company your father told you about?"

"Yes." He stood up from the chair and walked over to the delicious afternoon snack who was currently teasing the hell out of him.

"What have they found?"

Bret sat on the edge of the bed and squeezed one of the young woman's pert, soft tits. The woman's hazel eyes glazed over with desire. "Not much yet. I do have to go. I'll let you know when I find something out." He dipped his head down and flicked his tongue over the taut bud.

"Christmas is coming fast, and I want my grandson at our home."

"Uh-huh." Two of his fingers slipped into the young woman, and he groaned softly at how tight and firm she was.

"Are you listening to me?" His mother's voice raised higher, if that was even possible.

Just shut the fuck up! "Yes. I've already told you I have to go." He moved his fingers in and out of the luscious college student while his thumb circled her clit. As long as he lived, he'd never get tired of fucking a tight pussy or running his hands over a young woman's smooth, firm body.

"All right. Call me later. I don't want to let that bitch you married raise my grandson. And don't sign the divorce papers. You're a Carlton and we don't divorce."

"I have to run. Bye." Bret threw the phone across the bed then covered the giggling twenty-year-old's clit with his mouth.

An hour later, he stood by the window looking out at the Boston skyline wondering where the hell Savannah was. The young woman, fully dressed now, gave him a quick kiss on the cheek while squeezing his ass.

"I had a fun time. Call me if you'd like to hook up again."

"Yeah," he said, watching the snow flurries dance over the Charles River.

"Do you have the Coach bag you promised me?"

Bret grabbed his wallet off the table and handed her five one-hundred dollar bills. From the corner of his eye, he saw her frowning. "What the fuck's the matter?"

"I sorta wanted a tote bag, so I don't think this is enough."

He looked at her. "That's all I got on me."

She bit the side of her lip for a few seconds then smiled seductively while she wrapped her arm around his waist. "Thank you." She pressed her lips against his, then pulled back and stuffed the bills into her small handbag.

Bret heard the door close behind him, and he wondered what the hell her name was. She'd told him a few times when they'd met before, but her name escaped him at that moment. It didn't matter because he knew she'd be more than willing to hook up with him again. Maybe the next time he'd take her out for an expensive dinner at No. 9 Park in Beacon Hill. He liked her eagerness to please and her unabashed enthusiasm, and her pussy tasted sweet like cotton candy. He presumed it was whatever douche she used to make sure her mound was sparkling clean and fresh.

For the umpteenth time, Bret called Savannah, but it just went to voicemail. "Fuck!" he yelled out, slamming his fist against the thick window. "You're causing me a shitload of grief, bitch." If it were up to him, he'd have signed the divorce papers the minute he received them and be done with it. Of course, he wouldn't give her everything he had; however, he'd make sure she and the brat were comfortable, but it wasn't up to him. His mother had made it her mission to keep butting into his damn life.

If only Savannah hadn't lied to him about being on the pill. She had to have known that he wasn't fond of children and didn't really want any, even though he might have led her to believe they'd have a family when they were dating.

Bret closed his eyes and pressed his forehead against the hotel window; the cool glass felt good against his warm skin. Images of Savannah waiting tables at Luna's flooded his mind. *She was damn beautiful.* He'd been a senior at Harvard when he'd discovered Luna's and had first seen her. *She fucking knocked my socks off.* All his efforts had been focused on winning her over. Savannah had been reluctant in the beginning because she came from "the other side of the tracks"—her words, not his. It was true that she was from a working-class family but Bret hadn't given a damn about that. She was the most beautiful, funny, and genuine woman he'd ever known.

"We were happy, baby," he whispered, "then you took an enviable sexual relationship and threw it in the fucking garbage by getting knocked up." Once Savannah was pregnant, he couldn't stand how her body had changed, and then after Timmy was born, Bret found the idea of a sexually active mother disturbing. He just hadn't been able to connect with his wife again.

The buzzing of Bret's phone brought him back to the moment, and he placed it against his ear.

"Bret," Mary said. "I've left you several messages."

He knitted his brows when he heard his mother-in-law's voice. He wished everyone would leave him the fuck alone. "I've been real busy and haven't had a chance to listen to my messages."

"I heard from Savannah. I spoke with her a few days ago. She said they were both fine."

"Where is she?"

"She didn't tell me, and the phone number didn't register, so I don't have any way of getting a hold of her."

"When's she coming back?" The headlights from the traffic below looked like the glow worms he used to buy at concerts when he was a teenager.

"I don't think she is." Mary's voice quivered.

"She can't just disappear with my son." Anger flared up inside him, not from any fatherly love, but from the fact that Savannah was throwing him the middle finger in a big way, and no one did that shit to him.

"I know why Savannah left you."

"She told you about the affair?" The falling snow blurred the twinkling lights from the skyscrapers.

"Yes, she did. I haven't told Frank," she whispered.

Of course she hadn't; Frank would never understand. He was loyal to a sickening fault, and if that's what Savannah wanted, she should've married the plumber next door. Bret was a Carlton—the men cheated on their devoted spouses. His dad's numerous mistresses never meant that he didn't love his mother. *Mother knew Dad would never leave her. Why the fuck would he do that for a stacked bimbo?*

"Bret?"

"I lost you for a second. Savannah seemed to have forgotten about me once Timmy was born."

"I can't believe that. You two were so much in love. I know having a child is a lot of work, but she always wanted to be a mother and have a big family."

"Yes ... well ... here we are. She'll get tired of her little tantrum and come home, especially when the money runs out." Bret had promptly cancelled all her cards when he found out she'd left him. *No matter what you tell others, baby, we both know you love the lifestyle my money afforded you. You don't fool me for a fucking minute.*

"Savannah said she'd call me again real soon and that she won't be home for Christmas." Another quiver—it was getting annoying.

Mother's going to be livid. Fuck you, Savannah. "Try and get her to tell you where she is. I want to bring them back home where they belong."

"Are you finished with the woman you were carrying on with?" Mary's hushed voice irked him.

"Yes. It was just a fling—it didn't mean anything." And it didn't, but Savannah just didn't understand that. *You're the one who changed the dynamics, baby, then you got mad when it backfired.*

"I'll try and find out. Timmy needs both his parents. I can't believe they won't be here for Christmas." This time a small sob filtered through the phone.

Enough! "I have to go. We'll keep in touch." Bret slid the phone in his pocket then pulled on his overcoat. He was meeting some buddies for dinner before they headed over to one of the exclusive gentlemen's clubs. One of his friends' girlfriends was a stripper at the club. Declan was crazy mad for the stripper, and Bret and his pals thought Declan was acting the fool to jeopardize his marriage and reputation by falling in love with his plaything. That was something Bret had never done. At the end of the day, he still loved Savannah.

Bret wrapped the cashmere scarf around his neck and walked out of the Ritz Carlton Hotel into the cold night air.

CHAPTER SEVEN

A FTER FIVE SNOWY, dreary days, the sun finally peeked out from behind gray clouds. Timmy was beside himself and kept begging Savannah to help him build a snowman. The only problem with that was they could barely open the doors due to the high snow drifts.

"When can I go outside?" Timmy whined.

Ryder closed the iron grate, and the fire in the woodstove threw off a warm red glow as he looked over at the boy.

"The snow would swallow you up. I got some friends that'll be here in a day or two to dig us out."

"Brutus gets to go out." Timmy's bottom lip pushed out in a small pout.

Ryder fought the smile that tried to form on his lips. "That's different. He's gotta go outside, and I made an area in the garage for him to do his business. He's got a lot more insulation than you do. Anyway, he usually comes back in pretty quick 'cause it's so damn cold out there."

"I want to go in the garage too, like Brutus."

Before Ryder could answer, Savannah shook her head. "Timmy stop arguing with Ryder. You're being rude. It's too cold out there. I know you're antsy, honey, but he said things will be cleared soon. I wish we could go out on the front porch, but you can't even open the front door." She bent down and pulled out a cast-iron frying pan.

Ryder walked over and stood behind her, reveling in the now familiar scent that was all Savannah. He inhaled deeply then brushed against her, waiting for her body to shiver like it always did when he'd "accidentally" touch her. It was sleazy on his part, but if her body didn't react like it did, he wouldn't be doing it. The truth was, they were both damn attracted to each other—he saw it in her eyes, in the way her skin flushed, and her shallow breathing. He wanted to yank her to him and crush his mouth on her delectable lips, but he was afraid if he kissed her once, he'd never be able to let her go. Ryder was the interlude on her journey to a new life and he didn't want to mess that up. Besides, he didn't want a woman full-time in his life, but he had to admit that the blonde cutie tugged at something deep inside him. Something that he hadn't felt since Dana. *Why the fuck am I thinking about that bitch? Savannah's nothing like her.*

"Did you want something?" Savannah's soft voice pulled him from his thoughts.

"Yeah … there's a lot of things I want," he replied, his gaze locking hers. *There's that adorable pink blush coloring her face. Damn.*

She shifted in place then put the frying pan on one of the burners.

Ryder leaned over, loving the small catch of her breath when his arm brushed against the side of one of her breasts, and grabbed the handle of the pan. "I told you I was making breakfast. Go sit down and we can talk."

Savannah threw him one of her megawatt smiles—the ones that were slowly chipping away at the ice encasing his heart.

"Yes, sir." She touched her hand to her temple in a mock salute.

"Smartass," he mumbled as visions of her bent over his lap while he spanked her naked, round ass filled his head.

"Is this like the worst blizzard in Colorado history?" she asked as she slid onto one of the stools and watched him.

"Pretty much." He turned away and took out eggs, bacon, and a couple of potatoes from the refrigerator.

"Mommy, Brutus is kissing my hands."

Ryder glanced over and smiled; Brutus had really taken to the kid. "If you want to give him a treat, the dog biscuits are in the pantry." Watching Savannah pad over with Timmy at her heels touched him in ways he didn't want to think about. Ever since he'd lost everything, he'd shut himself away from the world, not wanting anyone to get close to him, especially women. His parents and siblings had finally caught on that he wasn't the same person who'd left for his last tour of duty a few years before. That man had a son who he adored, a beautiful and strong woman by his side, and a shitload of hope for the future. That man was gone, and the one who replaced him lived a solitary life caring only about meeting his basic needs. The only person he was close to was Hawk, and the last person he'd let into his life was a woman, but Savannah and her young son were wreaking all kinds of havoc on his emotions and his life. It surprised him because they'd only come into his world a short five days before.

It must be due to the snow and that we're housebound. Being in such close quarters messes with you. Ryder peeled the potatoes then grated them into a bowl. *And she's fucking hot.* He glanced over his shoulder and saw Savannah sitting on her haunches next to Brutus and Timmy. *Damn she's got a fine ass.* Timmy prattled and she laughed while running her hands over Brutus's thick fur. She was a picture of beauty and sexy femininity, and Ryder was mesmerized.

Then suddenly, as if sensing his gaze, Savannah craned her neck and looked him right in the eyes. A warm smile swept across her face, and he picked up a glint of desire in those sparkling blues. *Oh yeah, darlin'.* Timmy's chattering grew quiet in Ryder's ears, and everything around him seemed to slow down and fade. At that moment, the only thing that existed to him was her face and that smile. Ryder wasn't sure how long they held each other's gaze, but he didn't care because he was lost in it … in *her.*

"It smells funny in here." Timmy holding his nose plummeted Ryder back to reality and he looked down at the burnt bacon.

"Fuck!" He grabbed the handle of the skillet and moved it off the burner to avoid a grease fire. He switched on the overhead fan then stalked over to the garage door and opened it to try and clear the smoky haze. *I need to stop this shit and focus. It's like I'm some horny eighteen-year-old. Fuck.*

"What happened?" Timmy asked as Savannah tried to shush him.

"I burned the damn bacon." Ryder opened the fridge and took out another slab.

"Do you need any help? I can clean the frying pan," Savannah offered.

He gave her a sidelong glance. "I'm good," he snapped then felt a tinge of regret when he saw her face fall as she slinked away from him. After cutting the slices again, he placed them in another sizzling pan and refused to look or even think about the sexy woman as the rush of desire mixed with anger coursed through his body.

By the time they were ready to sit at the table, the anger had subsided inside him, but the desire was still there, always bubbling just beneath the surface, ready to boil over whenever Savannah was near.

"The breakfast is very good," Savannah said while she scooped another spoonful of hash browns onto her plate. "I figured you were a good cook since you have such a well-stocked pantry and fridge."

Ryder grunted then picked up his coffee and took a deep gulp. "You on some sort of timeline?"

"Yes and no," she replied.

"What the hell does that mean?"

Timmy giggled and Savannah threw him a stern look, and he went back to shoveling scrambled eggs into his mouth.

"It means that I'd like us to reach our destination by a certain date, but that date is somewhat flexible."

"Where you going to?"

She shrugged slightly. "Maybe northern California or Alaska."

Ryder jerked his head back. "There're a lot of miles between those states. I'm hearing that you aren't sure where the hell you're going."

Savannah stiffened in the chair and raised her chin up. "That's not true. I'm just trying to figure out where would be the best place to …" she lifted the glass of orange juice and brought it to her lips.

"Escape?" Ryder pushed his empty plate away from him.

She threw him a quick look then glanced down. "No."

"Are you sure about that?" he asked.

An awkward silence fell between them until Timmy's voice broke through it. "Can I play Super Mario Brothers?"

Ryder leaned back, not taking his eyes from Savannah. She nodded too vigorously and helped her son push back his chair. Timmy sprinted away with Brutus following behind him.

Savannah started to stand up, but he grabbed her hand, holding her in place. "You didn't answer my question."

"Maybe I don't want to," she whispered.

"I'm not stupid, Savannah. There's no way you're dragging your kid in a second-hand trailer just for the fun of it."

"I'm running away," she replied in a barely audible voice.

She suddenly seemed fragile and vulnerable, and as she looked up at him with those big eyes, an overwhelming urge to hold this woman in his arms and protect her rustled through him.

He kept his hand over hers and gently squeezed it. A small gasp fell on his ears and he scanned her flushing face.

"Do you want to tell me why?" he asked.

"I've left my husband. It's something I don't want to go into right now." She didn't pull her hand away from his.

"Okay," he answered, tilting his head. "But since you don't have an exact plan, and it's gonna take a week or two to clear the back roads, you and Timmy should stay here for a while longer." Her eyes widened at his suggestion, and he was pretty damn surprised by it as well. *Where the hell did that come from?* Ryder was a loner and hadn't wanted to get close to anyone, yet he had a strong inclination to protect her from whatever it was that had her spooked enough to run in the dead of winter. *And Timmy ... damn he reminds me of Colt—dark hair and all.*

"If you're sure it's no bother, Timmy and I would like that. Maybe we can go to the charity event where you're donating the train set. I'd love Timmy to see Santa Claus." She ran her other hand through her hair. "Christmas is going to be very different for him this year."

Ryder had expected her to balk at his suggestion, at least just a little bit, so it amazed him when she'd agreed so readily.

"Once the roads are cleared, I'd like to go into town and get some gifts for Timmy."

"I can take you, but it won't be for a few more days at least. Timmy can hang at Hawk's house. He's got a boy who's a year younger than Timmy."

"I'm not sure about that. I don't like him going to anyone's house if I don't know them. Maybe you can grab a bite to eat with him while I shop."

"You'll meet Hawk soon enough. He's cool. He's VP of the Insurgents. His old lady's a lawyer, and she comes from a rich-as-hell family here in Pinewood Springs."

Savannah's lips curved up into another one of her smiles that slayed him. "I'd like to meet them. What're the Insurgents?"

"A motorcycle club. I'm an inactive member, but I used to be an active one a lifetime ago."

"Do you still ride?" Her gaze drifted to his missing leg then back to him.

"Yeah. The ride is what keeps me going. There was no damn way I was gonna be a permanent cager. Hawk customized my bike so I could ride with this thing on." He tapped his prosthesis. "It works great. It took some getting used to, but I don't even notice the difference anymore when I'm cruising around the mountain roads."

"I know how you feel. I used to ride on the back of an old high school boyfriend's and my dad's bike. I loved the feeling of flying and the wind whipping around me. It's easy to see how people can get addicted to it." She slipped her hand out of his and pushed away from the table. "You cooked, so I'll clean up. I can make some hot chocolate if you'd like. According to Timmy, mine's the best he's ever tasted in all of his six years." She laughed, and it was music to Ryder's ears.

He hauled himself up and took his dish to the sink, and then walked into the family room and added a few more logs to the fire. He slumped on the couch and rubbed his skin; his stump was extra buzzy that day. Even though phantom pains still bothered him at times, they weren't nearly as severe as they used to be, especially that first year after the amputation. It was a weird feeling to look down and not see his leg even though it felt like it was there. In the beginning, it'd messed with his head, but after finding out that a lot of people dealt with phantom pains, he'd learned how to trick his mind from believing that the leg was still there. Most of the times it helped, but sometimes the damn stinging just wouldn't stop.

Staring at the fire, Ryder relaxed and applied pressure on his skin the way his therapist had taught him. *Savannah didn't seem disgusted about my missing leg.* When she'd confessed that she'd seen him that afternoon without his prosthesis, fear and shame ran through him all at the same time. *Fear* that she'd see him the way mainstream society often viewed the amputee—incomplete, and *shame* that she'd think he was less of a man like his ex-fiancée had. As far as he could tell, Savannah hadn't acted any differently since learning about the loss of his limb.

"Here you go. Do you want a shot of whiskey in it?" she asked him, startling him from his thoughts.

"That'd be good. The bottle's in the—"

"Third cabinet on the right." She smiled. "I know."

Ryder watched as she stood on her tiptoes and reached up high to gingerly take the bottle down from the top shelf. He sucked in a sharp breath as the hem of her top rose, revealing inch after inch of creamy skin. She closed the cupboard, pulled down her shirt, and walked back into the family room.

"How much do you want?" she asked, unscrewing the top.

"I'll pour it." He took the bottle from her. "Want some?"

"I'm not a whiskey gal." She giggled softly. "Don't give me that look—not everyone drinks Jack Daniels."

"I don't know why the fuck not." He poured a generous portion into his mug.

"I'm going to bring Timmy his cup. I'll be right back."

Ryder put the bottle down on the end table, amazed that it was still half full. Normally, he'd have gone through the three bottles of booze by now, and it surprised him that he hadn't.

"He's so engrossed in the game," she said, walking toward him.

Savannah sat on the opposite end of the couch with her fingers curled around the ceramic mug. Wisps of steam curled above it as she puckered her lips and blew softly.

Fuck … that mouth of hers.

Her body was angled toward him, but her gaze was on the crackling fire. He couldn't help but notice that the baggy shorts she wore slowly rode up her thighs. And they were beautiful thighs—soft but toned. They would be good for … well … a lot of things.

An exasperated sigh followed by fingers pulling down her shorts made him look up and capture her gaze.

"Really, Ryder?" Her tone was impatient, but a hint of desire shone in her eyes.

Holding his intense stare, his front teeth slowly bit his bottom lip. "What do you want from me? You're a beautiful woman, and I'm a man."

A pinkish flush crossed her cheeks as a small smile tugged at the corners of her mouth. "I'm very well aware that you're a man," she said before taking a sip of hot chocolate. "Anyway, I-um … I'll be leaving after Christmas. I have to make sure Timmy's enrolled in school for the next school term."

"Pinewood Springs has some excellent grade schools."

Savannah looked at him and smiled. "We can't stay here forever."

"I just meant until summer when the weather warms up and it's safer to drive." *What the hell's gotten into me? I'm sitting here practically begging her like a fucking pussy. And what am I asking her to do? I don't want a full-time family in my life. Being snowbound has me thinking like some lovesick asshole. Shit.*

"You may have a point there. I'll just have to think about everything."

"There're a lot of nice apartments or houses for rent in town." He wanted to make sure she understood that he wasn't a desperate and lonely wuss.

For a split second, a look of confusion fell across her face, then she tilted her head. "I'll keep that in mind," she said and shifted her gaze back to the spitting fire.

A comfortable silence stretched between them. Savannah leaned over and put the mug on the coffee table then leaned back against the cushion. Seeing her breasts rise as she crossed her arms behind her head ignited his desire. His gaze stayed with her every movement as she ran her fingers through her golden hair and licked her bottom lip with the tip of her tongue. He began to sweat as his excitement escalated.

Ryder adjusted his jeans as he stood up, mumbling that he needed to take a shower. The truth was that he had to get out of the room. His dick hadn't gone soft since Savannah had come back into the room, and he didn't put much trust into keeping his hands to himself. Ryder'd been fantasizing about her too damn much.

He dashed to the bathroom and started the water, then shed his clothes and put a large plastic bag over his prosthesis. Two minutes later, he stood under the warm jets, stroking his swollen cock as he imagined sinking into Savannah's hot, silky pussy. Seconds later, his balls roiled and constricted, and his lower back stiffened.

"Fuck," he murmured.

The top of his scalp prickled all the way to his toes. Pulse after pulse, threads of his release splattered on the shower tiles as he panted and leaned against the wall to keep from toppling over.

That woman is fucking killing me.

Ryder stood there until the blood finally rushed to his head, and his breathing grew steady. *Fuck, that didn't last long.* Grabbing the shower-head, he aimed it at the tiles and watched his spunk wash down the drain, wishing it were inside Savannah. *What a fucking waste.*

Later that night, Ryder escaped to his workroom and shut and locked the door. He didn't think he could handle another evening of Savannah's scent wrapping around him as they sat on the couch watching a movie. *Too close, yet too fucking far.*

He wanted his life back with his normal routine: thumbing through biker magazines, creating wooden toys, drinking until he passed out. Glancing at a worn wooden chest his father had given him years before, Ryder gritted his teeth as he stood up. If he wasn't so fucking stubborn, he'd ditch the leg and give his skin some time to heal. Even though Savannah had suggested it, he didn't want her to see him without his leg. *I know that's stupid as fuck.* But that's the way he felt.

Ryder bent down and opened the chest, then he pulled out a large cigar box and walked back to the chair. His insides twisted as he placed the box on the worktable and slowly opened it. On top of a stack of photographs was the Purple Heart awarded to him because a fucking landmine blew off his leg in Afghanistan. He ran his thumb over the gold-colored profile of President Washington, then moved it across the textured purple ribbon. *I can't believe you're gone, buddy.* Images of Jeremy's bloodied face and scattered chunks of his charred and red-stained flesh stabbed at Ryder's mind. *Why the fuck did you follow me? I told you to stay back. Fuck!*

Suddenly, gunshots erupted around him, and he felt the dust of the desert choking him as he yelled out to his best friend. More screams— explosions—chaos. His fist slammed down on the worktable, breaking one of the smiling wooden people he'd made for the train set. Gulping in deep breaths of air, Ryder tapped his arm repeatedly. "I'm in the workroom. I see my drills and saws. I see the unpainted train cars." He continued to say out loud everything that was in the room in order to ground him to the here-and-now. It was a technique he'd learned at one of the counseling sessions to combat PTSD.

After what seemed like hours, his body stopped shaking and his breathing returned to normal again. Ryder tucked the Purple Heart under a stack of letters, then he picked up a photograph of a grinning younger version of himself, holding a young boy in one arm and draping the other around a pretty dark-haired woman.

A soft knock on the door interrupted his memories.

"Are you all right?" Savannah's muffled voice drifted under the crack.

After a long pause, he rose to his feet and opened the door. Concern etched her face, and he wanted to pull her into his arms and hold her tight as if she were a life raft saving him from drowning in the memories of his past.

The photograph fluttered down from his hands and fell on the floor. Before he could move, Savannah had picked it up.

"Is this you?" she asked, pointing to the tall man in uniform.

Ryder nodded.

"Who's the young boy?"

Another long pause.

"He's my son." Icy fingers tightened around his heart, and he clenched his jaw.

"I didn't know you had a son. Is ... was this your wife?"

"No ... we were planning to get married." Not wanting to dredge up the past, Ryder snapped the photo from Savannah's hands and walked back to the table. He shut the cigar box and slammed down the top of the chest.

Savannah didn't ask any more questions, and he was grateful for that. He sat down and picked up one of the trees he'd made and stared at it.

Then her scent enveloped him, telling him she was near. Her soft hands fell on his shoulders as strands of her hair brushed the back of his neck.

"Come watch *How the Grinch Stole Christmas* with us. I'm making caramel corn."

Her touch, her laugh, and her kindness shone light into the darkest corners of his heart. He stood up and let her take his hand in her own as she led him out of the room.

CHAPTER EIGHT

S AVANNAH WRAPPED A blue twisty tie around her ponytail while she
looked out the window at the pristine snow sparkling under the
clear blue sky. Her thoughts were on Ryder, and even though she'd
wanted to ask a slew of questions about the woman and boy in the
photograph, she picked up that it wasn't the right time. There had been
so much pain, despair, and bitterness in his eyes before he turned away
from her. *I wonder what happened. Where's his son now, and why doesn't
he have contact with him?* She gently kneaded the side of her neck—
another one of her habits which drove Bret crazy. *Maybe she ran away
with the boy like I'm doing with Timmy.* Guilt assaulted her, and she
wondered if such rashness would ultimately end in Timmy resenting her
when he grew older. Bret's words—*I told you I didn't want the fucking
brat*—echoed through her head as if on autoplay. How many times had
he repeated that since Timmy was born? *No ... I made the right decision.
Bret is cruel, cold, and manipulative.* Squeezing her eyes shut, she
banished the images of the last time she'd seen him from her thoughts;
the memories of that day always loomed in the dark, shadowy corners of
her mind, threatening to crawl out and torment her.

The creak of the door was a life savior to Savannah, and she turned
around and smiled when she saw Timmy. He had a bright-red painted
firetruck in his hand, and he shuffled over to her and laid his head
against her leg. She buried her fingers in his hair and massaged his scalp
gently.

"What's going on, honey?"

"I miss Grammy and Grandpa," he said against her jeans.

She stood still and silent, her heart aching.

"When are we gonna see them?"

Inhaling sharply, she placed her fingers under his chin and tilted his head back so their gazes locked. "I'm not sure, sweetie. I know this is hard, but once we get settled, they'll come out to see us, okay?"

"Why can't they come now?"

"The roads are still blocked. How would they be able to drive here?" She held her breath then released it as the sadness slipped from her young son's face.

"Yeah. When the snow melts they can come."

"That's right." She bent down and kissed his soft cheeks. "Let's call Grammy and Grandpa. You can tell them all about the snow."

"And Brutus," Timmy added.

Savannah hugged him. "I love you," she whispered. "Where did you get that nifty firetruck?"

"Ryder gave it to me. He made it. It has lights and it makes noise. Look." Timmy dropped to his knees and turned on the toy. The headlights switched on and a siren blared from the wooden truck as it sped across the floor.

"That's awesome," she said, sitting on her haunches.

"He said he's going to build me a firehouse, too, with a pole and everything." Timmy's eyes shone with excitement.

"I can't wait to see it, honey." Savannah stood up and picked up the burner phone. "I'm going to call Grammy and Grandpa now. After we're done talking, you can go with Ryder and Brutus for a quick walk."

"Can we build a snowman later?"

"Yes, we can. After lunch, we'll get to it. Maybe Ryder will help us out."

"I think he will. He's nice."

Savannah's lips curved up as warmth rushed through her. Timmy held her soul in his heart, and her heart was forever his; she'd walk through hell and back to make sure he was safe and loved. A lump formed in her throat, and she cleared her throat several times before tapping in her parents' phone number.

"Hi, Mom. How're you and Dad?"

"I'm so happy to hear from you. We're all fine. How're you and Timmy?"

"Good."

"Let me speak to Grammy," Timmy said, tugging on her jeans.

"Timmy wants to say hi. Hang on." She passed the phone to him, then bent over and picked up the miniature firetruck, marveling at how well made it was.

After several minutes of conversation with both her mother and father, Timmy handed back the phone then left the room in search of Brutus.

"Who's this man you're staying with? Do you know anything about him?"

Savannah's stomach churned. *I'm* so *not into this right now.* Sucking in a breath through her teeth, she paused before answering. "He's helping us out. If it wasn't for him, we would've frozen to death in the blizzard."

"Not if you weren't so impetuous. Why couldn't you have reached out to your father and me before rushing into this crazy plan of yours? What if this man is a serial killer or a child molester? You don't know anything about him. You should be home with your husband. We're *very* disappointed in you."

"I'm sorry to worry all of you, but you have to trust that I know what I'm doing. And Ryder is a kind-hearted person."

"How do you know that?"

"I feel it. I'm good at reading people. *You* were the one who pushed me into marrying Bret—my instincts told me that it probably wouldn't work since so many of our core values were different."

"So now this is *my* fault? I just wanted what any mother wants for her daughter—to be taken care of by a decent man. Bret gave you a life that none of the losers you dated ever could."

Savannah heard her mother sniffling and her chest tightened. "Mom, please don't be so upset. I'm not blaming you for anything. I'm just asking you to have some faith in me. Once I get settled, I promise to tell you the *real* reason why I decided to leave Bret."

"Leaving is one thing, but turning your back on your family and taking Timmy away from his grandparents just isn't right. We never did anything but love and support you even when you gave us a hard time as a teenager."

Here it goes … "Is Dad there? I'd like to say hi to him."

"I'm just saying, you should've come home to us."

"I don't want Corrine to get her claws into Timmy. She's been sabotaging me since Bret slipped a wedding band on my finger. Timmy's her first grandchild, and she'll stop at nothing to take him away from me. I can't fight their money."

"Aren't you being a little paranoid? I just spoke to Bret a few days ago, and he's very worried about you. He misses you and Timmy."

"Just trust me," Savannah whispered. "I'd like to speak with Dad."

Without another word, she heard her mother say, "It's Savannah on the phone."

"Hi, Curly," her dad said.

Tears filled her eyes as a warm glow radiated through her. Ever since she was little, her dad always called her "Curly." Savannah figured it was because she had curly hair up until she was about four or five, then it relaxed into wavy hair. When she was a kid, it'd made her feel special to be called something unique. When she had gotten married, her dad told her that he probably should stop calling her Curly, and she'd made him promise to never stop. At that moment, it meant the world to her just to hear the familiar nickname.

"Hi, Dad. I'm so sorry about every—"

"No need for any of that. I know you had your reasons, and you'll tell us when you're ready. The important thing is you're safe, but I wish I could call you."

"Thanks for understanding, Dad. I didn't come to this decision lightly, but I had to get away. I don't want to spend another second with Bret. He's an awful man and a horrible father."

"You know him better than any of us. I wish you'd have told me or your brothers what was going on—we would've straightened him out."

Savannah laughed. "I don't doubt that."

She and her dad talked for a long time, and his reassurance, support, and love calmed her frazzled nerves. Before she hung up, her mother came back on the phone.

"We love you. Be careful and call us soon. Where are you at right now?"

"Near Pinewood Springs, in Colorado. I'll give you the number of my new phone in case you need to get a hold of me. But please, Mom, I'm begging you not to tell Bret where I am, and don't give him my phone number—I don't want to hear from him."

"Okay. Now let me get a pen and paper." Some shuffling in the background. "What's your number?"

After saying their goodbyes, Savannah stuffed the phone in her pocket as second thoughts about giving out her number pricked at her brain. *Mom means well, but I hope she doesn't give out any of my info to Bret. She just wants us to stay together, but that'll never be. It's over.*

She swiped on another coat of raspberry lip gloss and walked out of the room.

AFTER HELPING RYDER and Timmy build a kickass snowman, Savannah stood by the kitchen window waiting for the kettle to boil while she gazed at the ice man, wearing a purple-checkered scarf snug around his neck, standing vigil in front of the house. Timmy had been happy as he hunted for tree branches to make Freezy's arms in the small area Ryder had managed to clear. During the past two days, the heat from the sun had helped in melting a bit of the snow on the east side of the cabin.

A blast of chilly air swept around her legs as Timmy and Brutus rushed in.

"Brutus!" Ryder yelled. The dog's tail went between his legs as he padded back to the mud room.

Timmy froze in his tracks and stared at Savannah. "I forgot to take my boots and jacket off." He spun around and quickly followed Brutus.

"Do you want me to help you?" she asked.

"I can do it alone, Mommy."

"All right, but if you need help with your boots, let me know." Savannah grabbed a bunch of paper towels and wiped away the tracks the two had left on the floor. By the time she'd finished, Timmy, Ryder, and Brutus traipsed in. She glanced at Ryder and his gaze latched onto hers.

"Who wants hot cocoa?" she asked, looking at him.

"I don't, Mommy. I'm gonna play my game." Timmy yawned.

Breaking contact with Ryder, Savannah smiled at her son. "Building a snowman is hard work, isn't it?"

"It sure is."

Savannah laughed and watched him shuffle toward his room with Brutus following him. "Would you like some hot chocolate?" she asked him.

Shaking his head, he fixed her with an unwavering stare.

"What about some tea?"

This time, a slight shake of the head.

"I think I'll make myself a chai latte. I love the blend of spices." She opened a small cupboard and pulled out a box of chai teabags she'd brought with her from the trailer, then took out a carton of milk from the fridge. "There's something comforting about a cup of hot tea. All I need is a good book, and I'll be set." She giggled softly and glanced at him.

Ryder's tongue glided slowly across his bottom lip as the naked heat in his stare seared her. Muscles deep inside tightened as a thousand butterflies fluttered in her stomach.

The shrill whistle of the boiling teapot pierced the air. Savannah jumped and clutched at her throat as she tore her gaze away from Ryder and looked at the billowing steam above the screeching kettle. A nervous laugh escaped her lips as she removed it from the burner.

From the corner of her eye, she saw Ryder watching her as she poured hot water into the mug. "Dammit," she said as some of it spilled on the counter. Glancing up at him, Savannah froze as his eyes smoldered with lust. She put the tea kettle down, then picked up a napkin to wipe up the spill and turned toward him, her heart slamming against her ribcage. Savannah was pretty sure that Ryder could shatter her heart in pieces if she wasn't careful. She was more fragile than he knew, but he tempted her in ways she wasn't willing to admit.

"I don't bite," he said gruffly.

"It's not that," she replied, throwing the dirty napkin in the trash. "I just don't want to be hurt."

"I'm not gonna hurt you—I'd never do that."

"Famous last words of men." She hadn't meant to sound so bitter.

Ryder reached out and grabbed her arm and gently tugged her to him. "I'm not *men*, I'm me, and I'd never hurt you."

Savannah pressed her lips together as she stared at him, resisting for one long pause, her emotions tangled in a ball of confusion by this brooding and mysterious man. Then she leaned into him wanting his touch and so much more than she could articulate.

"You know we both feel it, Savannah—this fucking deep attraction between us. I've been trying to fight it, too, but it hasn't done any damn good. You're the most beautiful and genuine woman I've ever met, and the way you love your son is"—he ran his fingers through his hair—"so fucking honest and unconditional."

Savannah fixed her gaze on Ryder's brown eyes, the scowl that darkened his features, and the ever-present haunted look which kept his secrets at bay.

"I've never met such an intriguing man before," she murmured.

His grip on her tightened, and his hand burned into her skin, making her nerves snap and sizzle.

Ryder's thumb traced along her jawline and then her lower lip. "You feel the pull … the connection, don't you?" he asked, his voice was rough as sandpaper, a sexy rasp that sent tingles down her spine.

Savannah swallowed, trying to moisten her dry mouth. "Yes," she said in a breathy voice. Her knees wobbled and she gripped the counter to stop herself from keeling over. She felt like all the strain of the past few years was draining out of her.

Ryder's thumb stroked her cheek, and her insides turned to mush. Her pulse thundered in her head as she leaned in slightly and inhaled his earthy male scent and the spicy aroma of his cologne. He placed his hands on each side of her face and looked deeply into her eyes.

"I'm fucked up real bad," he said, his hot breath dancing across her cheeks.

"So am I," she whispered.

"If you know what's good for you, you'll pull away," he gritted, his gaze dark, mesmerizing, dangerous.

"Playing it safe is overrated," she replied.

A low growl escaped from his throat as he closed the gap between them and lowered his head. Her lids fluttered closed as she parted her lips, the anticipation quivering through her.

Then his mouth covered hers and it was like a million watts of electricity sparking between them. Savannah wrapped her arms around his neck and kissed him back with a ferocity she didn't know she possessed. It was a hot, fast, wild tangle of mouths. Her hands twisted in his hair, drawing him closer, needing more of that fierceness ... that passion. Goosebumps skittered over her and desire burned like fire in her veins. Images swarmed in her mind of them coming together, his wicked mouth scorching a trail down her body while his fingers pushed the right buttons inside her.

The kiss grew deeper, more frantic, as their lips fused together in raw hunger. Heat rippled off him as he ground against her, and she moaned at the intensity of that feeling.

Then he broke away and stepped back, her body immediately aching to be back in his arms. Disappointment rushed through her as she stared at him.

Savannah saw the muscles in Ryder's jaw pulse as he scrubbed the side of his face. "That shouldn't have happened." He shook his head.

"I'm sorry."

"Don't be. We—"

"I gotta do some stuff." Shoving his hands in his pockets, he sauntered out of the kitchen.

Savannah watched his retreating back, telling herself she was glad, and even relieved, that he pulled away. Yet, a long buried part of her wanted him to come back and kiss her again—to crush her against him as his strong arms held her tight, taking them further. She picked up the mug of cool tea and dumped it down the sink. *It's just as well he stopped. Taking anything further with him would be a huge mistake. I can't get involved with Ryder.* The man had a dark edge to him that scared and excited her at the same time. At this point in her life, the last thing she needed was a complication, and Ryder had "complication" stamped all over him. Even if he was sexier than sin and could kiss like no other man she'd ever met, she couldn't risk her heart—it already had too many cracks that still needed healing.

With Ryder's kiss still burning hot on her lips, Savannah filled up the teapot again and put it back on the burner. The last thing she wanted to do was obsess about what had happened and all the feelings twisting inside her, so she walked over to the pantry and rummaged through it. She found a box of lasagna noodles and several cans of San Marzano crushed tomatoes. Cooking had always been her refuge when stress threatened to shut her down. During her marriage, she'd become a gourmet cook, especially since Timmy's birth because that's the way she'd dealt with the slow disintegration of her marriage.

Making a hearty Italian dinner would occupy her mind for the next few hours, and that's exactly what she needed. She bent down and pulled out several pans and focused on creating the best meal ever.

"DAMN, WOMAN, YOUR lasagna trumped my mom's," Ryder said as he cleared off the dishes. "Do you have some Italian blood running through your veins?"

Savannah laughed, happy that Ryder had finally spoken to her. Dinner was awkward between them, but she focused on Timmy while Ryder's penetrating gaze during the meal ensured that she wouldn't forget he was there.

"I worked for a few years at a family-owned Italian restaurant in Cambridge. Luisa sort of took me under her wing. Her daughter had gotten married and moved to Oregon, and it killed both Luisa and her husband, Carlo, so I became their surrogate daughter. They were wonderful people, and I felt privileged that she shared her family's recipes with me. So you're Italian?"

"Yeah—on both sides. Last name's Rossi. Why'd you quit waitressing?"

"I got married."

"To Daddy," Timmy chimed in, and she smiled and ruffled his hair.

"That's right, sweetie."

Timmy turned back around and watched the Christmas cartoon, and Savannah followed suit. As she stared at the screen, she was acutely aware of Ryder's eyes on her. She pivoted her head slightly in his direction and caught him gazing at her chest. He quickly looked back to the TV and stretched out his good leg.

Savannah licked her lips and tried to concentrate on the show Timmy was watching. For the life of her, she had no idea what was going on and stared blankly at a slew of elves scurrying back and forth across the screen. She sneaked a peek at Ryder to make sure he wasn't looking then lowered her gaze to the big bulge pressing against his jeans. Blood rushed to her head in fear of getting caught, but she couldn't tear her eyes away. Then his hand dropped casually down on his thigh and she froze, knowing full well that when she looked up she'd meet his brown orbs. *I can't believe I let him catch me looking at his groin.* Her tongue ran across her bottom lip as she debated what to do.

"If you don't stop looking at my dick while licking your lips, there's gonna be trouble, woman," he said in a low voice.

Savannah snapped her eyes up and Ryder's gaze traveled over her body briefly before landing on her face. They stared at each other for a long while, the sexual tension crackling between them at a frantic pace. Then Ryder stood up and turned away quickly, muttering something about having to take Brutus outside. The poor dog was stretched out on the floor next to Timmy, and Ryder had to whistle at least three times before Brutus scrambled to his feet.

When he came back about ten minutes later, Brutus padded over to the same spot on the floor and laid down, and Ryder made his way to his bedroom. Savannah figured that'd be the last she'd see of him that night, and a part of her—albeit a very small part—was sorry they'd kissed earlier that day. Things were just becoming comfortable between them, and they had to ruin it by kissing. From his actions alone, Ryder had made it clear that it had been a big mistake, and *that* really stung.

After watching two hours of cartoons, two cups of hot chocolate, and several Christmas cookies, Savannah bent down and kissed her son's cheek. "Sleep well," she whispered as he yawned.

She closed the light and left the door ajar then went into her room and slipped between the sheets. In less than a second, she'd fallen into a deep sleep.

"No! No! Fuck!"

Savannah bolted up in bed—she was disoriented. It took her a few seconds to work out that she was not in the trailer but in the cabin because of the snowstorm. *Timmy!* She jumped out of bed and rushed into his room. The hallway light spilled over his bed in a rectangle, and she went over and saw his arm hugging his favorite stuffed tiger. She pulled the blanket over his shoulder and smiled. *I must've been dreaming.*

"Go back, Jeremy. Get the fuck away!"

Ryder! Savannah slipped out of Timmy's room and made her way to Ryder's as shivers tiptoed up her spine.

"No! Fuck no!"

Standing before the closed door, she swallowed then gathered the tattered edges of her courage and turned the knob. Darkness encased her and she waited until her eyes adjusted to the dimness of the room.

"I fucking shot a kid! Get back, Jeremy. I got this!"

Ryder's anguished-filled voice bounced off the walls, and she slowly approached the bed. "Ryder? It's me Savannah."

"I'm hit. Goddammit! Jeremy, go back! There're fucking landmines everywhere. Don't follow me!"

He was in the war. That's how he lost his leg. Oh, Ryder. Savannah climbed up on the bed and breathed in and out several times before she reached out and gently shook him.

"It's okay, Ryder. You're okay," she said in a calm, reassuring voice.

He groaned and cursed while tossing and turning, but she kept a steady hand on his shoulder and shook him several times. It seemed to have helped because he stopped yelling.

"Where are you?" he grunted.

"I'm here." She came closer and ran her hand over his sweat-soaked face. "You're okay."

"Where's Jeremy? Is he in the Medevac? Where the hell is he?" His voice began to rise again.

"You're in Colorado, Ryder."

"I'm in the fucking Chinook. Why won't you tell me where the fuck Jeremy is?"

Again she gently shook him, then leaned over and grabbed some tissues from the box on the nightstand, and mopped his face. "It's okay."

"Am I in a war?" he gritted.

"No, you're safe in your cabin. Brutus is sleeping on the floor, and I'm Savannah. Everything is just fine. We're all safe." She cuddled his head on her lap and rocked slowly like she did when Timmy had a bad dream—it always calmed him.

"Fuck," he said in a low voice.

"It's all okay."

"I'm in Pinewood Springs."

"Yes, you're home and you're safe, and nothing can hurt you."

Silence engulfed them as Savannah ran her fingers through his damp hair, still cradling his head in her lap. Seconds turned to minutes before he gripped her hand and tucked it under his chin. His heavy breathing told her he'd fallen asleep.

Slipping her legs under the sheets, she held on to him. There was no way she was going to let go. Ryder was a lonely and broken man, and she was an angry and scared woman. For a split, second she wondered if fate had brought them together to heal one another.

Maybe there's something to Christmas wishes.

Ryder's arm flung over her thighs as he let out a sputtering sigh. Savannah smiled and leaned against the headboard as his breathing quietly lulled her to sleep.

CHAPTER NINE

B RUTUS'S COLD NOSE pressed against Ryder's face, and he groaned as he cracked open his eyes. The dog's soft whine prompted Ryder to throw off the covers and push up. His good leg bumped into something warm and soft, and when he looked over his shoulder, his eyes widened as his body went stiff.

"What the fuck?" he said under his breath as he stared at Savannah sleeping peacefully beside him. He sat up, closed his eyes for a minute and then slowly opened them, expecting Savannah to be gone, but she wasn't. The sheet draped around her tempting curves, and the way her sweet lips parted enticed him to slip his tongue inside for a taste.

Shaking his head, he tried to figure out how the hell Savannah had landed in his bed. There was no way he wouldn't have remembered fucking her. The kiss they'd shared was still etched on his lips, so he was pretty sure slamming his cock inside her while he played with her tits wouldn't be something he'd forget.

Several whimpers from Brutus focused Ryder. He grabbed his crutches and hauled himself up, then he left the room.

A blast of cold air gushed in when he opened the door to let Brutus out. After closing it quickly, he crutched into the kitchen and leaned forward against the granite counter. The sun's rays bouncing off the snow made him squint as visions of Savannah swirled in his head: her arms wrapped around him as they kissed, the sliver of skin when she raised her arms, the way her shorts rode up and showed off her thighs, and her soft lips alternately sweet and wicked on his. His dick twitched against his boxers and he cursed softly. *If I can't remember fucking her, then I might as well pack it in. We must've done something 'cause there's no way she would've come into my room for nothing. I can't remember shit when I take those damn pain meds. Fuck!*

For the past week, Ryder had been jerking off to various scenarios that starred Savannah and him fucking in a variety of ways, and to think it might have happened without him remembering was a cruel kick in his balls.

As he shut his eyes against the sun's glare, blurred memories from the previous night started to come into focus: his unit in Afghanistan engaging in combat against militants, driving the sonsofbitches farther back in the province … the firing ceasing … he and several men cautiously moving in to clear the cluster of old Afghani houses … Jeremy following.

"Fuck!" Ryder hit the side of his head with the heel of his palm. Recollections of Savannah's soft, comforting words pulling him out of the war filled his mind. *She must've heard me screaming. That's why she came to my bed. Dammit!* He'd been trying so fucking hard to control the demons that lurked inside him, never wanting her to see the times they clawed their way out. Since Savannah and Timmy had come to stay with him, Ryder had been so careful to thwart any triggers that would threaten to expose how fucked up he was, but he'd failed. *I probably scared the shit outta her.* Then he remembered her soft hands on his face and the way she held him until he fell asleep.

Brutus barked at the back door, and Ryder hopped over to let him in. He grabbed the towel off the hook, then sank down on the bench and dried the dog off before heading back to the kitchen to fill Brutus's bowl with dried food. The room echoed with the dog's teeth crunching noisily as dread wove around his ragged nerves. *What if she pities me after last night's fucking display?* The one thing he hated was pity, and if he saw that look in Savannah's eyes, it would crush him for sure. *Why the hell did I have to lose it last night?*

The landline rang, stopping his thoughts as he hopped over to the wall and picked up the receiver.

"Hey, dude. Rags and me are gonna come by and dig you out,"

Throttle said.

"It's about fucking time," Ryder replied, plopping down on the chair.

Throttle laughed. "Did you run outta whiskey?"

"Believe it or not, I didn't."

"What the fuck, bro?"

"Been busy with stuff. What time are you guys coming by?"

"In an hour or so. We'll use two of our big-ass snowplows, so you should be able to take your four-wheeler out after we're done. Hawk and Animal are gonna come by and help out with the shoveling. Should we bring some Jack?"

"Yeah. I only have moonshine whiskey."

"Tom's?"

"Yep. It's all right in a pinch, but I miss the good stuff. I'll feed you fuckers. Chili okay?"

"Hell, yeah. Besides Jax's old lady, you make the best fuckin' chili."

"I heard Cherri's is kickass. I'll have to try it sometime," Ryder said.

"You gotta get in on poker nights when Jax hosts. That's when she makes it, and she always serves it with homemade cornbread. Fuck, it's good," Throttle replied.

Ryder heard a woman talking in the background, and he shook his head. It was still surreal for him to picture Throttle with an old lady. The man was a confirmed bachelor and loved the perks of hooking up with his choice of the many wild women who were so much a part of the outlaw biker lifestyle. If he'd taken bets on which of the Insurgents' brothers would never be tied down to one woman, Hawk and Throttle would've come to mind right off the bat, and Ryder would've lost the bet big time. His two brothers were both married, and Hawk even had a couple of kids. All at once, loneliness and a deep longing for something he couldn't articulate seized him, and he sputtered and coughed from the intensity of it.

"You okay?" Concern laced Throttle's voice.

"Yeah. Just swallowed funny. Is that your old lady talking to you?"

Throttle chuckled. "Yep. Kimber has a habit of talking to me when I'm on the fuckin' phone. Let me hang up and see what she wants. I'll see you in a bit, bro."

Ryder held the receiver in his hand for several minutes before placing it back in its cradle. For the last few years he'd relished his solitude, but since Savannah and her son had entered his life, feelings and thoughts he hadn't had for a very long time started poking at him, and he didn't like it. Having them around dredged up bad memories he'd long since quashed, or so he thought.

Brutus barked and Ryder jerked his head up to glance in the direction at which the dog was looking. Timmy's pajama-clad body hugged the doorway, and his messy mop of dark hair and sprinkle of freckles across his nose and cheeks reminded Ryder of Colt when he'd been about Timmy's age. Ryder's heart squeezed in his chest as he pushed himself up. "Where's your leg?" Timmy asked in a low voice, his eyes bulging.

"Lost it." Ryder went over to the island and reclined against it.

"Can't you find it?"

Ryder chuckled. "Nope. It's gone. The doc cut it off."

"Did it hurt?"

"Sure did, but not so much anymore."

"Oh." He scrunched up his face while staring at Ryder. "Did the doctor cut it last night?"

Ryder's face crinkled in laughter. "Nope. It happened several years ago. I have a fake leg."

"You do?"

"I'll show it to you sometime." Ryder was ready to ask Timmy if he wanted to come to his room to see, but then he remembered that Savannah was in his bed. "You hungry?"

"Uh-huh."

Ryder handed a banana to the boy. "Eat this for now, and I'll be back in a bit. Do you like pancakes?"

"They're my favorite. Mommy always makes a smiley face on them."

Damn, this kid is killing me. "I don't do that, but you're gonna like them anyway." He looked at Brutus. "Stay with Timmy, boy."

When Ryder entered the bedroom, Savannah wasn't there. He glanced at the open bathroom door and wondered if he'd imagined that she'd been in his bed. It wouldn't surprise him if he did since she's been on his mind so damn fucking much for the past week. He sighed and locked the bedroom door, not wanting her to see him without his leg. He sat at the edge of the bed and massaged lotion on his skin. A limb, especially an above-knee cut, took time to shape back into the fit of the prosthetic.

After almost an hour, Ryder was dressed and ready to make Timmy a stack of his killer pancakes. He snapped his fingers then remembered that Brutus was with the boy. Shaking his head, Ryder chuckled; the German shepherd had really taken a liking to the boy.

The scent of dark-roasted coffee beans wafted around him as he made his way to the kitchen. When he entered the room, Ryder found Timmy sitting at the table coloring a picture, and Savannah washing dishes by the sink. He sucked in a sharp breath and ambled over to the pantry.

"Morning," he said gruffly without even a sideways glance at her. He couldn't bear it if she had "the look" on her face: sad smile, eyes filled with pain, and sympathetic creases across the forehead.

"Good morning," she replied cheerfully. "I just made a pot of coffee. Would you like a cup?"

"Yeah." He scanned the shelves looking for the baking powder and flour.

"Black, right?"

"Yeah." He grabbed several items.

"Timmy tells me you're making pancakes. He loves them." A small laugh floated in the air. "I have to admit, I do too."

She's trying so fucking hard to be perky. He slammed the ingredients he needed on the counter. "I'm not much for small talk."

A soft hiss of breath. "Oh ... I'm sorry," she said.

For the next half hour, Ryder flipped flapjacks while Timmy watched in fascination and Savannah read the cereal box on the table for the tenth time.

The only one chatting and laughing during breakfast was Timmy, and he seemed unaware of the strained tension between Ryder and Savannah.

"I ate too much," Timmy said, putting his hands on his belly.

"Means you liked it," Ryder said, as he stood up.

"I'll wash the dishes since you made breakfast." Savannah started to collect the plates.

"Sit down. I'll do it. I got friends coming by to dig us out."

"That's good, but what does that have to do with me helping with the cleanup?" Savannah gathered the dishes and brought them over to the sink.

"I told you to sit the fuck down, woman." He looked at her and met her glare. It was the first time since he'd walked into the kitchen that he looked directly at her. He grunted and turned away.

"Can I leave the table, Mommy?"

"Yes, sweetie. Do you want to play Chutes and Ladders?"

"No. Maybe Qwirkle. Do you wanna play with us, Ryder? It's really fun."

He looked over his shoulder. "Another time. I gotta make some chow for my friends."

"Why don't you get the game out, and you and I can play it in your room?" Savannah said.

"Can we play here?"

"I think Ryder wants to be alone. We can set the board up on the floor in your room."

Savannah's soft and understanding voice grated on his nerves like sandpaper. "I don't give a fuck if you want to play here," he said through gritted teeth.

"Timmy set the game up in your room, and I'll be there in a few minutes."

Ryder heard the chair scrape against the floor then the soft thud of retreating footsteps. He opened the dishwasher and put the breakfast plates in.

"It's okay to be mad at me, but don't take it out on Timmy. I also don't appreciate you using bad language around him."

Ryder froze—the utensils in his hand—as licks of fury blazed through him. Pushing down his ire, he turned around to face her. Savannah glared at him, her cheeks flushing.

"Why're you so mad at me? Is it because of the kiss?"

Staring at her clenched fists, Ryder drew in a deep breath which didn't abate his anger one bit but gave the illusion of calm. "No—I've forgotten all about it." He felt some sort of perverse pleasure when she flinched.

"Then what's your problem?"

"I don't like being told what the fuck I can say in my own goddamn house." He watched her swallow, watched that beautiful mouth strain as she tried to form the words. Ryder didn't want to remember the feel of her in his arms or her soft lips on his. He scratched his unshaven face and huffed; he hated wanting her.

"Once your friends clear the area, Timmy and I will go to a hotel in town. I'm sorry we've been such an intrusion into your life," she said.

Bitter regret rushed through him, and he was furious with himself, with Savannah, *with everyone.* He watched her walk away but stood rooted to the floor as pride mixed with anger stopped him from calling out to her. Long after she'd left, he stayed there staring until something inside him twisted like barbwire.

The loud roar of snow plows cut through the crushing silence, and Ryder realized that he hadn't even started making the chili yet. As he chopped onions, garlic, and hot peppers, he realized that he was pissed at Savannah because she'd witnessed his PTSD episode the night before. Shame flooded through him at the thought of her seeing him at one of his most vulnerable moments. He hated the fact that he was helpless at times ... that he was weak. Her damn cheeriness that morning, pretending that he wasn't a fucking mess of a man the night before infuriated him. Anger was the fire; vulnerability was the fuel.

"Fuck it!" He threw the knife across the cutting board. "If she wants to go, that's fine. I don't need any woman feeling sorry for me." Then Dana's face popped into his head, and he staggered over to the kitchen table and crumpled onto the chair. Beads of sweat trickled down his forehead as memories flooded his mind. Ryder forced out painful thoughts and focused on the conversation he'd had with Dana while recovering at the hospital after the surgery.

"I'm not coming," Dana said sternly.

"This is the second time you've canceled. I need to see you, baby. I fucking miss you."

A too-long pause; uneasiness began to claw at him.

"What's going on?" Ryder held his breath.

"I can't handle this."

"This?"

"The loss of your leg. Thinking of you like that turns my stomach. I can't do it."

Her words were arrows to his heart.

Ryder cleared his throat. "I'm the same person. I need you to help me get through this. I need you and Colt."

"I'm sorry, but deformities … amputations, all that kind of stuff has always creeped me out. I know it makes me sound like a horrible person, but I can't help it. You have your family to get you through this."

"It's not the fucking same. You and I are going to be married for fuck's sake." His mouth felt like the Sahara Desert; he reached over and grabbed the glass and took a deep drink of water. "I need to see and hold Colt."

"I can't marry you. I'm sorry … I really am."

"Fuck you! You don't have to see me, but you're not going to deny me my son. I'll send two tickets. Your ass will come to the hospital, and the nurse will bring him in to see me."

Another pause.

"Okay. Send the tickets, but I won't change my mind about visiting you. It's over. Again … I'm sorry."

"You never fucking came," Ryder said out loud. "You took my son and left. I never got to say goodbye to him."

Brutus erupted in a barking fit when a loud bang on the window dragged Ryder from the past. He looked over and saw Hawk's grinning face. Ryder lifted his chin at him. *I gotta get a fucking grip on things. I'm blaming Savannah for Dana hurting me.* But truthfully, he was scared to death that Savannah now saw him as less of a man just like Dana had. *Dammit to hell!*

"Open the fuckin' door. It's cold as shit out here," Hawk said.

Brutus ran to the door barking as Ryder rose to his feet. "Brutus, calm the fuck down!" he yelled, turning the doorknob.

"How're you doing, buddy?" Hawk stomped his feet then shrugged off his jacket and gloves before kicking off his boots. Animal, one step behind Hawk, followed suit.

"Not bad. Thanks for helping out," Ryder replied.

"No worries." Hawk smacked him on the back. "Throttle said you're making chili. Why the fuck don't I smell anything?"

"Yeah," Animal added. "I was thinking about it as I shoveled."

"Just starting it now. Have a seat in the family room, and I'll join you guys in a bit."

Hawk and Animal put four bottles of Jack on the counter. "We need three glasses, bro," Animal said.

Hawk went over to the cupboard and took them down. "Throttle and Rags should be done in a few." He handed the tumbler to Ryder, and the three men clinked glasses together before throwing back the shot.

"Fuck, that's good," Ryder said, pouring more of the amber liquid in their glasses. "Jack's one of my best friends." The men laughed.

"I'm pretty sure we can all say that." Animal raised his arm. "Here's to Jack."

Taking two of the whiskey bottles with them, the two Insurgents sauntered into the family room and sank down on the couch while Ryder hurriedly browned the meat, spices, and onion mixture.

An hour later, a pungent, smoky aroma wafted through the air as the men sat in front of the fire, popping nuts and pretzels in their mouths and talking about motorcycles as the chili simmered on the stove.

"Do you have any bottled water, bro?" Animal asked, standing up.

"In the fridge," Ryder replied. Having his brothers around him was the best medicine for busting up his earlier self-pity party. *I couldn't have been any more pathetic.*

"Bring me one," Throttle said.

"Me too," Rags added.

Animal grumbled something under his breath, and the guys chortled.

"How's your dad doing?" Ryder asked as Animal handed him the water bottle.

"He's got his good and bad days. I ran by there earlier today, and he seemed in good spirits, but he's also good at faking it." Animal unscrewed the bottle and took a big gulp.

"Tell him I said hi." Ryder stared at the fire and a comfortable silence fell over the group. Animal's dad had it way worse than Ryder did—two of his legs had gotten blown to smithereens in Iraq.

"Who the hell's that?" Rags muttered.

Ryder looked up and saw his brothers staring over his shoulder. He craned his neck and his gaze fell on Savannah. She'd changed into a long-sleeved T-shirt and a pair of snug blue jeans. Her golden hair fell loosely over her shoulders in waves, and he wanted to reach out and bury his fingers in its silkiness.

"Hey, are you okay?" he asked, his voice a nearly silent rasp.

Savannah turned her head and looked at him. His breath caught in his throat when he saw her face; her eyes were a little puffy and red, and he could tell she'd been crying. At that moment, he loathed himself for doing that to her.

"I didn't mean to interrupt," she said softly. Their gazes locked for a few seconds, then she looked away.

Ryder pivoted in his seat to look right at her. "You're not." He pointed at Hawk. "This is Hawk." Then he introduced the others, ending with, "and this is Savannah."

The men's eyes darted from Savannah to Ryder then back to Savannah.

"It's good meeting a … friend of Ryder's," Hawk said, the corners of his mouth twitching.

"Yeah. We don't get to meet many of his wo—I mean friends." Rags grinned.

"Did you get my juice, Mommy?" Timmy said, stopping behind Savannah and peeking out at the bikers behind his mother's shapely legs.

"Who do we have here?" Hawk asked.

Timmy hid behind his mother.

"You gonna come over here and give us five?" Throttle asked.

"What's that?" Timmy whispered.

Hawk held out his hand. "Go ahead and hit it with yours."

"These are my friends," Ryder said. "It's cool."

Timmy shuffled slowly over and tapped his hand against Hawk's palm then he stepped back, his eyes wide.

"That a boy. How old are you?" Hawk leaned back against the chair's cushion.

"Six."

"My boy's five and our president's son is six. Maybe you can all play together sometime," Hawk said.

Timmy looked up at his mother. "Can I, Mommy?"

"We'll see. Let's go in the kitchen to get you some juice. I'm sure Ryder and his friends are busy visiting." She gripped his hand. "It was nice meeting you," she said before disappearing to the other room.

"I better check on the chili," Ryder said, standing up.

"Yeah, you do that." Animal guffawed, and the other men joined in.

"Fuck you," Ryder gritted as he made his way to the kitchen.

When he entered, he saw Savannah pouring a glass of apple juice in a mug while Timmy sat on one of the stools. Ryder went over to the stove and lifted up the lid, then he stirred the contents in the pot. He added more chili powder and a few dashes of cayenne pepper.

"Is that going to be our lunch?" Timmy asked.

Ryder glanced at the wall clock. "It's looking like it's gonna be more like your dinner." He chuckled and Timmy giggled.

"Here you go," Savannah said, going around to the other side of the island as if to avoid getting close to Ryder. She placed the mug down on the counter. "Do you want to bring it to your room?"

Timmy wiped his mouth with the back of his hand and shook his head.

"Then hurry up."

"There's no need to rush. You and the boy can stay in here if you want."

"I wouldn't dream of intruding." Savannah picked at her nail.

He walked over to her. "You're not. Don't mind the shit I said earlier—I didn't mean it."

She looked up at him with those eyes—so soft and blue, and he wanted to yank her to him and kiss her deeply, but he just stared back. A strand of hair fell across her cheek, and he reached out and brushed it away, his fingertips touching her delicate skin. He pulled away quickly, amazed at his self-control.

"We can go into town tomorrow. I know you want to get some things."

"Okay," she whispered.

Ryder turned to leave, but he stopped and held her gaze. "Are we all right now?"

"I don't know." Savannah blinked. "I did something to make you mad," she continued, her eyebrows squishing together, "but I don't know what it was. I wish you would just talk to me."

"It's me. I was having a bad day."

"Then talk to me."

He paused for a moment then clenched his jaw and squared his shoulders. "I'll let you know when dinner's ready." He ignored her exasperated sigh and walked out of the kitchen.

When Savannah and Timmy retreated back to the boy's room, Animal shook his head. "Now I get why you haven't been coming around for some pussy at the club."

The other bikers cajoled, and Throttle and Rags poked Ryder in the ribs.

"How long has this been going on?" Hawk asked.

"Nothing's going on. Get your fucking heads out of the damn gutter. I'm just helping her and her son."

"I bet you are," Animal said, and the men busted out.

"They were stranded on my property. She's driving this shit trailer, and they got caught in the snow storm. I didn't want to have to deal with two dead bodies on my property, so I invited them to stay until the blizzard passed. That's all there is to it."

"Bullshit." Hawk's deep blue eyes sparkled.

"We're just roommates." Ryder scowled.

"Fuckin' bullshit," Rags added.

"I never had a roommate like that," Animal said which made the men laugh.

"Brandi keeps asking 'bout you whenever she sees me. I told her you were trapped alone in the cabin, so she's ready to come by and do a fuckin' house call." Hawk shook his head. "Damn, bro. These past several days, I was fuckin' feeling sorry for you 'cause you weren't getting any." He poured whiskey in all the glasses. "You sly sonofabitch." He threw back his drink.

The men continued to rib Ryder while trying to dig for more information about Savannah, but he just sat there shaking his head and kept telling them he saw her just as a friend. He knew they didn't believe that bullshit for one second, and he didn't either, but he didn't want to talk about her to his friends.

For the rest of the night, Savannah and Timmy stayed away, but she was very much present in Ryder's mind. As the men ate, drank, and talked, he relived their kiss over and over: the softness of her skin, the curve of her ass cupped in his hands, and their tongues twisting and probing each other's mouths as her body pressed against his. Savannah drove him wild with animal lust between the taste of her sweet mouth and her soft moans, to the way she smelled so damn good. He was stiffening even now, just remembering it.

"Great dinner, dude." Throttle stood up and stretched his arms over his head. "I gotta get going. Do you wanna meet up with us at Ruthie's tomorrow for lunch?"

"Uh … I'm not sure," Ryder said, trying to focus on what Throttle was saying.

"He's got his mind on that hot blonde." Animal laughed.

Ryder glared. "I've got some things I gotta get done tomorrow. I'll let you know if I can join you. What time will you be there?"

"About one. Show up if you can. I'm beat."

Rags nodded. "Me too. Great chili, dude." He bumped fists with Ryder.

"Why don't you bring Savannah by our house so she can meet Cara? I think it'd be good for her son to play with Braxton. I can have Banger bring Harley by," Hawk said as he slipped on his jacket.

"That's a good idea. I know she wants to buy some Christmas presents for Timmy, so if he's occupied, it'll make it easier for her," Ryder replied.

"You're giving a shit about Christmas?" Throttle said.

"Haven't you been a fuckin' Scrooge about it for years?" Animal asked, slipping on his gloves.

"I'm talking about her and the boy, not me," Ryder growled.

"Gotcha." Animal smirked.

"So they'll be here for the charity event?" Hawk asked.

"Yeah. Probably through the new year." Ryder opened the door and hoped the frigid air blowing in would put an end to the conversation.

"Looks like Ruthie's isn't gonna happen for you, seeing that you're taking your *roommate* and her son to Hawk's tomorrow." Throttle wrapped his scarf around his neck.

"Another time." Ryder looked over at Hawk. "I'm gonna try and make the meeting at the VA next Tuesday. You gonna be there?"

"Yep." Hawk clasped his shoulder. "See you tomorrow around noon, okay?"

"Sure."

Ryder watched the men trudge down the walkway until they disappeared into the cold night. He shut the door and waited for Brutus to come back from doing his business, and he wondered what Savannah was doing right at that moment. The hour was late, so he figured Timmy had already gone to bed, and a strong urge to go to her room seized him.

Brutus barked and Ryder opened the door then locked it. He put out the fire in the fireplace and ambled down the hallway, pausing in front of Savannah's closed door for a few seconds. He quirked his lips then slowly walked to his room.

CHAPTER TEN

IT WAS JUST after eight when Bret fished out his cell phone from the pocket of his Armani terrycloth robe and thumbed through his contacts for Harry's number. A cup of tea steamed on the table alongside his chair, and he reached over and grabbed it. Bret took a sip and stared out the window over the roofs and lights of Beacon Hill. Across the street from his penthouse, a small park lay shrouded in darkness on the moonless night.

A low buzz on his phone cut him off before he'd been able to press the call button. He looked at the screen, and a thin smile pulled at his lips as he set the tea down then answered it.

"Hey, Boss. I see you called me earlier. I was working on another job, so I was sorta indisposed," Harry said.

"The bitch is in some fucking hick town in Colorado," Bret replied.

"How'd you find that out?"

"Her mother told me. She wants her and the brat home for Christmas."

Harry's deep chuckle rumbled through the phone. "And she thinks you're going to play romantic and bring her home for a damn Hallmark holiday."

Bret brushed off a piece of lint from his navy blue robe. "Yes ... something like that."

"Which town?"

Bret walked over to the computer monitor and squinted. "Pinewood Springs. It looks like it's not too far from Aspen. I might be able to salvage this fucking trip after all."

"Did you get the name of the hotel?"

A frown creased his forehead, and he narrowed his eyes. "Apparently some guy is helping her and Timmy out. From what Mary told me, they're staying with him. It seems like they got caught in that blizzard that was on the news."

"How'd she get there? I've checked all buses, trains, planes, and rental agencies," Harry said.

"It sounds like she used *my* money to buy a second hand ... *RV.*" His nose wrinkled in disgust. *"You can't make a silk bag out of a pig's ear."* Since he'd married Savannah, his mother had said that often enough to him. He slinked down into the cushy chair by the window and crossed his legs. *You were so fucking right, Mother.*

"How do you want me to handle this? I can bring them both back," Harry said.

"I'll have to go with you. I need to talk with her and clear up some things." Bret leaned back and closed his eyes. *This is a major pain in my ass. I have parties to go to and a few sweeties to fuck.* "I've got some obligations. Why don't you head over there and get a feel of what the situation is. I'll join you in a week or so."

"Sure thing, Boss. I just gotta wrap up this case, but I should be ready to go in a couple of days. Will that work?"

"It will. This is between you and me. There's no need to tell my father or mother that we know where they are."

"I understand. I'll touch base with you in a couple of days."

Bret put the phone back into his pocket and stretched out his legs. Harry's dad had been on the Carlton family's payroll for as long as Bret could remember. When the old man had keeled over while banging one of the strippers from Dirty Dan's, Harry had stepped in and taken over the business. Bret used him often—mainly to dig up dirt on competitors, board members, and anyone else who could become troublesome.

His phone pinged and he dug it out again and opened the text. He licked his lips several times as he stared at Denise's fingers inside her shaved pussy. His newest toy was turning out to be quite the adventurous vixen.

Denise: Wanna play, Daddy?

"Fuck, yeah," he muttered under his breath.

Bret: What do u have in mind?
Denise: Besides riding ur face & sucking u dry ... a lot of things.
Bret: If u fuck me good, I'll take u to Aspen with me.
Denise: Ohhh, Daddy!

He laughed. There was definitely something to be said about young college students who didn't have any money—it didn't take much to excite them.

Bret: I'll send a car to pick u up. Wear lingerie & put ur butt plug in.
Denise: The one with the shiny pink jewel?
Bret: Yeah. I like u in pink.
Denise: I've got a pretty pink pussy.

He chuckled.

Bret: Just the way I like it. Put ur plug in now. I want you nice and stretched.
Denise: OK, Daddy. I better go.

Bret tapped in the number for the Ritz Carlton and reserved the suite. Next, he contacted Emerson, his right-hand man, informing him that something had come up and he'd be late, and to push the following day's meeting from the morning to the afternoon. As Bret passed the dresser, his gaze landed on their marriage portrait. He stopped and picked it up. "We were so happy back then," he said in a low voice, his thumb grazing the side of Savannah's face. "We had a good thing going, so why'd you have to fuck us up? Wasn't I enough for you?" As far as Bret was concerned, the day Savannah had announced she was pregnant was the end of their marriage, so all bets were off. He was faithful for the two years they'd dated and, for the most part, during the six years they were married before she fucked everything up. "I loved you more than any woman I've ever known, but you blew it, baby. *You* broke up this marriage, not me."

For several minutes, he stared at Savannah's shining blue eyes, her bright smile, and her feminine curves, and then he placed the framed photograph face down on the dresser and made his way to the bathroom to get ready for a night with his twenty-year-old plaything.

CHAPTER ELEVEN

S AVANNAH PULLED INTO the garage, slid out of Ryder's Jeep, and walked around back to take out the bags from her shopping spree. She'd dropped Timmy over at Cara and Hawk's house earlier that morning and had a quick cup of coffee with Cara. At first, Savannah was uneasy about the idea of leaving Timmy at the house of the vice president of an outlaw motorcycle club. When she'd met Hawk at Ryder's cabin, the dark-haired man had intimidated the hell out of her, but Ryder assured her that his bark was worse than his bite when it came to his brothers and the people in their lives. But when Ryder took her and Timmy over to meet Cara and their son, Savannah took an instant liking to the friendly woman. They ended up talking for a few hours while Ryder and Hawk went over to the Insurgents' clubhouse. Timmy and Braxton got along fine, and their daughter, Isa, seemed to have taken a real shine to Savannah, which touched her and stirred up buried longings to have another child. At thirty-six and separated, she knew time was ticking away, but she didn't want to think that all hope was lost.

Savannah pushed open the door with her shoulder and set the packages down on the bench. She kicked off her boots and hung up her jacket then scooped up the bags and headed into the kitchen.

From the doorway, she saw Ryder sitting on the couch, his good leg propped up on the coffee table, and Brutus's head resting on his lap. The dog barked but didn't raise his head, then Ryder craned his neck, and those intense eyes that made her shiver bored into her.

"Must've been a helluva shopping trip," he said, his gaze still on her.

Savannah came into the room and dropped the bags on one of the overstuffed chairs. "It was." She smiled and sat down on the other end of the couch.

Since that night when she'd come into his room during his nightmare, Ryder had kept his distance. At first, Savannah had been hurt and disappointed, but as the days rolled by and she had time to get to know him better, she realized that he was embarrassed that she'd seen him like that. Silly, of course, but it made sense since Ryder had a real tough, independent edge to him. The guy was a biker, for Christ's sake, and for several years he'd been an active member of an outlaw club, which sort of scared the crap out of her when she really thought about it. The guys who came around were all members, and they looked like they wouldn't hesitate to cut a person's throat if they crossed them. But what blew her away was how they looked out for Ryder and each other. They came over often, brought groceries, and one of them called every day to make sure he was doing all right. She could feel the love, mutual trust, and camaraderie they all shared; she'd never seen such a bond or connection like that between a group of unrelated people.

"What did you get Timmy?" Ryder brought a mug to his lips.

"A couple of games he's been wanting for his Nintendo, some books, puzzles, and a whole bunch of other things." Savannah tilted her head. "I know, it's too much, but I feel terrible that he won't be home for Christmas. He misses my parents a lot."

Ryder pivoted toward her. "Does he miss his dad?"

"I'm sure he does, but he hasn't talked about him so much." She kneaded her shoulder. "My husband wasn't into having a kid."

For a few seconds, Ryder just sat there piercing her with his gaze. "I kinda gathered that. So is the dude your husband or ex?"

Savannah folded her hands in her lap. "Soon-to-be ex."

"So, you're divorcing him?"

"I want to. I spoke to a lawyer before I'd left Boston. I was planning to file the paperwork, but then he … let's just say things changed, and I had to get away sooner than I planned."

Ryder quirked his lips. "Do you wanna talk about what changed?"

It was a shameful secret lodged in her throat, ready to choke her every time she contemplated telling it. "Not really."

"When you do, I'm here. I'm a damn good listener."

A small smile fell across her lips. *And a damn good kisser. That's what came to your mind, Savannah? Really?* The truth was that she couldn't get their kiss out of her mind, and she was hoping he'd want to kiss her again. The way she'd been subtly flirting with him and patting his hands and shoulders, Savannah thought she was giving off signals that she wouldn't rebuke him, but he hadn't made a move. *He's probably not really interested, but he does look at me. A lot. Maybe he thinks "why bother" considering Timmy and I will be leaving after Christmas, and he's right. What would be the point in starting anything?*

"You look like you got something important on your mind. Care to share it?"

His deep voice took her out of her musings, and she tossed her hair over her shoulders. "I want to go to the tree-lighting ceremony. Cara told me about it when I dropped Timmy off at her house. She said it's a community thing, and the tree is lit in some square."

"They've been doing that since I can remember. The town council gets this big-ass tree and decorates it, then they have somewhat of a festival when the tree's lit. Main Square is where they do that."

"Do you still go?"

A crease lined his forehead, and his brows knitted. "No. Haven't done that shit in a long time."

"Why not?"

"I'm not into it—or any of the holiday cheer bullshit rammed down our fucking throats every December."

Savannah jerked her head back. "I guess you don't have the spirit of Christmas."

"No, I don't. It's just about spending money, putting on fake smiles, and pretending to like each other even though most are bitches and bastards the rest of the year. It's all bullshit." Ryder waved his hand toward the packages on the chair. "Look at all the money you spent.

Why the fuck can't people buy presents and show they care during the year, and not just reserve it for one damn day?"

"I can see your point about the commercialism, but it's nice to have a few weeks out of the year to really focus on our loved ones and those who aren't as fortunate."

"And forget the poor bastards the rest of the year?"

"Of course not. I guess it's good for people who need to be reminded to open up their hearts a little. For those who do it all year, it really doesn't matter if it's Christmas or the tenth of August, right? For me, it's about the family and the traditions. Traditions connect us to our loved ones who have passed away, and help to keep them alive for generations through honoring some of their traditions while adding our own for the future. Community events, like lighting the tree, brings people together for a night filled with fun and good feelings. We need that, especially in a world that is wrought with so much violence and sadness and loneliness. I don't know. When I think of Christmas, I think of family, favorite dishes to prepare, making cookies with Timmy, going to church, and taking a temporary break from all the ugliness in life."

"Good for you. To me, it's just another day of the year." He turned away.

"Didn't you like it as a kid?"

"I was a fucking kid, but then you grow up and see that life is full of shit."

"So, you always stay alone on the holiday?"

"Sometimes I go to my parents or my brother's house, but they know not to buy me shit or try and push me into the whole holiday trap." He threw her a warning look.

"Cara invited us over to their Christmas Eve party. Do you go to that?"

"Never been to it."

"Is it something that you'd like to go to?"

"Right now ... no, but you go if you want."

"It'd be nice to go to a party, and I know Timmy would enjoy it. I feel so bad about him not being with his Grammy and Grandpa this year."

"Then go."

Savannah nodded as she twirled a strand of hair around her fingers. "Would you like to go to the tree-lighting ceremony with us?" She held her breath.

Ryder shook his head. "You can take the Jeep and go, or I can ask one of the brothers to pick you and Timmy up if you don't want to drive on your own."

Disappointment mixed with sadness swirled inside her. "I was hoping you'd want to come with us. I know Timmy will love it."

Ryder turned away and stared at the fire. She saw a muscle jump in his clenched jaw.

"Is it okay if I decorate a little? If you don't want me to, I can decorate Timmy's room only."

A long pause stretched between them, and just when Savannah didn't think he was going to answer her, his deep voice said, "It's fine, but don't overdo this shit."

"Okay, thanks," she said softly as she rose to her feet. "I'm going to start wrapping Timmy's gifts before Hawk brings him home."

Ryder sat with clenched jaw, looking straight ahead.

Savannah picked up the bags and walked quietly out of the room. She took out three rolls of wrapping paper and a bag of bows then sat cross-legged on the floor and began sorting through the gifts she'd purchased. She opened a black box and stared at the sterling silver and white gold motorcycle chain bracelet with skulls that she'd bought for Ryder. She'd noticed that he sometimes wore a silver chain or a leather rope bracelet on his wrists, so she took a chance and bought him one for Christmas. She groaned and put the cover back on the box. Due to his Christmas rant, Savannah wasn't sure if it was appropriate to give him the gift. *If he throws it back in my face, I'd be mortified then pissed as hell, and that wouldn't be something I'd want Timmy to see.* She put it aside then began wrapping the presents she'd bought for Timmy.

After an hour, Savannah straightened up and moaned softly as her achy muscles stretched out. She glanced at the elaborately wrapped gifts and smiled just picturing how bright Timmy's eyes would be when he saw the gifts displayed under the tree. *The tree. Shit. Timmy and I can go get one tomorrow. I can ask Cara to help me with that.* Ryder was going to a counseling session at the VA. He'd told her how he missed seeing his buddies since the blizzard had shut everything down for over a week. He still hadn't told her what had happened over in Afghanistan. From what she could piece together from that night when she'd comforted him, he must have stepped on a landmine and someone named Jeremy was following, which had made Ryder very upset. Savannah wished he'd let her in, but then who was she to talk? She changed the subject the minute Ryder had asked her about why she ran away from Bret.

"No ... I don't want to remember that now," she said out loud as she wadded up the small bits of ribbon and wrapping paper. After hiding the presents in the closet, she picked up the bag of trash and left her room, heading to the bin in the kitchen.

When she entered the family room, she saw a pretty brunette sitting close to Ryder on the couch, too close in Savannah's opinion, and both of them were laughing.

"Oh," she muttered too loudly.

Ryder craned his neck and flashed her big smile.

"I didn't know you had company." Holding up the bag, she mustered a small smile. "I'm just passing through to throw this out." She skittered across the floor and went to the large receptacle in the garage. *Who the hell is she, and how long has she been over?* Not wanting to go back into the house, she leaned against the cold wall and waited until her trembling body couldn't take it anymore. *I'm acting like an idiot.* Her teeth chattered incessantly, and she walked into the mud room and sat on the bench as she tried to warm up.

A woman's soft voice lilted through the air accompanied by Ryder's deep chuckles. When Savannah finally stopped chattering and trembling, she pulled down her knit top and shuffled through the kitchen.

Hoping that Ryder didn't see her, she walked carefully behind the couch and almost made it to the hallway when his voice called out, "Savannah, come over here."

Dammit. She inched over toward the couch and the pretty woman with waist-length straight brown hair and big eyes of the same color met her gaze. The woman's berry stained lips spread into a smile.

"Hawk called and asked if it's okay for Timmy to stay for supper."

The woman's knee was pressed against Ryder's. Her top was daringly low, exposing more than a fair amount of cleavage, and the hem stopped just above the waistband of a short denim skirt. Turning her attention away, Savannah looked at Ryder. "That's fine. If you can give me Hawk's number, I can call him back."

"I'm Brandi," the woman said, placing her hand on Ryder's thigh.

"Savannah," she mumbled. Her emotions were so conflicting that it felt like she was being twisted, bent, and torn on the inside. Brandi was pretty and younger than her by at least ten years. *Of course, Ryder would have someone like her in his life.* Her heart twinged and jealousy ran amok all over her body.

The young woman leaned over and whispered something in Ryder's ear then laughed as her big breasts pressed against his arm. For one cold moment, seeing Brandi cozying up to Ryder while he gave her a lazy smile brought back the dreadful memory of Bret pulling his young lover to him and kissing her passionately in front of Savannah. Her heart hammered and Savannah willed herself to calm the hell down. Ryder *wasn't* Bret and, even more importantly, Ryder didn't owe her anything. They weren't involved, perhaps a tinge of flirting; a single kiss between two lonely people didn't count. *I can't be that naïve to think that he didn't have a woman in his life. I'm being ridiculous and letting the past dictate my present feelings.*

Avoiding his stare, Savannah stood up. "I have some things to do," she said and shuffled away toward her bedroom. Once inside, she closed the door and wiped the tears trailing down her face. The truth was that Savannah hated seeing the younger woman laugh and lean against

Ryder. She was jealous, and as much as she tried to talk herself out of it, realized that she liked the rough biker more than she wanted to admit. The images of Brandi and Ryder kissing and touching freely on the couch, now that Savannah had left, raged inside her mind.

A knock on the door had her scrambling to find a tissue to wipe her face and blow her nose. The last thing she wanted was for Ryder to see her crying. She fluffed her hair with her fingers, took several deep breaths, and then opened the door. He filled the doorway, his dark eyes boring into hers. Without saying a word, he closed the door and yanked her toward him, then he shoved her back against it and crushed his mouth on hers. At first, Ryder's lips were warm and soft, and a small moan slipped between them. His tongue invaded the recesses of her mouth, plunging and swirling, until she leaned into his embrace, realizing that she could never have enough of his kisses. Then he deepened their connection and kissed her harder with a fervid, possessive need she'd never known before. She knotted her fist in his shirt, pulling him against her.

"Fuck, Savannah," he rasped on her lips.

Every square inch of her body dissolved into his. Savannah's temples throbbed and her heart exploded while she gripped his hair and tugged hard. Never had she wanted a man like this. Ever. His hands slid down her body and then back up, and when one of them cupped her breast, a million sparks singed her nerves, sending delicious sensations from her nipple to the ache between her legs. All she wanted was Ryder—to feel him inside her, his mouth hot on her skin, and his tongue blazing a trail down to her needy sweet spot.

"Ryder," she murmured, slipping her hand under his shirt. The feel of his muscles rippling under her fingertips threatened to make her come just like that. It'd been so long since she'd had feelings for a man or even had sex for that matter. Then Bret's cruel smirk cut through her arousal, dousing it like a bucket of ice water. Savannah broke away slightly and stared at Ryder's quizzical face, at his lips that glistened from their kiss.

"What's going on?" he asked, stroking the side of her face with his finger.

"You have a guest waiting out there." Not exactly the truth, but Brandi *was* waiting for him.

"Don't worry about her. She just came by to see me. We've got nothing between us."

"She doesn't act like that."

"Brandi just got all possessive when she saw you. Club girls do that shit. She's just a good friend." Ryder gently kissed her. "You're the one who's getting to me." He leaned in closer and pressed his erection hard against her.

"You're getting to me, too, but whatever Brandi is to you, it's rude to leave her alone."

Ryder slowly nodded then stepped back. "You're right."

"And I still have to call Hawk."

"I'll do it." He opened the door and walked out.

For a long time, Savannah stood in the hall listening to Brandi and Ryder chat. Each time Brandi suggested that they could have some fun, Savannah's stomach would clench then relax as Ryder repeatedly turned her down. From what she gathered, Brandi and Ryder had some sort of relationship that involved sex. *Maybe a friends-with-benefits type of thing?* She wasn't sure, but there was definitely more between them than what he'd previously stated. Before she jumped into anything with Ryder, she had to be sure of what was going on between him and the pretty brunette.

Savannah went back into the bedroom, shut the door behind her, then sank down in the chair and looked out the window. The sky was a dove gray with thin wisps of sunlight filtering weakly through the clouds. The evergreens sparkled, their branches bejeweled with frost while the arms of the bare aspen trees hung low with the weight of the snow.

"It's so beautiful here," she said under her breath. "Ryder's beautiful, in a rough way." She smiled when his rugged face filled her mind. *And his* kisses *make my fucking toes curl. He's wonderful even though he doesn't want anyone to tell him that. He has a kind heart. I can't imagine him ever treating a woman the way Bret treated me.* The irony was that Ryder acknowledged that he had issues, but Bret thought he was perfectly reasonable in his actions toward people, including her and their son.

She rubbed her temples. "I should've left you a long time ago." But she'd decided to stay for two reasons: in hopes that Bret would come around and love his son, and for fear that she couldn't make it as a single mom. Timmy had a charmed life, at least financially, and he'd go to the best schools and have the best opportunities his wealthy status would afford him. Savannah knew how hard it was to climb the societal ladder, and she wanted so much more for her son than her parents could ever have given her. So she stayed. Bret and she lived separate lives, but the unspoken rule between them was that they'd treat each other with respect and play the happy family to the outside world. Even though Savannah was lonely without the love and intimacy from her husband, she learned to live with it. For the most part, things were going all right until Bret had begun to yell at Timmy and say crude things to her. She'd gone to a divorce attorney after several months of that behavior, and had decided that she was ready to leave him, even though she knew it was going to be a nasty, spiteful divorce. She had no doubt that Bret would ask for sole custody of Timmy to hurt her and to please Corinne. *He* always *made sure to please Corinne. She was the one who came first in his life.* Savannah geared herself for the challenge, deciding she'd file for divorce after the first of the year, but her plans derailed in a big way.

She leaned her head back and closed her eyes, afraid of the memories but knowing she had to confront them.

Savannah had parked her BMW in front of their mansion, cursing herself for forgetting the clothes for the tailor. She'd walked up the spiral staircase, and when she approached the master bedroom, the sounds of moans and groans were coming from inside. Her stomach twisted and her head pounded. For a long time, Savannah suspected that Bret was cheating on her, but she never imagined he'd bring the woman to their home.

Pushing the door aside, she saw a woman who barely looked of legal age, bouncing up and down on his dick. Bret glanced over, and instead of being mortified at being caught, he smirked at her then grabbed the young woman's breasts and tugged them. The girl craned her neck, and when she saw Savannah, she cried out and had the decency to scramble off of him. Savannah spun around and headed down the stairs, angry tears filling her eyes.

"Wait, Savannah," Bret called out at the top of the stairs.

Ignoring him, Savannah continued her descent to the marbled foyer. She heard his footsteps behind her, then the clack of heels as the young lady rushed past, her eyes cast downward.

The solid cherry wood door shut, and Savannah whirled around.

"How dare you bring one of your women to my home!" He laughed and reached out to touch her, but she cringed and pulled away. "I can't believe you!"

In two long strides, Bret grabbed her, his hands vices around her arms. "I pay the fucking bills around here, so I can do whatever the hell I want. And don't act so goddamn sanctimonious. I'm pretty sure you've got some pathetic loser servicing you."

"Does it make you feel better to think that?"

"Not really. If I do find out who you're fucking, I'll take care of him so he'll be singing in the boys' choir."

"I'm not cheating. Unlike you, I was raised to honor my wedding vows." She tried to pull away. "Let me go. Your touch is making me sick!"

"You're the one who fucked up our marriage, and you want me to honor my wedding vows?" He jerked her close to him and pressed his mouth against hers. She twisted in his grip, but he held her steadfast while pulling her to the ground.

"Stop it, Bret. Stop!" she yelled, but he ignored her; instead, anger plastered across his face as he pinned her to the cold floor. The hollow sensation in the pit of her stomach coiled into a lump of fear. "Please, let me up."

He hiked up her skirt and roughly pushed aside her panties before brutally shoving into her. Pain shot through her as he grunted.

"You're so damn dry, and loose as hell because of the fucking brat." More grunts, more thrusts. "Your skin's not young and firm like Zoe's. She's so much sexier than you are, and you're wondering how I could bring her to

our bed. How the fuck could I resist?" He laughed wryly.

Savannah tried to push him off but his arm was a crowbar across her chest. He grunted like a pig a few more times then shot his load inside her, his contorted face reminding her of a demonic troll she'd seen in a horror film back when she was in high school. Without a word, he pulled out, straightened his boxers, and walked up the stairs, leaving her spread eagle and dripping on the marble floor—humiliation burning through her.

Several minutes later, she heard the thud of his shoes on the marble stairs and scrambled to get up, but her hand slipped and she fell back on her elbow. "Shit," she muttered under her breath then froze when the scent of his expensive cologne assaulted her nostrils.

Bending down on one knee, Bret brought his lips to her ear. "Don't wait up for me tonight—I'll be home late. He stood up.

Still dazed from what had happened, Savannah avoided looking at him. She heard the jangle of keys and the heels of his thousand dollar shoes.

"On second thought, I may not be back until morning." There was a low chuckle, then the footfalls started up again until she couldn't hear them anymore.

Savannah crawled over to the banister and heaved herself up. Shock still held her, along with a plunging sadness. She had to get out of there right away. The thought of spending another minute in the house she loved with the husband who had become a monster disgusted her.

The first sexual contact she'd had with her husband in over five years had been a brutal rape and he didn't even think he'd done anything wrong.

A loud knock on the door.

"Savannah? Are you all right?"

She heard the knob jingle, and for a moment she wasn't sure where she was.

"If you don't open this damn door, I'm gonna break it down." Concern laced Ryder's voice.

"I'll be right there." Savannah pushed back the hair from her face then took several deep breaths before walking over to the door and opening it.

"What's wrong?" Ryder asked, his dark eyes panning her face.

"Just tired."

"Bullshit." He pulled her to him and embraced her, resting her head against his chest. The beating of his heart was comforting, and she tightened her arms around him. "Do you want to talk about it?"

Savannah shook her head. "Not now."

"Okay." Ryder kissed the top of her head.

They stood in the hallway clinging to each other, and it felt so right. This bitter and broken man had taken a hold of her heart when she wasn't even looking.

"Do you want to get a tree after dinner at Hawk's?"

Savannah tilted her head up and locked her gaze with his. "We're eating over there too?"

Ryder kissed the tip of her nose and smiled. "Yeah. Afterward, we can go to the tree lot with Timmy, and he can pick one out."

"But you hate Christmas," she said, swallowing past the lump in her throat.

"You don't though, and neither does Timmy. Who knows, I may end up liking the damn thing once it's up."

A warm glow spread through her, and she drew his head down. "Thank you," she whispered before pressing her lips against his. His noble act of selflessness touched her deeply.

Brave. Modest. Sexy. Maybe my wish for the best Christmas ever will come true.

Savannah tucked her hand into his as they walked into the family room.

CHAPTER TWELVE

A LL THROUGH DINNER, Ryder couldn't keep his damn eyes off Savannah no matter how hard he'd tried. There was no way Hawk and Banger didn't notice it, and he braced himself for the ribbing that would follow when the men retreated to the den while the women cleaned up.

What the hell am I doing? I don't need a woman and her boy to muddle up my life. He speared a piece of sausage with his fork and placed it in his mouth, chewing slowly. *She's a great kisser, I'll give her that, but it'd be a lot easier for me to pay Brandi a visit next time I go to the clubhouse.* Brandi. The memory of Savannah's jealousy over the club girl made him chuckle.

"You want to let us in on it?" Banger asked.

Ryder looked at the Insurgents' president and shook his head. "It's nothing. Just thinking about something Brutus did earlier today." He looked down at his plate and twirled the spaghetti around his fork.

"That's why we should get a dog," Cara said. "Braxton's been dying for one, and I think it would be good for him to have a pet. It helps a child be responsible."

"Can I have one, Daddy? Please ... can I?" Braxton's dark eyes sparkled.

"Harley loves Patches to death, doesn't he?" Belle said, looking at Banger, who nodded.

Hawk shook his head slightly. "It seems like I'm being ganged up on."

Ryder glanced at his buddy and it seemed like he was trying to suppress a smile. "I've always had a dog. It's a good thing for a kid." He picked up his beer, and his eyes locked with Savannah's. *Beautiful. Damn. She gets to me.*

"Well … we'll see," Hawk replied, but Ryder knew that meant Braxton was probably getting a puppy for Christmas. When Cara leaned over and kissed Hawk deeply, a pain stabbed at Ryder's heart. *I almost had a family, but Dana crushed all that.*

A slight nudge against his leg made Dana fly out of his mind, and he snapped his gaze to Savannah, who licked her lips while running her foot up and down his calf. *Fuck, woman.* Ryder shifted in his seat and adjusted his jeans the best he could without being caught with a burgeoning hard-on. Savannah had the uncanny skill of making him so damn hard whether she was around or not, and it made him feel like a damn teenager—raging hormones and all. *Double fuck.*

"Did you see the Christmas tree?" Timmy asked Savannah.

"Yes, it's beautiful. Ryder's promised to take us to get a tree later tonight," Savannah answered.

Ryder's muscles stiffened, Hawk choked on his beer, and Banger clucked his tongue. *Triple fuck!*

"That's wonderful," Cara replied.

"Are you going to Holly's Christmas Trees?" Belle asked.

"They have gorgeous ones. That's where we bought ours," Cara chimed in.

"I'm not sure …" Savannah said. "Ryder?"

"Yeah, that's where we're going. Can you pass me another roll, Belle?" Ryder was stuffed to the gills, but he wanted the tree conversation to end, so he buttered the roll and forced it down his throat.

After dinner, Timmy, Braxton, and Harley ran off to play a video game with a curly-haired Isa toddling after them. Belle, Cara, and Savannah cleared the dishes and disappeared into the kitchen, and Hawk motioned Ryder and Banger to follow him to the den.

A fire crackled in the fireplace, and Hawk poured each of them a couple shots of whiskey. Ryder settled back on the leather couch while Hawk and Banger each sat down on the wing chairs.

"So you're doing Christmas this year?" Banger asked, a twinkle in his eye.

Ryder took a sip of the premium whiskey. "Before you guys start your shit, I'm only doing this for Timmy. He's only six fucking years old, and he's away from his grandparents and cousins. I feel for the kid."

"And the mom?" Hawk asked.

"She made the choice to leave, not Timmy."

Banger set his tumbler down. "Let me get this straight. This sudden interest in decorating has everything to do with the boy and nothing to do with the sexy mom?"

"You got it." Ryder downed the rest of his drink.

"What a load of shit," Banger said while Hawk guffawed. "Just admit you got the hots for the mom. It's natural as fuck. Two good-looking people." Banger paused and looked intently at Ryder's face. "Well … *one* good-looking person and one not so much, stranded in a cabin in a snowstorm. Hell, it's right from one of those fuckin' sappy movies Belle watches this time of year."

Hawk busted out laughing, then stood up and brought the whiskey bottle over to fill up the glasses. "It's okay to want to fuck her, dude. I see the way you're both hot for each other. You deserve this."

"Yeah, she's hot and all, but she's heading out soon after the beginning of the year," Ryder said.

"Then have some fun until she does. You never know what may happen," Hawk replied.

"And this is coming from a man who fought falling in love with Cara?"

"He's got a point, bro." Banger laughed.

Hawk scowled. "I'm just saying to go for it. You got this hot chick in your cabin who seems more than ready to spend some cozy nights with you. It fuckin' beats the club girls."

"Yeah … well … we're just friends," Ryder replied.

"Make it with benefits, and you've got a great holiday." Hawk grinned.

Banger cleared his throat. "As fun as this shit is, we gotta talk serious now. We've got some assholes making noise in our territory. They call themselves the Twisted Kings. Skinless was at a dive bar …" He snapped his fingers.

"Brown Barrel," Hawk said.

"… the Brown Barrel," Banger continued, "and he saw these three fuckers wearing their colors. The prospect said what got him was that the bottom rocker said *Colorado*." Banger's face flushed red and his nostrils flared.

"What the fuck?" Ryder said. "Are they asking for trouble?"

"They're asking for a beatdown, and if they keep it up, then their families will be visiting Horan's Mortuary to pick out coffins," Hawk replied.

"No one fuckin' wears the Colorado property rocker in Insurgents' territory." Banger held out his glass and Hawk poured him another shot, then he tipped the bottle toward Ryder. Ryder shook his head, so Hawk put the bottle back on the table. "We gotta address this, pronto." Banger leaned back in the chair.

"You need my help?" Ryder asked.

"If you want to be in on it. You told me a month ago that you're itching to be involved in some of the club's enforcement, so we could definitely use you. You want in?" Hawk asked.

Ryder slowly nodded, excitement weaving through him. It had been a long time since he'd done a mission with his brothers, and it would prove to him that he still had what it took to be an outlaw. "I'm in. When do we roll?"

"We wanna do it before Saturday. What about Wednesday?" Banger asked.

"Can't—the fuckin' tree lighting is Wednesday," Hawk replied.

"That's right. I don't want Belle, Harley, Ethan, and Emily going alone to that. No fuckin' way," Banger said.

"Same with Cara and the kids. I gotta be there to make sure my family's protected." Hawk glanced at Ryder. "Are you doing the tree shit too?" A smile tugged at the corners of his mouth.

"Savannah said Cara had mentioned it." Ryder rubbed the top of his thigh; his residual limb was hurting like a motherfucker.

"Is that a yes?" A full-blown smile broke out over Hawk's smug face.

"Yeah, we're going. Fuck, dude," Ryder answered.

"Then we'll move on Thursday. The prospect said these three assholes hang out at that bar from Thursday through Saturday. Chas, Wheelie, and Animal are gonna find out how many of these bastards are playing MC. We'll just introduce ourselves to the fuckers at the bar. The way they're gonna look after we're done with them will be the warning to the other ass-wipes." Banger glanced at his phone.

"How many of us are going?" Ryder asked, his adrenaline already starting to pump.

"Figure eight of us should do the trick. Maybe ten, in case some shit happens that we aren't expecting. Hawk will get the posse rounded up tomorrow, and we'll meet at the clubhouse before heading over to the dive. Sound good?" Ryder nodded along with Hawk. "Good." Banger stood up. "I gotta get going. I promised Ethan I'd take him and his friends skiing in the morning. The shit we do for our kids." Banger laughed as he headed out of the room.

Gritting his teeth, Ryder stood up. "I better go too."

"Yeah, you got a tree to pick out." Hawk playfully smacked him on the back. "You okay, bud? You need some aspirin?"

"I'm good. It's just been a long day. Thanks, bro."

After they said their goodbyes, Ryder found himself doing something he never thought he would—going to buy a Christmas tree. He'd given up on holiday cheer after Dana had left him and took Colt with her. Even though he acted disinterested and downright gruff, he smiled inside when he saw how excited Timmy was from picking out a tree.

"Make sure you got enough stuff to decorate that big tree," he said to Timmy, who pointed at a large one.

"Ryder's right, honey. Let's get one that's a bit smaller." Savannah walked over to a six-foot Douglas fir. "This one is nice." Timmy rushed over and jumped up and down in place, making Ryder laugh.

Snowflakes floated down from the cloud-laden sky, dancing and swirling as a cold wind carried them toward the trees and the customers. Savannah tugged on Ryder's scarf, wrapping it closer around his neck then buttoning up the top of his leather jacket. It was the same thing his mother would have done, and for some reason, Savannah's thoughtfulness pissed him off. It angered the hell out of him because deep beneath the steel casing of his heart and his rough exterior, her gesture touched some starving part of him, the part that needed the warm and loving arms of a woman he could call his own. It had nothing to do with fucking; it had everything to do with need.

After Dana had shattered his heart, he swore he'd never again care about another woman, but Savannah stirred up feelings inside him that had been dormant for over six years. Ryder couldn't remember the last time he'd encountered that swell of emotion as he did with Savannah. It was crazy as hell—he'd only known her for ten days—yet his feelings were real, as much as he didn't want to admit it to anyone, even himself.

"Nice choice," the cashier said cheerfully as he pulled his cap down over his ears. "That'll be ninety-five dollars—seventy-five for the tree and twenty for the stand."

Out of the corner of his eye, Ryder saw Savannah opening her purse, so he grabbed her hand.

"I'll get it," he said.

"Definitely not. We're the ones who wanted the tree. I insist on paying." She pulled her hand away.

"Leave it be, woman." His voice brooked no argument, stopping the mad rush for her wallet, because she just stared at him and let her purse hang loosely from her shoulder.

Ryder paid the man then hauled the tree over to the jeep. One of the lot boys rushed over and helped him secure it, and in no time, they were headed back to the cabin. Timmy and Savannah chattered the whole drive, and by the time Ryder had opened the garage door, the snow was falling at a very fast clip.

"Let me help you with that," Savannah said, sliding out of the vehicle.

"I've got it. Go inside with Timmy and get warm."

"Are you sure you don't need any help?"

He grunted and threw her a stern look, and then satisfaction settled on his face when she turned around and walked into the house.

After setting up the tree in front of the picture window, Ryder popped a pain pill into his mouth and sat down on the couch. If he were alone, he'd take off his leg and massage capsaicin cream on his sore stump, but there was no way he was doing that in front of Savannah. Silly? Perhaps, but after Dana had spewed all that hurtful shit, it made him feel like he wasn't the man he used to be. It took Ryder a few years to shirk off that notion, and he didn't want to go back to that dark place again if Savannah looked at him with disgust in her eyes. *I'm probably being stupid as fuck. She hasn't even mentioned that night I lost it.* That had earned her major points from him, but actually *seeing* him without his leg was another thing entirely, at least that's the way he felt about it.

"Timmy was so exhausted that he fell fast asleep. He had such a great day. Thanks for helping to make that happen," she said.

Savannah was beaming, literally glowing with excitement. Ryder's heart tripped over itself at the sight of her blonde hair in loose waves around her shoulders, with no makeup, and wrapped in a green robe that hugged all her curves. It took every ounce of restraint not to scoop her up in his arms and whisk her off to the bedroom. Damn, he wanted her. Ryder couldn't remember ever wanting anyone as much as he wanted Savannah at that moment.

"I'm going to make some hot chocolate. Do you want some?"

"You're fucking obsessed with that drink." He chuckled.

She giggled. "I am—I never realized it. Although I think tonight I'll try it your way with a shot of whiskey."

"In that case, I'll have one too, but make it a double shot."

"You're so bad." She ran her fingers through his hair, and he grasped her hand and kissed it.

"You look beautiful," he said, his voice thick.

Savannah withdrew her hand gently and smiled. "You're good for my ego." He watched while she padded away, groaning as her hips swayed just right in the sexy-as-shit robe.

Actually, it was just a standard flannel robe that he wouldn't even have looked at twice, but the way it clung around her curves got his dick punching against his jeans. He tossed a throw pillow on his lap and shook his head and smiled. *Damn that woman.*

When she came back, she put his mug on the end table next to him, and hers on the coffee table. The front of her robe fell open, and he heard her suck in a breath. There was a pause then the slightest quirk to the corner of his mouth as his gaze fixed on the edges of her lacy bra. Savannah quickly pulled the robe together and tied the sash tighter before she sat down.

Ryder grasped Savannah's arm and jerked her to him, his mouth smothering her words as he kissed her hungrily. He just couldn't get enough of her tempting lips and addictive scent as her body pressed against his—he couldn't get enough of *her.*

They kissed for a while until Savannah pulled away.

"The cocoa is gonna get cold," she whispered, pushing her robe together again. As soon as she leaned over, the robe fell open at the bottom and revealed her shapely leg, which made Ryder press the pillow down further onto his lap.

His eyes stayed glued to the flexing muscles of her calf until she cleared her throat, and when his gaze snapped up, he noticed a flush of pink crawling across her cheeks. He'd been staring at her again. *Fuck!* There was something about Savannah that had him so damn off-center. She picked up her mug from the table then sank back against the couch. After carefully tucking her legs under her ass, she took a sip of the hot chocolate. Ryder watched her movements as they played havoc with his dick and roused his desire even more.

Savannah put her drink down and Ryder reached over and drew her to him. He lowered his lips to hers for a sweet, lingering kiss, just to enjoy how warm and soft they felt on his. She tasted like sugar and cocoa, and it took every ounce of willpower to break away.

"That was nice," she said softly, picking up the mug again. "Aren't you going to take a sip?" She pointed to his mug.

He picked it up and licked the froth from his lips. "Damn, that's good." The pillow had fallen to the floor, and his gaze followed hers as it landed on his noticeable hard-on. Savannah looked away quickly and fumbled with the robe's sash.

"Don't mind me, darlin'. A gorgeous woman just kissed me." He took another sip then stretched out his legs.

"Uh … can I ask you something personal?"

Ryder stiffened. *There's no way I'm talking about Afghanistan or Dana. Not tonight.*

As if sensing his discomfort, Savannah tilted her head to the side and scrunched her face. "I don't mean to be nosy or anything, but since we've been … you know … kissing, I wanted to know some things about you."

Brandi—that's what she wants to know. He relaxed. "Go ahead and ask." He watched as she squirmed and then tugged at the sash of her robe before she fixed her gaze on the table lamp behind him.

"Do you and Brandi date? You told me she's a club girl, but I'm not sure what that means. She seemed really into you, and you weren't exactly acting like a stranger." Her gaze shifted to his.

"We're friends with benefits sometimes. She lives at the Insurgents' clubhouse, and she's one of several women there who … have fun with the club members. It's nothing serious at all. I've never taken her on the back of my bike." Shrugging, he splayed his hands on his lap.

Savannah's brows knitted as a look of confusion etched her face. "Is that a big deal to have a woman on the back of your bike?"

"Fuck yeah, woman. A lot of bikers don't let just any chick on their bikes, only the ones who matter."

"How many have *you* taken?" she asked softly.

"One, but that was a long time ago."

Her eyes widened. "Really?"

"Yeah."

"How often do you and Brandi meet up?"

"Not that often. Sometimes she comes over here, but usually it's when I go to the parties at the clubhouse. The brothers have parties like all the fucking time, but I only go once in a while. I like being alone."

"What do the club girls do at the clubhouse?"

Ryder shook his head as he scrubbed his face. "Are you sure you wanna know? Most citizens don't get it when they find out."

"I'm presuming I'm a 'citizen,' but try me anyway."

"They service my brothers here as well as brothers from our other chapters and different MCs. Even if there isn't a party, they're expected to be available whenever a brother wants them. The Insurgents don't force a club girl if she doesn't want to fuck, but it's sorta one of the conditions in order to get free room and board and a monthly stipend. The girls want to be there. They choose that life."

"I see."

Ryder couldn't read Savannah; he didn't know if she was repulsed by what he said or what. "Are you disgusted?"

"No. Why would I be? Everyone knows the score. It's not like a member forces himself on one of them. That would be disgusting and unconscionable."

He saw tears well up in her eyes, and she turned away, rubbing her eyes as if pretending that something was in them.

"Are you okay?"

"Why wouldn't I be?" Severity had crept into her voice.

"I hope I didn't upset you. I want you to know that Brandi was nice to me after all the shit went down with my leg. It took me a long fucking time to even think about being with a woman, but we don't have any feelings other than friendship."

"I think she likes you a little more. I could tell by the way she looked at me."

Ryder reached over and held Savannah's hands. "I don't want you thinking that you gotta compete with her because since I laid eyes on you, I haven't thought about her for one fucking second. She came here because she wanted to know why I hadn't come over to the club. I told her I was interested in you, and I am. I know it's crazy, but I feel something for you even though we've only known each other less than two weeks."

"It'll be two weeks tomorrow," she whispered. "I feel something for you too, and I keep telling myself that this whole thing between us is insane. I've never been one to act recklessly."

"Maybe playing it too careful is making us both miss out on something great. I don't know, but I *do* know you're driving me fucking nuts, darlin', and it pisses me off."

Savannah laughed. "What I'm feeling for you pisses me off too."

Chuckling, Ryder scooted over and wrapped his arm around her shoulder, drawing her close as he leaned back against the couch. She rested her head on his chest, and he inhaled the vanilla scent of her shampoo while his fingers played with her hair, lightly sifting through and entwining the strands around them. *Her hair's so damn soft—like satin or velvet. Fuck.*

"This is nice," she murmured.

"Yeah." He thought about asking Savannah why she'd run away from her husband, and if she was going back after she got whatever it was out of her system, but he didn't want the answer to that, at least not right then. He had no desire to find out whether he was a rebound, and that she possibly could be heading back to Boston to rekindle her love with the man she'd married.

Not now.

That night, Ryder simply wanted to take all of her in—from her tantalizing scent, quiet breaths, and silky hair, to her sweet taste and natural beauty.

Even though she was a strong woman, there was a vulnerability and frailty about her that seduced him.

Despite the fact that his whole body raged with a burning desire and lust for Savannah, Ryder wasn't going to push her. He wanted her to open up to him.

He could wait.

He was a patient man.

Deeper breaths accompanied by light snores made him smile as he looked down at Savannah's peaceful face. He dipped his head down and lightly brushed his lips over hers, then tightened his arm around her shoulder and stared into the slowly dying fire.

CHAPTER THIRTEEN

HARRY POPPED THE tab on a Pepsi he'd bought in the gift shop of the Pinewood Springs Hotel and plopped down on a chair in his hotel room before tapping in Bret's number on his cell phone.

On the third ring, Bret answered. "Any news?"

"Not yet. I've scoured this whole damn place but no sign of her or your son. Is your mother-in-law sure that your wife said *Pinewood Springs?*"

"Yes. Mary's good at details and she wouldn't have reached up her ass for that name—meaning, the town fucking exists." Irritation laced Bret's voice.

"It's just strange that there's no sign of them anywhere."

"Mary said some dude befriended them, remember?"

"It's my fucking job to remember." Heat rose up Harry's neck as he swallowed a large gulp of soda, letting it slide down his throat and abate his anger.

"Maybe the guy lives outside of Pinewood Springs." Impatience had replaced irritation in Bret's tone.

"I know what the fuck I'm doing. I've been to more damn small neighborhoods and areas, trudging through piles of fucking snow, and I still got zip." Harry crushed the can in his hand and tossed it in the trash. "There's a community thing going on tonight. Some tree-lighting ceremony. I'll check it out and see if I can spot them there."

"If Savannah's anywhere near that damn hick town, she'll be there with Timmy. She'd never let Timmy miss something like that—she's *always* thinking of the kid and putting him first." Bret gave a dry laugh.

"Kids like those things." For a brief second, Harry's three children filled his mind, and a short jab of pain hit his gut. His wife had walked out on him two years before, and he hadn't blamed her; he was never home. Harry sighed loudly as he scratched his chin and glanced out the window at people rushing around the streets, many of them carrying Christmas-themed bags. It was during the holidays that losing his family hit him the hardest.

"Are you still with me?" Bret asked.

"Yeah. The phone just faded out a bit. Anyway, I'll check it out tonight and get back to you. No sense in you coming here if your family's not here."

"They're there. Just fucking find them."

The phone went dead and Harry clenched his jaw. "If you didn't pay me so well, you fucking prick, I'd tell you what I really thought of you," he muttered, slipping the phone in his pocket. Bret's father was a gentleman. Wayne always treated him with respect and not as if he were a bumbling, incompetent idiot the way Bret did. A large part of him understood why Bret's wife took off with their son, but it wasn't his job to judge. Harry's job was to find them and let the man take it from there. The large sum of money he was paid allowed Harry to push away his contempt for the spoiled asshole and focus on his job.

Just then, his stomach growled.

Harry stood up and grabbed his jacket and the room key, then left.

CHAPTER FOURTEEN

"I THINK IT needs to be moved over a little more," Savannah said, pointing to the right of tree and trying to suppress a giggle as exasperation masked Ryder's face.

"This is the last damn time I'm moving this monstrosity, woman."

"Then I guess you better get it right." She threw him a big smile to his scowl.

Shaking his head, he grabbed hold of the tree and inched it over.

"Perfect." She clapped her hands.

"*Now* can we decorate it, Mommy?" Timmy asked.

"We sure can!" Savanah walked over to the boxes of lights and ornaments she'd bought earlier that morning at Walmart. She wished she had some of the beautiful bulbs her grandmother had given her before she died, but she'd left everything behind when she ran away that fateful day.

"I've done my part," Ryder said, walking over to the couch.

"Just point me in the direction of a ladder and we're good," she replied, untangling a string of lights.

For a few seconds, Ryder's eyes darted from the tree to her then back to the tree, and then he mumbled something inaudible—most definitely some cuss words—and stalked back over to the tree, taking the lights from her hands. Without a word, he started wrapping them around the tree from the top down. Warmth spread throughout Savannah while she watched him, and she felt as though her heart was dancing around in her chest, filling a hole no one had ever done before. To think that Ryder was a complete stranger just a couple of weeks before, and now she couldn't imagine him not being around. It just blew her mind.

Savannah scanned the room, her gaze landing on the three stockings hanging from the mantel, the snowmen and Santa decals on the glass panes, and the string of lights around the kitchen window. *The man who hates Christmas did this all for us.* As if he sensed Savannah's eyes on him, Ryder turned around and looked back at her, a string of lights dangling from his hands. The faint glimmer of the afternoon sun ghosted over his olive skin, and there was something so beautiful in those brown eyes, something so safe and warm.

Savannah padded over to him and stroked the side of his face then kissed him sweetly on the cheek. "Thank you for doing all this for me and Timmy," she whispered in his ear.

A low growl emitted from his throat, and he wrapped his arm around her waist and pulled her in close.

"No worries, darlin'. I'm under your fucking spell." He brushed his lips across hers.

Giggling, Savannah pushed away. She wanted to kiss Ryder passionately but didn't want to confuse Timmy. He had taken a real liking to Ryder. The two of them had spent quite a bit of time together in the workshop with Timmy trying out each toy Ryder had made. Outside, they'd had fun snowball fights, made at least five snowmen, and had built a really cool snow fort. Ryder had spent more time with Timmy in just two short weeks than Bret had in the entire six years of Timmy's life. Savannah didn't want to get Timmy's hopes up about Ryder and herself, especially if things didn't work out between them—a thought that made her heart ache.

After Ryder had finished wrapping the last strand of lights, he looked over his shoulder at Savannah, who was perched on the edge of the couch placing hooks on the ornaments.

"That's the last thing I'm gonna do with this tree—the rest is your job." His tone was gruff, but his eyes were twinkling.

"And mine!" Timmy danced in place, and Ryder and Savannah laughed.

"You do the bottom half, sweetie, and I'll do the top. After we're done, I'll serve the sugar cookies we made this morning."

An hour later, empty boxes were in the garage, broken bulbs in the trash, and the floor was spotless as the three of them sat on the couch—Timmy in the middle—eating cookies, drinking hot chocolate, and watching the colored lights reflecting off the bulbs.

"It's the most beautiful tree we've ever had," Savannah said.

"I got to help. It's the best," Timmy replied.

And it was because they all did it together. It was the first time in years that she and Timmy had decorated a Christmas tree. They'd always had decorators come into their Boston home and deck it out to the nines. Bret told her it was what the Carltons did, so he employed the same company that did his parents' home to do theirs as well. It was breathtakingly gorgeous, but it felt too perfect and lacked the homey feel of the holidays.

"This is your first *real* Christmas tree," she said softly then kissed the top of his tousled hair.

"No shit? I mean … no way," Ryder replied.

"Daddy had people do it for us. I like this better." Timmy took another bite of his cookie.

From the corner of her eye, she saw Ryder put his arm on the back of the sofa, and her body tingled in anticipation of his touch. His warm fingers lightly caressed the back of her neck, and she raised her hand and placed it on his, squeezing it lightly.

Savannah sat staring at the tree as Ryder and Timmy talked while Brutus was sprawled next to Ryder's feet. *This is perfect. Maybe a bit more screwed up than a Norman Rockwell painting, but perfect nevertheless.*

IT WAS A Winter Wonderland of sparkling lights, glowing sculptures, animated displays, and an array of brilliant colors. Booths surrounded the perimeter of Main Square, selling homemade baked goods and cups of hot cider and cocoa.

Savannah stood next to Ryder, her arm looped around his, and watched as Timmy sat on Santa's lap telling him what he wanted for Christmas. Several good-looking men wearing leather jackets with the Insurgents' name and logo on the back came over to Ryder and bumped fists with him. She recognized just a few of the men: Hawk, Banger, Throttle, Rags, and Animal. The majority of the others were strangers to Savanah, but they lifted their chins to her when Ryder made the introductions.

"Santa gave me this," Timmy said, holding up a multi-colored sucker.

"Let's leave it for tomorrow," Savannah said, placing it in her purse. Timmy was already bouncing from all the sugar he'd ingested since they arrived at the festival a couple of hours before.

"When are they gonna light the tree?" Timmy asked.

"Real soon, so we should head over to it," Ryder answered.

As they stood listening to the mayor give his holiday speech, Savannah leaned against Ryder's arm, and he looked sideways at her and smiled. He'd placed Timmy on top of his shoulders so the boy could see the festivities over the heads of the adults crammed in front of them.

Suddenly, an uneasy feeling quivered in Savannah's stomach and the hair on the back of her neck stood up. *Someone's watching me.* The feeling overwhelmed her, and she knew whoever it was stood just behind her. Gripping Ryder's upper arm, she slowly looked over her shoulder and met the steely eyes of a man whose face looked as if it'd been rearranged a few times. A thick scar ran from his left temple to the middle of the cheek, pockmarks peppered his skin, a big bump lay atop his crooked nose, and his thin lips reminded her of those on her brother's lizard from when they were kids.

Savannah shuddered. *Do I know him?* She wracked her brain, but nothing came up. *I'm sure I'd remember seeing someone that creepy.* Angling her head slightly, she noticed that the man was still behind her, watching.

"Don't make it obvious, but have you seen that guy behind me before? I'm just wondering if he lives here," she said to Ryder.

"Is someone bothering you?" A hard edge marked his voice.

"No … that's not it. I'm just wondering if you've seen him around town."

Ryder glanced backward then shook his head. "Don't know him, but I don't go into town very often." His gaze landed on a tall, built man in a leather jacket. Ryder raised his hand and gestured him over.

The tall man looked at Savannah then at Ryder, lifting his chin at him. "What's up, dude?"

"Have you seen this guy behind me? The one whose nose looks like it's been broken a few times."

The brown-haired biker turned around and stared at the man. "What the fuck are you looking at?" he asked him.

"The tree," the man said.

"Bullshit," Ryder added, turning around slightly.

Savannah's chest tightened. *What are they doing? I just asked about him, I don't want to be the cause of any trouble.*

The young biker took a couple of steps toward the stranger. "Where the fuck are you from?"

"Here."

"Wrong answer. I saw you come out of the Pinewood Springs Hotel last night."

Soon, two other muscular Insurgents wandered over, joining in on the banter with the tall man.

"Ryder, I don't want any trouble. I just asked you a simple question," Savannah said in a soft voice.

"Man checks out a woman when she's with another man has to expect some trouble," he answered.

"Jerry, what's going on?" a pretty blonde asked as she came toward the small group.

"Kylie, go back over to your dad. I'll be there in a minute."

The blonde tossed her hair and shook her head. "I don't want you to start something. We came to have a good time. Let's go back together."

The stranger crossed his arms. "Listen to the girl—she's talking sense."

"What the fuck did you say to me, old man?" Jerry clenched his fists.

"Rock, Clotille wants you to help out with James," Kylie said.

"Tell her I'll be there," Rock said, and Savannah noticed his dark eyes never left the stranger's face.

"Ryder … think of Timmy. Please stop this from going any further," Savannah pleaded.

His jaw seemed to soften a bit, and tenderness pushed away the anger in his brown eyes. "Brothers, leave it be." He then pivoted toward the man, Timmy's small hands buried in Ryder's hair. "Move away and there won't be trouble. Staring at a man's woman is gonna get your ass kicked."

The blond-haired man's eyes shifted from Ryder to Savannah then to Rock and Jerry before he gave a slight shrug and walked away. Savannah exhaled slowly through her nose as her nerves calmed down.

"I know where that sonofabitch is staying," Jerry said.

Savannah shook her head. "This is a misunderstanding. I just wanted to know if that guy lived here because he … looked like someone I thought I knew." *Why am I protecting that creep. He* was *watching me— not checking me out like Ryder thinks. No … it was something else.*

"This is Savannah," Ryder said, breaking in on her thoughts. "This here is Jerry, and that's Rock."

"Nice to meet you. I'm sorry I caused this confusion."

"No worries. When a brother needs something, we're there," Rock said, clapping his hand on Ryder's back. "Later, bro." The two bikers walked away and disappeared into the crowd.

"Is the whole club full of intimidating men like them? Wait, it is— Hawk and Banger fit that bill too," Savannah said.

Ryder laughed. "They're pretty typical. Rock's the club's sergeant-at-arms. Jerry's old lady is Banger's daughter."

"That pretty blonde?"

"Yeah—Kylie."

"What's the sergeant-at-arms?"

"The heavy of the club. He's in charge of clubhouse security along with enforcement of club rules and regulations. He's the only one who can reprimand the president, should he fuck up, but Banger never does." Ryder grinned.

"Look, they're going to light the tree!" Timmy cried out.

"Awesome," she said as she playfully pulled at her son's boot. The boy giggled then riveted his gaze on the twenty-five foot tree. She snuggled against Ryder and watched as the mayor dramatically flipped the switch, lighting the tree decked out in tinsel, ornaments, and thousands of twinkling lights to welcome the Christmas season.

Timmy clapped his hands and laughed, darting his eyes from her face back to the spectacular tree.

"It's beautiful," she murmured.

"You're beautiful," Ryder said, planting a kiss on her lips.

Savannah stroked the side of his face with her gloved fingers, her body tingling all over.

"How did you like it," Cara asked as she came over, Isa and Braxton in tow.

"I loved it. I'm so glad we came, and Timmy is having the time of his life," Savannah replied.

Ryder lifted Timmy up and off his shoulders, and as his little body pressed against Savannah's leg, he and Braxton high-fived each other.

Cara's eyes switched between Savannah and Ryder, then she tightened the multi-colored scarf around her neck. "I'm having a little Christmas sleepover party for Braxton, Harley, and James—he's Clotille and Rock's son. I'd love it, and so would Braxton, if Timmy could come." Again she glanced at Ryder then back at Savannah. "Clotille's coming by to help out with the boys for a while, then it'll just be me and Hawk. Believe me, we'll keep a very good eye on them."

"Yeah, their house is tighter than Fort Knox." Ryder laughed.

"Can I, Mommy?" Timmy's upturned face, full of hope and excitement, touched Savannah's heart.

"So you were listening to us." She put her hand on his shoulder and drew him closer to him. "I think it sounds like a lot of fun, so … sure."

"Yippee!" Braxton and Timmy yelled in unison. Cara and Savannah laughed.

"When is the party?" Savannah asked.

"Tomorrow night. You can bring Timmy over around three thirty or four. Is he allergic to peanuts or anything?"

"No."

"Do you like macaroni and cheese, Timmy?" Cara asked.

"That's my favorite. My mom makes it the best."

"I know I won't beat your mom's mac 'n cheese, but I make a pretty good one too. Do you think you'll want to try it?"

"Uh-huh." Timmy bobbed up and down.

"Mommy, can we have meatballs too?" Braxton asked.

Ryder laughed. "You can tell he's a *paisano*. Italian-American kids gotta have their meatballs. Speaking of that, Savannah makes the best lasagna. Ever," he said to Cara.

"I waitressed at a mom and pop Italian restaurant a million years ago," Savannah replied to Cara's curious look.

"You about ready to get going?" Hawk asked as he swept Isa up in his arms.

"It's time we head out too," Ryder said, grasping Savannah's hand. The two bikers bumped fists before parting ways.

On the ride back to the cabin, a mix of '80s metal music played at a low volume as the vehicle heated up. Savannah rested her head back against the seat and stared at the darkness in front of them. The face of the stranger flashed through her mind, and suspicion trickled down her spine. *Something doesn't seem right.* Worry niggled in the back of her mind as she recalled her mother's declaration from their conversation earlier that day at how she was "pretty confident" Savannah and Timmy would be home for Christmas. After her mom had said that, she'd thought it was just her mom's way of subtly guilting her into returning to Boston, but after seeing that man, Savannah wasn't too sure about her mother's statement. *Did she tell Bret where we are? She wouldn't … or would she?*

Ryder's hand covered hers and drew her away from her thoughts. She looked at him and smiled then peeked into the back seat where Timmy's head lolled to the side as he slept.

"He's pooped out," she said.

"It was a big day," Ryder answered.

"Was it horrible for you? I mean, for someone who isn't into Christmas, you had the holiday cheer rammed down your throat today. I bet after the season, you probably don't ever want to see another decorated tree."

Ryder brought her hand to his mouth and kissed it. "It was a bit much, but I didn't mind it. I liked seeing how happy you and Timmy were, but I draw the line at incessant Christmas music."

She laughed softly. "I promise not to blast it throughout your house."

"Then we won't have a problem."

"Your family's not into Christmas either?"

"They are. My mom's all about the food and the traditions, and she's been baking up a storm with my sisters, aunts, and cousins since Thanksgiving. Last time I was over there, they had pizzelle all over the damn place."

"I love those cookies. I haven't had them since I worked at Luna's. I bet they're so good."

"I'll have to bring some to you."

"So, your family doesn't go in for the tree lighting?"

"Some years they do, others years they don't. I was surprised my brother wasn't there. His daughters like that kind of thing." He glanced at her briefly and shrugged. "Maybe they had something else to do."

"I didn't know you were an uncle," Savannah said.

Nodding, he stared straight ahead. "I got three nieces and a nine-month-old nephew. My brother's got two girls, and my sister has a girl and the new baby."

"Do you see them very often?"

"Depends—I go in cycles. Most of the time I want to be left the hell alone, so they back off. It works." Ryder veered the jeep onto the narrow road that led to his cabin. "What about you?"

"I'm the second oldest of five—two brothers and two sisters, and only one grandkid for my parents—Timmy." Savannah looked down and played with the fringe on her scarf. "That's why I feel bad about taking Timmy away right before Christmas. It's so selfish, but … I had to get away."

"Did you tell your mom that?"

"I did, but she doesn't really understand." She shook her head when his features hardened. "But I don't blame her—I didn't tell her the whole story." She leaned over and kissed him on the side of his mouth. "I appreciate you helping to make this Christmas nice for Timmy. I know he misses his grandparents," she said softly in his ear.

"Both sets of grandparents?"

"No"—she pulled away and reclined back in the seat—"just my parents."

Ryder hit the button and the garage door opened, and he pulled the vehicle inside.

"I'll carry Timmy to his room," Ryder said, opening the jeep's back door.

Savannah followed after him and pulled back the covers when they entered Timmy's room. She slowly took off her son's boots, mittens, hat, and jacket. Ryder squeezed her shoulder and retreated from the room, grumbling something about taking Brutus out for a walk.

After Timmy was snuggled in bed, his arm wrapped around Furry, Savannah switched off the light and walked into her room to change and wash up. By the time she sat down on the couch, Ryder had just come in from walking the dog; his cheeks were red and he rubbed his hands together as if warming them up.

"Do you want me to pour you a shot of whiskey to warm you up?" she asked. Her breath caught as his gaze slowly roamed over her then lingered on her mouth, making her burn.

"I got some other ideas about how to warm up, but a shot of whiskey's a good start."

Tingles skated over her skin, and she looked away from him. "Did you want me to start the fire?"

"I'll do it after I get out of these wet clothes." His footsteps faded down the hallway.

Savannah rose to her feet and padded into the kitchen to retrieve two glasses. She'd bought the premium black label of Jack Daniels for Ryder and a bottle of Bailey's Irish Cream for herself when she was in town the day before. She took down two tumblers and poured a hefty portion of whiskey in his and Bailey's in hers, then made her way back into the family room. Savannah took a sip of her drink hoping it would calm down her nerves. Ryder made her nervous and aroused more than she liked, and it didn't help one damn bit that he oozed masculinity from his every pore. The way he wore his tight-fitting flannel shirts gave her an idea of how wonderfully chiseled he was. She'd seen hints of ink rising up from underneath his shirt collars, and the ink on his arms intrigued and excited her. Savannah could never imagine Bret or any Carlton sporting a tattoo, and even though Bret once told her the vine of purple clematis flowers tatted right above her pubic bone was sexy, she knew deep down he thought it was trashy.

What worried her the most was that she was incredibly attracted to Ryder, not just physically, but intellectually and emotionally as well. It was like they complemented each other in some broken, twisted, and dangerous way.

The sound of a match striking snapped her eyes upward and in the direction of Ryder, who was by the fireplace throwing matches at the logs and bunched-up newspapers.

"I didn't even hear you come in," she said.

Without answering, Ryder looked over his shoulder and caught her in a heated gaze before turning his attention back to stoking the fire. A tremor vibrated along her body.

"Where's Brutus?" she asked.

"With Timmy." He chuckled.

Savannah watched him as he bent over and tossed another log into the fireplace, making his shoulder muscles ripple under the long-sleeved black T-shirt. *So damn sexy.* Ryder straightened up, placed the poker back in the iron stand and closed the mesh fire curtain, then he strode over to the couch.

"Does your leg hurt?" Savannah asked when she saw him grimace as he settled on the cushion.

"It's no big deal."

"If it's more comfortable, you can take it off." She held her breath, knowing this was a touchy topic with him.

Ryder paused for a few seconds, then he reached over and picked up his drink. "I'm good." The way he said it told her that it was the end of the conversation.

Savannah stretched out her legs, and he pinched her toes playfully. "You like fluffy things, don't you?" he asked tugging at her candy cane striped fuzzy socks.

"They make me feel warm and cozy."

"They're cute like you."

"Oh please … I'm too old to be cute."

Ryder tilted his head back. "How old are you?"

"Thirty-six," she groaned.

One corner of his mouth hitched up in a cocky smile. "I never had the hots for an older woman before."

Savannah lightly kicked him.

He laughed and squeezed her foot. "I like it though."

"Like I believe that. Why would you want me when you could have younger, prettier women falling at your feet? Brandi's at least ten or twelve years younger than me."

"Are you fucking kidding me? You're gorgeous and sexy in a way that drives men wild."

Bret didn't think so.

Ryder shook his head. "I'm not interested in young girls, and before you roll those beautiful blue eyes at me, I already explained about Brandi." He knocked her feet off the couch and moved toward her. "Give me your sweet lips, darlin'." Heat rippled off him.

Shivers zinged through Savannah's body, her pulse beat rapidly, and her stomach did somersaults as she leaned forward and fell into his arms. She touched his perfectly carved lips, and in an impatient gesture, he clutched the back of her neck and crushed his mouth against hers. He tasted of whiskey and peppermint from the candy cane he'd chomped on during the ride back, and she loved it.

Savannah pressed herself firmly against him, her muscles straining to get as close as she could. Aching to touch his heated skin, she pulled at his T-shirt until it lifted up from the waistband of his jeans, then she glided her fingers underneath the hem, pressing them against the corded muscles of his back. He groaned into her mouth, and the sound shuddered through her.

Ryder's mouth moved past hers and down to her jawline, where he planted soft kisses. Each brush of his trailing lips ignited flames along her skin.

"I want you so fucking bad. Now. I know you want me too," he rasped between kisses.

His words and touch sent carnal tingles down her spine. "I do want you. I ache for you, but—" The muscles in his back stiffened under her fingers as he broke away, his eyes meeting hers.

"But what?" Lines spanned across his forehead as he scowled.

"I want to be with you, but"—her gaze dragged away from his as she glanced at the hallway—"Timmy may come out. I don't want that to happen. As it is, everything that's been going on these days is confusing enough for him."

Ryder didn't respond right away, and Savannah expected him to pull away from her and tell her to go to hell before stalking out of the room. Instead, he swept his tongue across her lips then held her close.

"I understand, darlin'. Timmy's still thinking about his dad." His warm breath slipped over her skin and the place between her legs twinged with a dull throb.

"Tomorrow night we'll be alone," she whispered. "Timmy's going to a sleepover, remember?"

"That's right. Fuck baby, right now, tomorrow feels like it'll never get here." He bit her neck and she yelped. "I could just eat you all up."

"I'm going to have a mark there," she said, pulling away as she moved her hand to cover her neck.

"The next ones will be where no one but you and I can see them." Ryder winked at her and sat back.

The idea of her pale skin being the canvass for Ryder's love bites turned her on more than she cared to admit ... especially to him. "We'll see about that." She pushed off the couch. "Do you want another drink?" When he nodded, she scooped up his glass and walked into the kitchen to pour them each another.

Savannah sagged against the counter, staring out at the shards of moonlight highlighting patches of snow outside. The thought of them making love the following night threw her nerves into overdrive. She wanted it badly—it'd been so long since a man had desired her, but she worried it would change things between them. *Maybe he doesn't really want to ... I mean I'm the one who suggested tomorrow night. Could I have sounded more desperate? He didn't bring up the sleepover ... I did.*

"You need some help with those drinks?" Ryder asked.

Savannah hurriedly filled their glasses and handed a tumbler to him before sinking down on the other end of the couch; she didn't trust herself to be too close to Ryder.

Ryder took a large drink, placed his glass down and stared at her with those intense dark eyes that made her fluttery and intimidated at the same time. A few minutes passed before he shifted in his seat and faced her.

"Does Timmy ask a lot about his dad?" he said.

Savannah let out an audible sigh. "Not really. Bret didn't spend a lot of time with him."

"Even so, it must be hard on the boy and even harder on his dad."

Irritation pricked her skin. "I don't think so. Timmy's dad would never win a Father-of-the-Year award, and Timmy's used to not seeing very much of him." She took a sip of her drink. "Don't judge or presume things you don't know anything about."

With his gaze fixed on hers, Ryder paused for a few heartbeats then said, "Why don't you tell me?"

"Tell you what? How insensitive and cold Bret was to his own son?"

"Why you ran away from him."

Blood rushed to her head and her heart pounded so loudly in her ears that she was sure he could hear it. Covering her face with her hands, Savannah breathed in and out deeply until the panic clawing at her subsided. Ryder didn't bombard her with platitudes or ask what was wrong, he just sat there, and his silence comforted her. Slowly, her fingers slid down her face.

"He raped me," she said in a soft, steady voice. Then she told him about her assault, the details spilling out of her like gum-balls from a broken candy machine.

As she told him about her marriage and how Bret had see-sawed from charming to manipulative until the cruel side of him took over after Timmy was born, it was like she was dissolving layers of anger, numbness, shame, and hate. It was liberating. Ryder was the only person she'd opened herself up to completely. Deep down inside, she knew he wouldn't blame her for not pleasing her husband enough or not being the required perfect wife of a rich financier.

After several tissues, she leaned against the arm of the sofa, worn out. At some point during her monologue, Ryder had scooted over and placed Savannah's legs on his lap, but he gently pushed them down and then drew her close as he encased her in his arms. She tilted her head back and gazed into his eyes.

"The pussy you're married to doesn't appreciate you one fucking bit. He's a goddamn asshole. You deserve good things—like love, support, and happiness."

Tears rolled down her cheeks again, but he wiped them away and planted a tender and loving kiss on her lips. His unconditional under-standing buoyed her and helped to loosen the stranglehold of humiliation. He put his hands on each cheek and kissed her again, only this time it was more passionate, more possessive.

Ryder pulled his mouth away from hers. "I'd like just thirty minutes with that fucker to teach him a lesson. Goddamn sonofabitch," his said in a low voice.

Savannah curled her fingers around his wrists. Every time he held her face between his hands, it felt like he was untying all of her knots.

"I just want to move on with my life, but I'm so damn afraid of him and his money. I'll never let him take Timmy from me."

"Come here," he whispered.

Savannah pivoted around. Ryder put his arm around her, and she settled into the hollow of his neck. His body radiated warmth.

"I know he doesn't give a shit about Timmy, but Corinne, his mom, is such a mean bitch. She won't let this go."

Ryder kissed the side of her hair. "You gotta face this. I'll help you, and Cara can guide you with legal advice. No one's taking Timmy from you—I won't let them."

Savannah wanted to ask about his son and why he let the mother of his child take Colt away, but she didn't have the strength for it; she'd used up all her energy reliving that horrible day.

"I'm so happy I met you." Wrapping her arm around his waist, she squeezed it. "I know this sounds cheesy, but I really feel like you are our Christmas wish come true. I don't know what would've happened to us if you hadn't come into our lives."

Savannah didn't expect Ryder to say anything—that wasn't his way, but the way he held her tight and peppered kisses on her hair spoke volumes.

She burrowed deeper into the crook of his arm and closed her eyes.

CHAPTER FIFTEEN

RYDER PERCHED ON the edge of the bed and placed the suction liner over his cone-shaped stump as doubt snaked through him. What the hell was he thinking? If he undressed, Savannah would see it and probably cringe or pretend that it was okay, which would be even worse than if she ran away from him. *"You're not the man you used to be. I need a whole man."* Dana's words echoed through his head, and he smacked his fist against it trying to make them stop.

Savannah wants me—she knows about my leg. For fuck's sake, she held me while I freaked out that night. She's not Dana. He hung his head down and ran his fingers through his hair; he couldn't risk triggering an episode—not when his life seemed to be getting back to normal. Savannah was the first woman he'd been interested in since Dana left him. *What a fucking mess.*

Grabbing his prosthesis, he fit his protected flesh into the inner socket then stood up and pulled up his jeans. He'd learned long ago that it was easier to slide his jeans on over his artificial leg before putting it on. After buttoning his shirt and pulling on his boots, he opened the door to the sweet aroma of cinnamon and brown sugar curling around him.

When he entered the kitchen, Savannah was by the sink with her back to him. Her fine rounded ass moved in time to the beats of "Jingle Bell Rock" as she sang out loud while stacking pans in the chrome rack.

Ryder smiled and quietly walked over to put his arm around her waist.

"Oh!" Savannah craned her neck then giggled. "You scared the hell out of me."

"Don't stop dancing, darlin'," he said, his mouth barely touching her ear. He swept her hair to one side and gently sucked her earlobe between his teeth then kissed a trail to her shoulder. She moaned and cocked her head to the side, and her sweet ass wiggled against his hard-as-fuck dick.

"I like the way you move, baby," he rasped. His hand inched its way down toward her crotch until the jarring sound of the oven timer startled him. Savannah kissed his chin and broke away, then grabbed a pair of potholders before opening the oven door. She took out a sheet of bubbling cinnamon rolls, some of the gooey filling oozing onto the pan, and Ryder's stomach growled.

"Those smell fucking awesome, woman," he said.

"Are they ready yet?" Timmy asked as he walked into the kitchen. Brutus padded behind him, stretched and shook himself, then he circled several times before dropping to the ground.

"They will be real soon—I just have to ice them. Go ahead and sit down," Savannah said.

Ryder pulled out the chair for Timmy then slid into the one next to him. He bent down and ran his hand over his dog's thick fur.

"What have you and Brutus been up to?" he asked Timmy.

The small boy shrugged as he watched his mother spread icing over the warm rolls. "Mommy and me took Brutus for a walk."

"Mommy and *I*, not *me*, sweetie," Savannah said.

Timmy shifted his gaze to Ryder. "We went to our trailer."

A sharp pain hit him low and hard in the gut, and his heart clenched. "Why did you do that?" he asked, his focus on Savannah.

She pushed back the hair from her face with her wrist. "I had to get some things—like this cookie sheet, and I wanted to run the engine, but I couldn't get it to turn over."

"It's broken," Timmy added.

"I can take a look at it later. You planning on going somewhere?" He twisted his mouth. Damn, he hated to ask the question, but he had to know if Savannah and her boy were moving on as much as he'd dreaded the answer.

"Not really. I just thought I should run the engine. My dad used to pound that in our heads when we were teenagers."

Ryder let out a ragged breath. "Yeah, it's good to do that on cold days. It probably just needs a battery jump."

"Here you go," Savannah said as she placed the plate of cinnamon rolls in the middle of the table." She placed one on Timmy's plate and did the same for Ryder then poured coffee in his mug.

Ryder ran his hand up her thigh then winked at her when she looked down at him with a mischievous glint in her eyes.

"Is that all you're having for breakfast, champ?" Ryder stirred a dash of milk into his coffee.

"I had yogurt and bananas, strawberries and … what else did I have, Mommy?" Cream cheese frosting smeared across his face.

Savannah wiped a damp paper towel over his mouth and chin. "Blueberries and pineapple."

Ryder chuckled and picked up his roll then put it back on the plate. "Damn. I forgot to feed Brutus."

Savannah placed a hand on his shoulder. "I already fed him. Do you want some fruit salad? I picked up a bunch of frozen fruit at the store the other day."

Nodding, he watched her take down a bowl and spoon the colorful mixture into it. *How the fuck could her pansy-fuck-of-a-husband not cherish her? How could he do what he did to her?* All Ryder could think about was bashing the asshole's face in.

"When do I go over to Braxton's?" Timmy asked.

"Not for a few more hours. Do you want to do some puzzles?" Savannah wrapped her hands around the mug.

Why the fuck is everything this woman's doing driving me so damn crazy? Holding a fucking coffee cup is giving me a hard-on. What the hell? Ryder shifted in his seat to try and get more comfortable, but it didn't work. There was no way he was going to have Savannah see how hard he was. He grabbed a few more napkins from the holder and put them on his lap, breathing a sigh of relief when she stood up and walked over to the sink.

Ryder quickly shoved down the fruit salad, plopped another roll on his plate, and jumped up.

"I gotta finish up some stuff before Saturday night's Toys for Tots." Not waiting for her to respond, he hightailed it out of there with Brutus by his side.

He locked the door behind him and sat at the chair behind the worktable. After finishing his second roll, he tapped in Hawk's number then stared out the window as he waited for the biker to pick up.

"Hey, I was just getting ready to call you. Tonight's ass kicking is postponed until tomorrow night."

"Why's that?" Ryder was going to use the excuse of club business as the reason for Savannah and him not to fuck.

"Skinless said the douchebags got some concert they're going to tonight."

"How does a prospect know so much about these guys?"

"The bartender over there is his cousin."

"Are they still wearing the Colorado bottom rocker?"

"Yep. I can't wait to teach these punks a lesson. Fuck, dude, there's no respect anymore with these young guys. What happened to the days when an unspoken understanding among bikers was the one thing that bound all of us together?"

"It's gone, bro, and it's not just obsolete in the biker world," Ryder replied.

"I remember the new assholes on the block always used to contact us and ask permission to start a club in the area. Ah, hell ... those were the good days."

Ryder guffawed. "You act like you're an old man, bro."

"After staying up half the night with Isa, and the other half satisfying my old lady, I feel like one." Hawk chuckled. "How's it going with you and Savannah?"

"Good. Hey, I wanted to ask you a favor. Savannah's got a sonofabitch husband who's soon to be her ex. I told her to talk to Cara about it, but that's a different story. I wanna know who this fuckface is."

"Did he hurt her?"

"Yeah. I can't say too much about that, but I just want to know what he's capable of."

"Sure. What's the fucker's name?"

"Bret—one *t*—Carlton."

"Got it. I'll do some digging later tonight."

"Are you gonna be home for the sleepover?"

"Yeah—I wouldn't leave Cara alone with all that. Banger's coming over for a bit to go over some club business."

Ryder sucked in a sharp breath. "Have you found out anything about Colt?"

"Sorry, bro, but I can't find shit. I put it out there on the grapevine, but so far, nothing's come back."

"Maybe … with it out there, I may get lucky."

"Maybe. I can't believe the bitch did that to you," Hawk gritted.

"I don't get why she took Colt away like that and never let me know where he was. She acted like I purposely stepped on that goddamn landmine." Heat flushed his face as he clenched his fist.

"Let it go. Don't let this trigger an episode. Just breathe in and out—deeply. I'll keep count."

Ryder followed Hawk's advice, and by the time he was done, his anger and anxiety had dissipated.

"You're a good friend," Ryder said in a low voice.

"We watch out for each other."

"Yeah." But Ryder knew it was so much more than that. Their war experiences tied them together, but the brotherhood—the love and loyalty one brother felt for the other—was what bound them together for life.

"You want me to come by and pick up Timmy?"

"Nah. Savannah's gonna bring him. She wants to do some more shopping in town. Damn, that woman can drop some serious cash."

Hawk chuckled. "Sounds like Cara. We better not let those two go shopping together."

"That's for damn sure. Let me know about tomorrow night. See you, bro."

Ryder jammed the cell phone in his pocket, then he swiveled around in the chair and picked up one of the buildings in the train set to paint it. Woodworking was a detailed craft and required a lot of focus, and that's exactly what he needed at that moment to keep his thoughts off of Colt, along with that horrible day he'd lost his best friend, and how he'd have to turn down Savannah's advances later that night. Leaning over, he turned on the CD player and lost himself in the music of Suicidal Tendencies—one of his favorite bands. When he heard knocking on the door, he ignored it and hiked up the volume then went back to painting the wooden town he'd created.

THE SMELL OF whiskey, tobacco, pot, and pussy washed over Ryder as he entered the Insurgents' clubhouse. A small silver tree with blinking lights was out of place amid the framed posters of half-naked women on motorcycles. He glanced around and saw several of the members in various stages of fucking. Some of the club girls—Lola, Wendy, and Charlotte—were sucking some of the members' cocks, while Tania and Kristy sucked dick while being fucked at the same time. Yep ... a pretty normal Thursday night at the clubhouse.

Ryder hoisted himself on a barstool and told the prospect he wanted a double Jack. One of the prospects' jobs was to tend bar, and it was required that they knew what the members drank and had the drink ready and on the bar before a brother asked for it. Since Ryder was an inactive member and didn't go to the clubhouse much, he didn't expect Skinless, Hog, or Dagger to remember what he drank.

"Good to see you, bro," Axe said, clapping Ryder on the back. "It's been too long."

"It has. How's your boy doing?"

Axe chuckled. "Jagger's good. He just turned five months last week."

"What the hell are you doing here?" Animal asked as he settled on the stool next to Ryder.

"Stopped by for a drink and some company."

"What about your blonde roommate?" Animal picked up his beer bottle.

"Yeah … that's right. I heard you had a *roommate*." Axe nudged Ryder's arm.

Ryder narrowed his eyes. "She does her own thing."

"I thought you had something going with her. You two acted like it the other night in Main Square," Animal said.

"Just leave it the fuck alone, okay?" Ryder swiveled around and stared at Lola bouncing up and down on Helm's cock, her big tits swaying and her blonde hair flying. *Why am I hiding out here like a goddamn pussy? I'm a fucking biker—an Insurgent. Fuck!*

"I gotta go. I promised Baylee I'd stay with Jagger while she went out to dinner with a couple of her friends," Axe said as he put his empty glass down on the bar. "See you on Saturday." He bumped fists with Ryder then ambled away.

"Hey, baby." Brandi's sweet-smelling orange scent wafted around him. She leaned into him, her large breasts pressing against his chest, and planted a big kiss on his lips. "I'm so happy to see you."

A small smile tugged at the corners of his mouth as Ryder gently pushed her away. Her eyes widened and confusion marred her face.

"I just came by for a drink," he said.

Brandi's face fell. "Oh, I was hoping we could have some fun."

"Not tonight." He picked up the other drink the prospect put on the bar for him. "Did you help with putting up the tree?" Stupid question, but he wanted to break the awkwardness between them. She bobbed her head. "It's nice."

A wide grin broke over her face. "Thanks."

"Brandi, bring me a bottle of Coors," Smokey's deep voice boomed.

She looked over her shoulder and winked at the dark-haired biker. "I gotta go," she said to Ryder. "Take care of yourself and don't be a stranger." She rubbed against him as she picked up the bottle of beer then spun around and walked over to Smokey, her hips swaying wickedly.

After a few hours of motorcycle talk and playing pool, Ryder strode out of the club into the crisp, frigid night air and hauled himself up into the jeep. At that moment, he wished the roads weren't so damn icy so he could go for a long moonlit ride. He craved the serenity riding his bike always gave him, and if he still had his left leg, he'd already be on his Harley, taking a chance on the backroads.

The twinkling colored lights shimmered and cast a kaleidoscope of color on the snow, and he wondered if Savannah would be waiting up for him. After she'd returned from dropping off Timmy and shopping, he'd told her he was headed out to the clubhouse to hang with his brothers. He ignored the surprised, then pained, look that flashed across her face and, without saying anything more, he'd walked out of the house. It was a shitty thing to do, especially since she'd told him how her ass-wipe husband's penchant for twenty-year-olds made her feel insecure about her aging body. Ryder knew that he was giving Savannah mixed signals, but he couldn't stomach the look of disgust, which would most definitely be in her eyes, when she saw him without his prosthesis.

Brutus whined then barked gleefully, and Ryder shushed him before coaxing him outside. The German shepherd didn't stay more than fifteen minutes; the night air was even too cold for him. Ryder dried him off then walked out of the mud room.

He glanced into the family room, and there was no sign of Savannah, only the lit tree and the dying fire in the fireplace gave off any light.

"Come on, boy," Ryder whispered, gesturing to Brutus to follow him. When he passed Savannah's room, a thin sliver of yellow light seeped from under the closed door. Pausing at the door, he strained to hear any noise from within the room, but Brutus's panting was the only sound in the cabin. Turning away, he hastened to his room.

Ryder had just switched off the table lamp when a knock on the door startled him.

"Ryder?" Savannah's soft voice drifted through the door and wrapped around him. "Are you awake?"

He sat there, bedcovers clenched in his hands, and stared.

The brass knob jiggled, then the door opened slowly, and Savannah's silhouette appeared against the dim light of the hallway. And what a sexy outline it was: curvy, full tits, and mighty fine legs.

Brutus jumped up and barked.

"It's okay, boy." His voice sounded hollow and hoarse.

"Did I wake you?" she asked.

Her soft voice had a bit of rasp to it and was making his dick wake up.

"Nah ... I was just ready to turn in."

Without asking, she came into the room and slinked toward him. Ryder swallowed several times, his mouth felt like it was stuffed with cotton, and he wiped his sweaty palms on the comforter. Savannah stepped closer and the scent of her caressed him, the sound of her quick breaths stoked a fire deep down in his belly as desire for her raged through him.

"Do you want some company?"

Ryder didn't answer as she closed the space between them. Every turn of her head and sway of her hips mesmerized and enticed him until all he wanted to do was ravage and claim her, but he didn't move a muscle, he just sat there breathing harshly. The bed shifted slightly as she perched on the edge of the mattress. Lust twisted in his gut when her cool hand glided down his hot face, but when her tongue licked along his bottom lip, all his restraint vanished and he grabbed her, his fingers digging into her arms as he yanked her close to him. Hard and rough, he ground his lips to hers. Their mouths dissolved together, wet and hot and wild.

Ryder pulled away, breathless. "Fuck, darlin'," he growled, then he kissed her again, his hands still gripping her tightly. Dragging his lips down her chin to her neck, he bit her hard, and Savannah gasped and clutched him, fueling his lust even more.

"Ryder," she moaned.

He ran his hands over the soft fabric of Savannah's robe, his gaze holding hers, as he impatiently pulled at the sash and loosened it. Heat flickered in her deep blues, and when he heard the quick and soft catch of her breath, he cupped the back of her neck and lowered her mouth to his to capture it. Savannah ran her fingernails down his neck and shoulders, and it surprised him that he had to fight off a shudder at the feel of her fingers on his skin.

Grasping the front of the robe, he jerked it off her shoulders and molded his hands around her firm round tits that spilled a little out of his palms. The minute he touched them, greed took over and all he wanted was to devour them.

Savannah lifted up and arched back and her breasts jutted out.

"You're killing me, baby," he growled.

Ryder pulled her back to him and buried his face between the swell of her tits, then ran his tongue down over her soft skin, skimming the top of her lacy bra. With one fluid movement, he unhooked her bra and slid the straps down her arms, loving how her skin pebbled under his fingertips. She threw her bra on the floor and bent down. He dragged his mouth over the areola, nuzzling her, then seized one of her nipples between his teeth and gave it a sensual tug, which incited small gasps. His mouth teased one nipple while his fingers tormented the other, tugging, flicking, and pinching.

"That feels so good, Ryder," she moaned, burying her hands in his hair and yanking it hard.

The room was dimly lit, and he wanted to see her in the light, but he didn't want her to see *him*.

"Hang on," she whispered.

Savannah broke away and stood up, and he could see the outline of her magnificent tits swinging as she bent over and reached for the table lamp.

Apprehension assaulted him.

"What the fuck are you doing?"

Savannah's movements stopped as if she were frozen. "Turning on the lamp. I can't really see you."

"I don't want it on." *Don't try and get me to fucking talk about it.*

"Don't you want to see my body?" A thread of insecurity wound around her voice.

"Of course I do, it's just—"

"That's good." Relief replaced uncertainty. "I want to see you too. I bet you don't know that I've been whipping myself into a frenzy imagining how sexy you look under your flannel shirts."

Ryder smiled.

"I can put a scarf or something over the lampshade to mute the brightness if you'd like."

"It's a three-way bulb," he said thickly.

"Then let's see how we do at the lowest wattage."

The click reverberated in his ears, and then a gentle yellowish glow filled the room. Ryder's gaze fell on the most gorgeous tits he'd ever seen: big with pink areolae surrounding luscious nipples—red and taut from his attention.

"Fuck," he murmured under his breath.

Reddish streaks painted her cheeks as she folded her arms over her naked breasts.

"Don't cover them—they're fucking awesome."

Her arms dropped to her sides, and he drank in the sensational sight of her: smooth ivory skin, electrifying blue eyes, perfect breasts, and soft curves with a little belly pudge. As if ashamed, Savannah covered her belly and shook her head.

"I used to have a flat stomach before Timmy, but everything I've tried hasn't helped to get rid—"

"Hush, darlin'. A lot of men like curves, it's feminine as fuck. I know I like having something soft to cuddle. You're a stunning woman." Ryder's eyes drifted to the tattoo disappearing beneath her lacy panties. "And that tat is sexy as fuck. Come over here, woman."

When Savannah was in reaching distance, he yanked her to him and she fell on top of his chest, laughing as she propped herself up. Ryder went for her tantalizing tits again, bringing them close together and sucking both her nipples at the same time. She gasped and moaned and her hair fell down over him, tickling his face and shoulders.

As he feasted on her, she slipped her fingers under his T-shirt, and scratched her way down over his muscles. He hissed in a sharp breath as she rubbed her fingertips over his skin while biting his shoulder.

"Take this off," she whispered, tugging at his shirt. He whipped it off over his head and smirked when she gasped as she took him in.

"Like what you see?" he asked, as he pinched her tits.

"Oh, yeah. I knew you had a fantastic build, but it's even better uncovered." She lowered her head and brushed her lips against the macabre skulls and black roses decorating his chest. "I like these," she murmured, tracing the tribal symbols curling around his biceps. "And this one." He watched her tongue lightly lick the tangled barbed wire circling around his forearm. There was something so fucking sensual about Savannah touching and exploring his tattoos.

Savannah looked up at him, the tip of her tongue resting against her upper lip and he wanted to suck the shit out of it. Taking her plum-tipped finger, she outlined his lips, teasing him as he tried to capture it in his mouth, then she very slowly ran it past his chin and down his throat until it rested on his chest—on the face of a melting skull.

Savannah lowered her head and place a soft kiss on his inked skin. "Your tattoos are so intricate"—she kissed his right pec—"and very"—she kissed his left pec—"very sexy"—she swirled her tongue over his nipple and bit it—"like you."

Desire burned and crackled inside him, a voracious wildfire scorching a trail to his hard-as-hell dick. He grunted when her tongue slid up his throat and their mouths melded—passionately, deeply, and demanding.

"I want you so badly," she smothered on his lips.

"You've got me, darlin'," he rasped.

His hand glided down her side, landing on the waistband of her panties. Looping the elastic around his finger, he tugged at it until it revealed a bare ass cheek. Digging his fingers into her soft flesh, he bit the bottom of her lip and a small yelp erupted from her mouth.

"Fuck, woman. I've been jerking to fantasies about touching your ass."

Savannah helped him take off her panties then she raised up a bit and began to pull the covers down. Ryder tensed and grasped the comforter away from her.

"Please don't do that. I want to see you."

He sucked in a sharp breath. *I'm not ready for that. I bet my shriveled stump isn't in your fantasy.*

"Please?" She peppered his face, jawline, and neck with feathery light kisses, and then she traced his ear with her tongue before drawing the lobe into her mouth.

Fuck! His hold on the sheets loosened, and he lost himself in the scent and feel of her as she rubbed her body against his. The rush of cool air snapped him back to the moment, and he grabbed at the bedcovers, but it was too late—she'd pulled them off, exposing him.

Without taking her lips away from his flesh, Savannah dragged down his boxers, and then wrapped her fingers around his erection; they felt amazing as they gently traced the veins up and down his cock, tickling the rim and gliding over the sensitive mushroom head.

"Do you like that?" she asked softly.

"Yeah," he hissed, stroking her hair.

Ryder watched her face as she met his gaze then, without breaking eye contact, lowered her mouth onto his cock and took him in deep. His abdominal muscles tightened as he gripped the edge of the mattress and bit the inside of his mouth; as he watched her head move up and down, her mouth was hot and unyielding.

"Fuck, darlin', you gotta stop 'cause you're gonna make me blow."

She sucked harder and deeper.

Ryder leaned over and placed his hands on her face, pulling her off him. "I want to come inside you." He opened the nightstand drawer and took out a condom then hurriedly tore the package with his teeth. Savannah snapped it away from him and took out the sheath and glided it on him. *Damn that was sexy.* "Come on and ride me."

Savannah spread her knees apart and straddled him, bending over deeply to press her mouth against his. Ryder pushed his tongue inside while tweaking her nipples, and then she broke away and reclined on her heels.

"Fuck, you're wet," he said as he looked at the shining folds of her sex.

She was totally shaven down there, and the vine tattoo curved wickedly low, just barely touching the top of her swollen lips. Reaching out, his fingers parted those lips, revealing the tempting, glistening flesh beneath.

"Your pussy is perfection, darlin'," he said, his eyes fixed on the tiny pearl at the top, which was barely peeking out from beneath its hood.

"The way you're staring at me makes me want to come right now," she said, reaching around and running her fingertips over his balls.

"Fuck," he whispered. "Come closer." His hands gripped her hips and brought her up as he slid down on his back and then positioned her over his mouth. The heady scent of her arousal swirled around him, drawing him closer until his tongue slid into her folds. She moaned then gasped when he ran it up the entire length of her opening.

"You taste so damn good, woman."

His fingers explored her flesh, moving upward, circling around her ever-growing nub without touching it directly, and then down, past her heated slit until they tickled the soft flesh around her puckered rosebud.

Savannah whimpered and bucked slightly, and he buried his tongue in her folds while sliding two fingers inside her. Her walls cocooned them with their wet heat, and he twisted them while flicking her hardened sweet spot with the flat side of his tongue.

"Oh, shit," she whispered before rocking against his mouth and fingers.

Closing his mouth around her erect nub, he sucked it gently while thrusting his fingers in and out of her. Glancing up, he watched her tits bounce and listened to her hoarse cries as she climaxed, collapsing on top of him like a blanket. He watched the aftershocks of her orgasm pulse through her, and he couldn't resist rolling one plump nipple between his thumb and forefinger. *Fuck, she's beautiful.* She was all soft and flushed and relaxed.

After several minutes, Savannah tilted her head back and smiled at him, her eyes misted over.

"That was incredible," she said, scooting down to kiss his Adam's apple.

Before he could say anything, she sat up and positioned her hips over him. "Your turn." Her lips tugged up into a devilish grin as she leaned down and pressed them to his, her hard nipples caressing his chest. Pushing back, she curled her fingers around the base of his dick and guided it inside her.

"Damn, you're big," she said as her flesh wrapped around him and started to eat him up.

"So damn wet and good," he gritted, controlling her movements with his hands until he filled her up, her pussy sucked tight to his dick.

"Oh, fuck," she moaned, looking at him.

Ryder kissed her face and ground his hips, thrusting up into her as she dropped back down on him. Over and over, Savannah slowly lifted off him until he almost escaped her, and then she'd push back down, burying him inside her heated walls while she moaned softly. It was fucking unbelievable, and it took all the strength he had not to blow his wad.

He reached out and worked his finger on Savannah's clit as she picked up the pace and bounced on him.

"I'm gonna fuck you hard, darlin'," he gritted as he thrust up, his hand moving her up and down as his finger kept stoking the side of her turgid nub. Savannah moaned long and loud, her sweet ass smacking against his thighs as she rode him.

Driving into her harder and rougher, he felt her insides squeeze around him and he knew he wouldn't be able to hold out much longer.

A light sheen coated her face and she threw her head back. "I'm coming!"

As she cried out, he could feel it: a thousand fingers gripping him at once and stroking his dick. He watched as she writhed on him, then his balls retracted and his cock began to pulse, and a moment later, he joined her with a chorus of growls, grunts, and groans, shuddering his own release.

"Savannah," he panted, sliding his hand through her silky blonde hair.

"Ryder," she croaked.

He coaxed her to roll next to him, and he pressed her close. Warmth spread through him as his heart beat erratically. It'd been a long time since he felt anything toward a woman, and Savannah complemented him very well. Where he was rough, she was smooth. Where he blew his top, she kept her cool. Where he was introverted, she was extroverted. She was the part that made him whole, and he wasn't quite sure what to do about it.

Then she rested her hand on his withered limb and he tensed. "You don't need to do that to prove something to me," he said.

"I know," she whispered. "My hand just went there. I wasn't thinking—I forgot how touchy you are about it. I'll move it if you want me to." Savannah started to withdraw it, but he grasped her hand and held it firm against his flesh.

"Thank you for letting me in," she said softly.

Ryder grunted and held her tighter. Everything about her threw him off center, and he wasn't sure what to do about it. He knew that what they'd just shared went beyond two lonely, broken people fucking, but he didn't want to think about it. His past relationship taught him that he couldn't count on women, but Savannah was so gentle, so honest.

Her deep breathing told Ryder that she'd fallen asleep. He kissed the top of her head then buried his nose her hair and inhaled her scent. He didn't want a single day to go by without her fragrance filling his nostrils.

And with that thought weaving through his mind, he drifted off into a deep sleep.

CHAPTER SIXTEEN

BRET CARLTON OPENED the crystal decanter and poured himself a drink before answering the vibrating phone on the end table. Harry's name flashed across the screen and for a split second, Bret debated about letting the call go to voicemail, but his mother's stern face popped into his mind, and he brought the cell phone to his ear.

"I found your ex and your son," Harry said.

"She's not my *ex*—we're still married." Bret took a sip of the brandy, welcoming the smooth, warm burn as it slid down his throat.

"Whatever. I spotted them at that community tree ceremony."

Bret shook his head and took another sip of his drink. "Savannah's so fucking predictable. Where's she staying?"

"I don't know, Boss. She's not staying in town."

Bret's fingers gripped the glass tightly. "You already established that days ago. Where the fuck is she staying with my son?"

"I'm not sure."

"That's not a ten-thousand-dollar answer, Harry." Heat rose up his neck.

"She's staying with some dude, and from the looks of it, they're more than roommates," Harry said, hardness creeping into his voice.

"What the fuck does that mean?" Bret sat down on the wingback chair next to the fireplace.

"They acted like they had something going on, and your son seemed pretty friendly with him."

Bret paused, trying to take in what Harry was saying. *That's why the old bitch ran away—she's been having an affair. What a sanctimonious hypocrite.* "Who's the guy?"

"A biker with an outlaw club."

"What?"

"He's involved with the Insurgents—they're based in Pinewood Springs."

"That figures. I wonder where the hell she met him. Are there any of *those* people in Boston?"

"No—only in the west. Didn't your mother-in-law say Savannah met him when she got stuck in the blizzard?"

"Yes, but that's only been a little more than a couple of weeks ago." When he and Savannah had first begun dating, it took him forever to get inside her pussy, so he doubted that she'd take up with a stranger so soon.

"I just call it like I see it, Boss."

"Did you follow them home?"

"Uh … there were so many damn people, they got lost in the crowd. I'm keeping my eyes open around town. I'm sure your wife will want to do some Christmas shopping. When I spot her, I'll follow her."

"Yes—do your fucking job. I want to know where the hell this dirt-bag lives, and who the bitch is shacking up with. I can't believe she'd be doing this with my son there."

"I'll find out everything. I know what I'm working with now."

"I can't get away until after the weekend. Before I go to some damn hick town, I want all the information on this asshole, and I don't want any fucking excuses why you don't have it."

"I'll have it all for you."

The cell phone landed with a thud on the end table as Bret stood up and paced around the den. The thought of Savannah with another man infuriated him, and he couldn't wrap his head around it. *She* had *to have met him in Boston, but where the hell was she that she'd meet someone like him?* Bret knew Savannah's schedule—he made it a point to keep tabs on his wife, and she rarely veered off from her daily routine of fundraising meetings, lunches with her girlfriends, and taking care of Timmy. Bret cracked his knuckles. *Of course, Timmy was the focal point of all your days.* The thought that she would take up with someone she'd just met didn't sit well with him, so Bret had to convince himself that Savannah had been cheating on him and that's the reason she'd left. *It was all an elaborate plan, and calling your mom and telling her you were stuck in a blizzard was genius, bitch, but you didn't fool me, did you?*

The grandfather clock against the maroon-painted wall across from the picture window chimed loudly as it counted eight strokes. Restless as hell now, Bret swiped through his electronic black book. He wanted a young blonde with big tits, a fake tan, and a nice rounded ass. His gaze fell on Kim's number with a notation "Loves raunchy sex." *Just what I need.* He'd planned to stay in and have a quiet night catching up on some of the television shows he'd recorded, but Harry's call ruined all that, and now he planned to fuck Savannah right out of his head.

Bret tapped in the number and smiled when Kim's enthused voice cried, "Daddy! It's been too long."

"I'll send a car to pick you up. Wear the filthiest lingerie you got, babygirl."

"I can't wait to play with you," she gushed.

"Make yourself pretty for me. See you in an hour."

Once he secured the driver and the hotel suite, a rush of adrenaline surged through him. Kim was the perfect woman to help him forget about his old wife and her biker lover. As he ran the electric shaver over his face, the image of Savannah when he'd first seen her years before waiting tables at Luna's floated through his mind, and then Timmy's face with his spattering of freckles and dark eyes replaced it, and Bret's muscles tensed. *You changed the game plan, Savannah, and now I find out you've been cheating on me? Fuck that.* He pounded the porcelain sink with his fist. *No one makes a fool out of Bret Philip Carlton. No fucking one.*

Impeccably dressed, he walked out of their penthouse and rode the elevator down to the parking garage. As he drove to the hotel, loneliness gnawed at his gut, and he cursed his renegade wife. Bret's knuckles whitened as he gripped the steering wheel hard.

"You want a fight, bitch? You got it," he said out loud.

Then he sped up and merged into traffic on Tremont Street.

CHAPTER SEVENTEEN

C OLD SLIVERS OF light flecked through the kitchen window casting watery stripes across the hardwood floor. The coffeemaker buzzed on the counter and the air carried the rich aroma of roasted dark beans. A bar of light from the walk-in pantry formed a rectangle on the floor in front of the half-opened door, and a rendition of "Jingle Bells" filtered into the room. Ryder smiled as he stood listening to Savannah sing as she rummaged through the pantry shelves. He walked over to the island and waited for her, not wanting to intrude on her private moment.

Savannah closed the door with her foot, her arms loaded with boxes and cans.

"Let me help you," he said, and her head snapped up as if startled to hear his voice, and then she beamed. Ryder took the bag of flour from her hands and the cans of pumpkin and evaporated milk and turned around to place them on the counter.

"You planning to stay in and cook all day?" he asked.

Setting the other items down, she nodded. "I'm going to make Christmas cookies, pumpkin pies, and waffles. The waffles are for breakfast, but I wanted to bake a pumpkin pie and make up a tin of cookies for Cara and Hawk. They've been so nice to me and Timmy." Her sparkling eyes hit him right in the groin.

Ryder drew her to him, his lips capturing hers. They were warm and soft and a small moan slipped past them. His tongue invaded the recesses of her mouth, plunging and swirling, until he felt her body lean into his embrace.

"You're something special, woman," he said, his hands gliding down her jeans and landing on her ass. Cupping her cheeks, he pressed her closer to him.

"You're not too shabby, either." Savannah swept her tongue across his lips and he caught it, sucking it inside his mouth, tasting it.

"Spearmint—I like it," he muttered as he broke away a bit. He ground his hard dick against her, lust shooting through him. Grabbing her hand, he pushed it against his rigid bulge, and she moved it up and down. "That feels real good, darlin'"—he dug his fingers into the denim fabric—"but it'll feel a lot better inside your sweet pussy," he growled, nipping at the base of her throat.

"Mmm … I know it will, but Hawk already dropped Timmy off"— she threw her head back, and he ran his tongue up her throat—"and we already had a hot turn in the sheets before Timmy came home."

"That doesn't mean shit, baby. Now that I've tasted you, I want more. I've always been a greedy sonofabitch." And it was true. There was something about Savannah that made him want to lose himself over and over in all those luscious curves, to lick, suck, and fuck to oblivion. And he wanted them to belong only to him.

Savannah cocked her head to the side, and Ryder lavished kisses all over the side of her neck, loving the way she kept stroking his encased dick and becoming more aroused by the millisecond. The sounds of her whimpers and hushed moans was enough to make him mess up his pants right there and then.

Ryder heard Brutus's familiar footsteps, and he stiffened then pulled away. "Timmy," he whispered at a confused Savannah. He followed her gaze toward the doorway and saw Timmy shuffle in.

"I'm hungry," he said. "I think Brutus is too."

Ryder laughed, pinched Savannah's ass and walked over to the bottom cupboard and pulled out a bag of dried dog food. A flurry of barks and yelps ensued as the dog jumped up on his hind legs, his tailing wagging furiously. Ryder filled the stainless steel dog bowl, and Brutus nudged against his leg to get at the food.

"See—he was hungry," Timmy said, standing next to the island.

Ryder ruffled the boy's head then put the large bag back into the cupboard. "Did you have a good time with your friends last night?"

"It was the bestest," the boy said, his head bobbing.

"It was the *best*, honey, not the *bestest*," Savannah said.

Ryder winked at Timmy. "Your mom said you got in early this morning."

"Yeah. Mr. Benally said he had stuff to do. Everyone went home early."

Hawk's at church ironing out the details for tonight. He glanced at Timmy and Savannah talking.

"… waffles. They'll be ready in about fifteen minutes."

"Did you buy out the grocery store?" Ryder asked picking up the box of waffle mix.

She lightly punched his arm and snatched the box from his hands. "Smart aleck."

He swatted her ass as she passed in front of him, the island hiding his action from Timmy, who was now seated at the table.

"Do you want to help me decorate some cookies for Isa and Braxton?" Savannah asked her son.

"Okay." Timmy yawned.

"Maybe after we eat, you want to lie down for a nap."

Timmy shrugged, his gaze fixed on Brutus chomping away on the bully stick Ryder had just given him.

The mixing bowl slid on the counter, and Savannah put a dishrag under it then resumed stirring the batter. Ryder watched her every move—along with the way her tits swayed with each turn of the spoon. His dick twitched. *I can't believe I'm getting a hard-on watching her make waffles. Shit. This woman has me turned so fucking inside out.* He turned away and pulled out two cups from the cupboard.

"Do you want a cup of coffee?" he asked.

She glanced at him and smiled. "That'd be great."

A gulp of the strong java hit the spot. He stood staring out the window, looking at the snow dusting the pine trees, the snowmen he and Timmy had built over the last week, and the deer as they cautiously walked over the snow-covered terrain then disappeared into the forest of trees. The ping of his phone drew his attention, and he glanced down.

Hawk: *We'll meet at 9 at clubhouse.*

Ryder: *Cool. Who's going?*

Hawk: *Besides us – Throttle, Wheelie, Axe, Rock, Jax, Animal, Smokey, Helm.*

Ryder: *See you then.*

"Waffles are ready," Savannah said.

"Yippee!" Timmy giggled.

Ryder picked up the pitcher of orange juice and brought it over to the table. Then he sat down and rubbed his hand up and down Savannah's thigh as she put three waffles on his plate. The scent of— clean, floral, and a touch of vanilla—wrapped around him, and he wondered how he'd managed without her for so long.

ICE CRUNCHED UNDER the Insurgents' boots as they made their way to the clubhouse parking lot, their breaths vapor in the frigid air. They slid into SUVs, cursing the ice and snow that stopped them from taking their bikes to their destination. Ryder cupped his hands in front of his face and blew into them, his breath warming his cold face.

"It's like the fuckin' North Pole out here," Wheelie said as he opened the back door of Hawk's SUV.

"I'm freezing my balls off 'cause some damn punks don't know shit about respect," grumbled Smokey as he scooted across the seat.

"Kimber was curled up on the couch in front of the fire when I left," Throttle said, closing the car door. "I'm gonna kick those bikers' asses real good for taking me away from my woman."

Hawk chuckled and Ryder nodded, knowing too well how Throttle was feeling. He'd rather be back at the cabin getting cozy with Savannah than out in the dark, but if he was being real honest with himself, it felt good as hell to be back on a mission with his brothers. He'd missed the action, and for the past few years, he'd let himself disengage from the brotherhood too much. Hawk had pushed him to start hanging out more at the club the year before, and Ryder had seriously considered giving up his inactive status and getting back into the thick of things.

"We ready to roll?" Hawk asked, looking behind him. The men lifted their chins, and he put the SUV in gear and followed the caravan of cars in front of them.

The parking lot was practically full when the bikers arrived at the bar. With heads down and hands jammed in leather jackets, the men walked across the lot then opened the scratched-up wooden door and went inside.

Brown Barrel was a classic dive bar: no karaoke, no bar trivia, only drinking as the main activity. An unruly mess of a bar in the seedier part of town, the place boasted five-dollar mugs of beer, a free jukebox with an eclectic musical selection—which included Elvis Presley, The Bee Gees, and Lamb of God—and a place where the patrons could smoke inside without any hassles.

The men pushed through the crowd and walked up to the bar, their eyes scanning the room for anyone wearing a three-piece rocker with Colorado on it. Ryder smiled when he saw the scuffed formica bar, which brought back memories of the hours he'd logged in there the summer he'd graduated from high school. He'd been bearded and had enough of a sturdy, muscular physique back then that he could get into the bar, no questions asked. The first time he'd legally ordered a beer and engaged in a philosophical conversation with an old biker, he knew he was hooked, and thus began his love affair with bars, motorcycles, and the Insurgents.

An old, unremarkable television tuned to the local news sat on a corner shelf next to the bar, but no one was watching. A steady stream of men going to the restroom confirmed that key bumps were still worth a visit to one of the filthiest bathrooms Ryder could remember. A few men decked out in faded denim vests, gripping the hands of worn-out women with gaunt faces and stringy hair, sauntered down a hallway, and Ryder remembered the time he'd fucked an older woman on top of one of three washing machines in the back room of the bar. The owner had let customers both wash clothes and have sex in the room. Ryder would bet his leather cut that the washing machines were still there.

"Here you go, bro," Helm said, handing Ryder a mug of frothy beer.

"See any chicks you want to hit on after we kick some ass?" he asked.

"Nah. What about you?" Ryder replied, lifting the mug to his lips.

"That redhead by the jukebox swaying to the Tina Turner tune looks hot." Helm pushed his shoulder length hair over his shoulders. "What do you think?"

Ryder glanced at her and gave a half shrug. "She doesn't look like she fits in here. As a matter of fact, there're quite a few people in here who look like they belong in West Pinewood Springs."

"But do you think she's hot?" Helm said.

"I guess." The only color hair that was on Ryder's mind was blonde, and the only woman on his mind was Savannah. No other woman compared to her, and he couldn't wait to get home and fuck her hard and fast. Just thinking about it made him squirm, and he had to concentrate on the ceiling stain that was in the exact same location as it was seventeen years before.

"Why are there so many shits in here who should be in the bars downtown? They're giving dives a bad name," Animal said as he sidled up to Ryder.

"I was just noticing that. I think they're just fucking bored living in their safe and controlled neighborhoods. That shit can be soul-killing, so they come here for some danger," Ryder replied.

"They're gonna get it real quick," Jax said jerking his head toward the door.

Ryder looked over his shoulder and saw four men wearing leather jackets with a Twisted Kings' patch. Two of the men looked to be in their mid-twenties, while the other two appeared to be in their late twenties or early thirties. Two were very muscular, one was short and scrawny, the other, medium height and stocky.

"We can easily take these fuckers down," Jax said.

"Hell, I could take them down by myself," Rock said.

"Shouldn't be a problem," Ryder replied, turning back around.

Hawk came over to the brothers, his gaze fixed on the four men making their way over to the bar. "We need to see their rockers before we approach them," he said.

The men agreed, and Ryder watched as the bikers leaned against the bar and talked to the bartender. It'd been a while since Ryder had been in a fight. Once he'd returned to Pinewood Springs and built his house, he turned the basement into a gym and worked out six out of seven days for years. He wanted to keep his strength up, so when Joey—one of the vets in the counseling sessions—told Ryder that he trained at a mixed martial arts studio, Ryder had to check it out. All he wanted was to be able to defend himself and hold his own, which he proved on a few occasions that he could do just that. It was a long, grueling process to get where he was now, but standing among his brothers as an equal, all the hard work had been worth it.

"The one asshole just took off his jacket, and he's got the Colorado bottom rocker on the back of his cut," Animal said.

"Let's go," Hawk replied.

As the group of Insurgents made their way over to the members of the Twisted Kings, people moved out of their way; some of the more seasoned dive patrons made a beeline for the back of the bar or down the hallway. The yuppies continued drinking, playing pool, and ordering more beer, seemingly oblivious to the impending conflict.

A young woman bumped into Ryder, spilling her beer all over him.

"I'm so sorry," she said, her perfectly manicured fingers wiping at his jacket. "I tripped." Ryder followed her gaze down to her open-toed heels. "Not the best choice in footwear, right?" She smiled sweetly.

Ryder jerked back and grabbed the napkin she offered him. "Shit's about to get real, so you better haul your privileged ass outta here. Go out back or something," he said, mopping up the liquid.

"You want to go out back with me?" Her eyes ran over his body then landed on his face. "Okay … cool."

"You're in the wrong fucking bar, lady. I'm telling you to get out because you might get hurt." Ryder whirled around and stalked over to the bikers.

"You fuckers enjoying yourselves?" Throttle asked as he reclined against the bar, pinning one of the guys in.

The stocky man turned around, his eyes widening at the outlaws surrounding him and his buddies.

"We got a real problem here," Hawk said as he jerked his head at the bartender.

Ryder saw the man raise his hands to a group of clueless patrons as if saying that he was done serving drinks for a while. He walked to the end of the bar and stood there, his eyes fixed on the Insurgents. Ryder, not worried that the dude would call the badges, focused his attention back to Hawk.

"What is it?" the taller Twisted King asked.

"Your bottom rocker's laying claim to an occupied area. You're in Insurgents' territory."

"So?" the other member said.

"Fuck, Tag, this is serious," the scrawny member said.

"Better listen to the dude, *Tag*, this is fuckin' serious." Hawk leaned in real close so that his chest laid against the back of one of the members.

"We're just dudes who like to ride," the scrawny one said, his eyes darting to each of the Insurgents and back like a ping-pong game.

"We know that's fuckin' bullshit," Rock said.

"Take the fuckin' rocker off now, or we'll do it for you," Smokey gritted.

"You sonsofbitches don't know shit about respect," Ryder said, putting his foot up on the bar rail.

The stocky guy cleared his throat. "We should've asked your club for permission to wear it. We made a mistake. We'll take care of it."

"Duke is right," the scrawny man said.

Tag glared at them, and from the way his brothers scowled at him, Ryder knew Tag was going to regret the day he ever affixed the Colorado bottom rocker to his cut.

"Shut the fuck up, Pencil," the other tall man said.

"Let's just take the damn thing off, Gear," Pencil replied.

"Enough of this pussy bullshit!" Hawk grabbed Tag by the back of his neck. "We're gonna teach you how to show some respect.

"Then if you wanna keep wearing the patch, there'll be an outright war. It's pretty fuckin' simple," Axe said.

"It's not just us. We got a lot of members," Tag said, a slight tremor lacing his voice.

"We know, and we're gonna deal with them after we're done teaching you a lesson," Wheelie replied while the other Insurgents grunted their agreement.

"Let's go," Hawk said.

Wheelie, Axe, and Jax took hold of Gear and dragged him toward the door while Ryder, Smokey, and Animal escorted a squirming Tag out of the bar. Hawk, Rock, Helm and Throttle joined them in the alley with Pencil and Duke in tow.

"No one lays claim to Insurgents' territory." Hawk glanced over at Ryder and gestured him forward.

Ryder swung his good leg and it landed in Tag's belly and the man fell to his knees. Then the Insurgents descended on the four men who failed to show them the appropriate respect.

Boots stomped.

Fists punched.

Chains whipped.

Bones cracked.

Cries echoed.

Blood flowed.

At the end of it, the four men lay on the cold pavement beaten to a pulp, their patches sliced off their cuts. The outlaws weren't sure which ones belonged to the fallen Twisted Kings, but the two they took bore the Twisted Kings' logo.

Rock bent down low. "Your fuckin' club no longer exists."

Ryder helped Axe, Wheelie, Throttle and Smokey put the bikes on Throttle's flatbed pickup. Ryder handed the patches over to Wheelie, who lifted his chin as he crammed them in his pockets; the patches would be burned and the bikes stripped down for spares or resold.

"What about the other fuckers? Are we going over there now?" Ryder asked.

Wheelie shook his head. "We decided at church to teach whoever walked into the bar tonight a lesson. If the other fucks continue to wear the rocker and act like a club, we'll wipe them out."

Nodding, Ryder inhaled deeply. He seriously doubted the others would be a problem, but if they were, he and his brothers would take care of them. They had to because the punks broke the rules and failed to see the Insurgents as the dominant controlling club in Colorado. The Insurgents had to make an example of the Twisted Kings to show that the outlaw club wouldn't tolerate *any* disrespect in their territory. Wars started when clubs failed to follow territorial rules, as the Insurgents knew all too well, and those wars quickly escalated out of control and could go on for years, causing more agony and bloodshed than what was done that night.

Ryder swung his legs into the SUV and rested his head back. All he could think about on the drive back to the clubhouse was Savannah; he couldn't wait to hold her in his arms.

He stretched out his legs and stared out the window. Shades of trees appeared like smudges in the landscape as darkness yawned behind them.

Soon he'd be home.

CHAPTER EIGHTEEN

S AVANNAH PEEKED OUT the curtain, her eyes adjusting to the darkness as they strained to see if someone was out there past the trees watching her. Nothing.

"Are you looking for Ryder?" Timmy asked.

She glanced behind her and saw Timmy fitting a piece into a puzzle. "Yes, but he's not back yet."

"How come?"

"He said he may be late. How's your puzzle coming along?" The curtain fell from her hand, and she walked over to where Timmy sat on the floor, his elbows propped on his knees.

"It's going good." He picked up another piece and tried to fit it in a space that was a tad bit too small.

As Savannah watched him, her nerves jumped at every sound in the cabin; she never noticed before how much noise a house could make. She'd seen the man from the tree-lighting night when she and Timmy went into town to see the Christmas displays in the windows on Main Street. She didn't have the heart to ask Ryder to do *yet another* holiday outing with them, especially since she knew he wasn't a fan of the yuletide season.

It'd been about thirty minutes before she'd had a feeling that someone was watching her. Sure enough, she'd glanced behind her shoulder and that man was there again, his deep-set eyes boring into her. Savannah had prodded Timmy along, making sure to stay with the large crowd that walked from window to window, and when they'd finished, she literally dragged poor Timmy to the SUV and threw him in.

Not wanting to go home quite yet, Savannah had driven to Ruthie's for a snack, and fear curdled in her stomach when she saw *his* two sharp eyes staring at her out of the darkness. He had continued to follow them, at least she thought it had been him. Too petrified to turn onto roads that weren't familiar, Savannah drove back to the house using the only route she knew, and then the car that she'd thought was his drove right past the road.

But if it was him, now he knows the road. All he has to do is come back and take it and it'll lead right to us. A fit of barking erupted from Brutus, and Savannah cried out and jumped up from the floor.

Timmy laughed. Brutus kept barking. Savannah's heart pumped against her throat.

"Brutus! Calm down," she said.

"I think he wants to go outside," Timmy said, pointing at the dog, who stood by the front door with his ears erect and his body stiff.

Shit! Wait ... Ryder has guns coming out of his ass. He told me where the bullets are. She folded her arms against her chest. "Timmy, don't move. I'll be right back. Don't let Brutus out or anything, okay?"

"Uh-huh." Timmy rolled around on the floor.

"Please promise me you won't move."

"I promise, Mommy."

Savannah dashed to the master bedroom and retrieved four bullets, then she ran into the workshop and took a rifle down off the wall. Her father had taught all his children how to shoot, and she quietly thanked him for that as she loaded the gun. Hurrying back into the family room, Savannah slowly walked toward the front door, which Brutus was now scratching frantically.

"He needs to go to the bathroom, Mommy."

Terror raced through her veins as she crept on weakened legs toward the door.

"Stay where you are," she said to Timmy. She put her clammy hand on the knob and held the rifle tight in her other one. Again, she looked outside through the peephole, and once again, nothing but darkness.

Slowly, she turned the knob as Brutus went wild beside her. When it was opened just enough, Brutus darted out, his sharp barks fading as he disappeared into the night. She slammed the door and locked the deadbolt, then sagged against it while gulping in breaths of air.

"Where did Brutus go, Mommy?"

"I don't know." *Maybe he heard a deer or something.* She glanced down at her phone: 12:00 a.m. *Where are you, Ryder?* She'd texted him a few times and never received a reply, but she knew he was out on "club business"—whatever that meant—and that's all he would say about his clandestine outing.

"When's Brutus coming back?" Timmy lay on his back on the floor, yawning.

"When he's ready." She put the gun down near the door then shuffled over to Timmy. "Come on, honey, lie down on the couch. It's too cold on the floor." If she wasn't scared out of her mind, she'd have taken him to his room and tucked him in bed, but she didn't want Timmy to be away from her.

Then the doorknob jiggled. Timmy closed his eyes, and Savannah swallowed down breaths to keep from crying out. Tiptoeing across the floor, her gaze stayed fixed on the door, and as she reached for the rifle, the door flew open. A blast of icy air froze her to the spot, and she let out a blood curdling scream.

"Mommy!" Timmy leapt up from the couch and she watched him, as if in slow motion, scamper toward her.

She tried to tell him not to come near—to run away, but she couldn't speak. All Savannah could do was watch her son come closer and closer to the unimaginable.

"What the fuck's wrong?"

Ryder! Oh God, thank you!

He wrapped an arm around her and crushed Timmy to him with the other as Brutus darted into the house barking excitedly. Ryder's warm kisses opened the torrent of tears, and she rested her head in the crook of his neck and sobbed in relief.

"What the hell's going on around here?" he murmured into her ear, but she couldn't answer him. He guided Savannah and Timmy to the couch and sat down, each of them collapsing against him.

"Mommy ... what's wrong?" Timmy's hand stroked her face. "Why's Mommy crying?" he asked Ryder.

"That's what I'm trying to figure out. Did something bad happen while I was gone?"

Through her tears she saw Timmy scrunch up his face then shake his head.

"Darlin'? Can you tell me what's wrong?" Ryder handed her a wad of tissues, and she wiped her cheeks and blew her nose.

"I'm sorry," she said. "I just got freaked out, that's all." She crumpled the tissues in her fist.

"About what?"

"Later," she whispered, her gaze drifting to Timmy.

"Okay."

For a long time the three of them sat on the couch, she and Timmy snuggled on each side of Ryder, his arms wrapped around them like a security blanket. Savannah felt nice and warm next to him ... like sitting in front of a wood-burning fire on a frosty morning. "Mommy and me went to see the elves," Timmy said, breaking the silence.

"That's right. How'd you like the windows?" Ryder asked.

As she listened to Ryder talk with Timmy about the boy's night, she craned her neck and kissed him quickly on his jaw. Never once had she heard Bret ask Timmy anything about what the boy liked, let alone carry on a conversation with him. *Ryder's everything Bret isn't. I can't believe that I'm giving my heart to a man I just met, yet it seems like I've known him forever.*

"Feel better now?" Ryder kissed the top of her head.

"Yes. Sorry for the meltdown."

"Don't be." Another soft kiss on her head.

Savannah pulled at Timmy's pajama bottoms. "It's way past your bedtime, sweetie." Yawning, he nodded.

"Let's go," she said softly.

"Can Ryder put me to bed tonight, Mommy?"

Her eyes looked to the biker and found a big smile spread across his face. "Yes, honey." She scooted away from them and gave Timmy a goodnight kiss, and then watched as her son flung his arms around Ryder's neck and rested his tired head on his broad shoulders. In all of Timmy's six years, his own father had never put him to bed.

Savannah walked over to the door and picked up the rifle, shoving the bullets into the pocket of her robe, and then placed the gun back on the wall in the workshop. On the way to the master bedroom, she heard Ryder's deep voice reading one of Timmy's favorite bedtime stories, and a surge of desire rushed through her for this gruff, yet gentle, man. She walked away, and after putting the bullets back in their place, she went to the kitchen to make hot chocolate.

Resting her hands against the sink while waiting for the milk to boil, Savannah didn't hear Ryder's footsteps until he was right behind her and he snaked an arm around her waist.

"Thanks for putting Timmy to bed," she said softly.

"No worries. He was out like a light after I read the second page."

His breath was hot against the curve of her neck. Pressed up against her back the way he was left no space between them.

"I couldn't wait to get back," he said hoarsely. "What happened to spook you like that?" he asked while pushing her hair over her shoulder, and his tongue danced over the nape of her neck.

Arousal followed where he touched, and she didn't want to think about the man and how scared she'd been. "Just jittery without you, plus Brutus kinda went crazy," she murmured, reclining against him. She'd tell him the next day, because at that moment, Savannah only wanted to get lost in the wonderful feelings skittering through her.

"Brutus can get that way." Soft kisses grazed her upper back. Ryder jammed his thigh between her legs and, even through his jeans, his dick was a bar of steel searing itself onto her ass. Savannah inhaled deeply, and it was all Ryder: leather, whiskey, and heated male. Tilting her head back, she nestled in that scent, in his raw lust. He moved his mouth down her neck, alternately kissing and biting a trail to her shoulder. She moaned and her knees buckled a bit, but he held her tightly while his delicious mouth and tongue blazed a trail over her flesh.

"Ryder," she murmured.

"Fuck, baby, I can't keep my hands off you." His voice sounded thick.

The milk bubbled and hissed as it overflowed onto the burner, and she jerked away and rushed to the stove.

"Dammit … I burned the milk," she said, pouring it into the sink.

"That's okay, darlin', I'd rather spend the time loving you than sipping hot chocolate." Savannah dropped the pan in the sink when Ryder swung her around and crushed his mouth on hers. For a long pause everything stopped around her except for the delicious surges of aroused desire pushing through her as their tongues tangled and their lips ground.

"I need to be with you," he said.

"Me too. Let's go to my room just in case Timmy wakes up, he can find me."

Ryder didn't let go of her once during their short trip from the kitchen to her room, and desire swirled around inside her, heightening her senses until she was downright giddy by the time she closed and locked the bedroom door.

Holding Savannah's hand tightly, he led her to the bed, and his body heat infused into hers through their connected palms, sending shivers of anticipation racing down her spine. Breaking away from her, Ryder perched on the edge of the bed and stared at her with the same intensity as when they'd first met, but unlike those times before, she met his eyes straight on, her body humming with arousal.

He gestured her to step back as his gaze roamed over her, lingering on her hips, her breasts, and then her face. "Take your clothes off for me, darlin'."

The rasp in his voice and the simplicity of his request went straight to her core, and she gave him her best seductive smile while slowly untying the sash around her robe. Underneath, she had on the sexy pair of red satin boxer pajamas with lace piping that she'd bought in the intimate apparel shop on West Fir Avenue. Savannah had fallen in love with it, and she had a pretty good idea that Ryder would love the look. The hunger in his eyes from the second she slipped the tight-fitting robe down her arms told her she was right.

Never taking her gaze off him, she unbuttoned her top, pausing between each button, and the only break in her stare came when she whirled around and swayed her hips as her top fell down on the floor. The sharp intake of Ryder's breath urged her on, and she turned back around—arms crossed over her chest—and locked eyes with him.

"Fuck, baby," he said hoarsely.

With one arm still covering her breasts, Savannah grasped the waistband of her boxers with her other hand and pushed it down. Wiggling as the silky fabric slid down her smooth legs, she flung the garment off her ankles with the flick of one foot. Her hand flew over her tingling sex, and she inched slowly toward him, her gaze fixed on his face.

"Damn you're sexy, woman," he said in a low voice.

When Savannah came closer to the bed, Ryder reached out and grabbed her, and she fell into his arms, clutching him tight. Then fingers were on her everywhere at once, dancing over her nipples, on her belly, above her mound, tickling her inner thighs, and pressing against her anus. Their mouths fused as she melted into him, and when she leaned against his chest, Ryder fell back onto the mattress. For a long time she lost herself in the sensations of their kiss until his hand glided in between them, and she felt his fingers on her mound. All her attention shifted to the digit swirling around her clit and the other ones inching their way into her slick heat.

"You're so damn wet for me," he said.

"You have a way of doing that to me." Her body trembled from his well-placed teasing fingers, and her hips rocked with a desperate desire for him.

Two digits pushed inside her and she moaned as her senses, her body, her arousal converged into a bonfire of indescribable pleasure. Writhing on top of him, the tension grew inside Savannah as she tugged at Ryder's belt in a desperate attempt to get at his gorgeous dick, but a shattering orgasm short-circuited her efforts. She stuffed her fist in her mouth to muffle her screams as her climax exploded; it was like tangling up a bunch of Christmas lights inside her, then blowing a fuse.

Ryder's hands skimmed over her ass, her hips, and her back as she panted and jerked from the subsiding eruption. He shifted under her and let out a low grunt, and reality pushed away the orgasmic afterglow.

Lifting up, Savannah scanned the grimace of pain in his face. "You're not comfortable," she said as she gestured to him to sit up.

"It's okay," he said in a low voice.

"It's not. I want you to enjoy yourself too." She unbuttoned his shirt, and after the last button, she pulled his shirt wide open and kissed his chest. Gliding her hands down, her fingers found his belt, and she fumbled with it until it fell free.

"Savannah, you don't have to—"

"Shh," she said, placing her lips against his. "Relax." Her nimble fingers grasped the zipper and pulled it down, and then curled around his hard dick; it was warm and smooth with a bit of wetness on the tip of its crown.

"Fuck," he grunted.

When Savannah started to pull his jeans down, Ryder straightened up and gently pushed her away. Without saying a word, she sat up then hooked her arms around his neck and kissed him deeply.

"Please don't shut me out. I want both of us to enjoy each other tonight, not just you pleasuring me."

The muscles on his face tightened as his brows pulled in, and his gaze ping-ponged around the room. Savannah didn't say anything, she just waited for the conflict inside him to settle, hoping that Ryder would let her share this part of him.

After what seemed like hours, he nodded, his face still taut, and she moved away while he stood up and let his pants drop. Savannah thought she'd be prepared for it, but she wasn't, and a wave of sadness for him coursed through her, but she couldn't let him see it, or what they had between them would be forever altered.

Biting the inside of her cheek, she reached out and touched the mechanical leg. "Does it hurt?" she whispered.

"Now it does. The end of the day's a killer," he replied in a low voice.

"Do you need me to get anything for you from your room?"

"My crutches and the ointment in the top drawer of the nightstand would be great."

"Okay," she said numbly, picking up her robe from the floor. As she shuffled out of the room, he called out to her and she looked over her shoulder.

"Bring a few condoms too." His smile was devilish, but worry still lingered in his eyes.

"Sounds like I'm in for a fantastic night." She threw him her most endearing smile then hurried into his room, wiping the tears as they fell down her cheeks. *I have to get it together. Ryder's injury happened years ago, and he's coping with it. I can't let him see how sorry I feel for him. I won't.* Taking deep breaths, she retrieved the items he wanted and walked back to her room.

Ryder was under the sheets, the prosthetic and a plastic cone-shaped object sat next to it. He'd turned the lights off with only the illumination coming from the ensuite bathroom. "It's now or never," she muttered under her breath as she ambled over to the lamp and switched it on, then turned off the bathroom light.

"I want to see all of you, and I'm pretty sure you want to see all of me." She slipped off her robe and sashayed over to him. Bending down, she kissed him deeply while drawing the sheet away.

Savannah looked down at his shrunken limb and her heart lurched. "Where does it hurt?" She ran her hand over his skin. "It's so soft," she murmured. "Which lotion do you use?"

"Mostly a jojoba or coconut oil at night and a silicone-based lotion during the day—it helps my liner from rubbing and pinching me so much throughout the day." His eyes stayed fixed on her.

She unscrewed the cap and poured some of the ointment in her palms and rubbed them together.

"I can do it," he said.

Placing her hands on his limb, she massaged the oil into the skin. "I've got it." At first she shied away from the bottom of his stump, but she noticed it was very red in spots. Inhaling a deep breath, she inched her fingers downward until they grazed over the scars.

Ryder hissed and she snapped her gaze up and met his. "Is this where it hurts?" He nodded, his eyes never wavering from hers.

For a long while Savannah gently massaged his sensitive skin until his hands stopped hers.

"Thanks," he muttered.

Without a word, she rose to her feet and walked to the bathroom to wash her hands. When she returned, the damn sheet was draped over him again. She sat on the edge of the bed and ran her fingernails down his chest and past his navel. When she reached the top of the sheet, she gripped it and pulled it off. Lowering her head, she covered his stomach with feathery kisses then lavished them on his residual limb.

"Savannah," he groaned, crushing her to him with such force that it took her breath away.

Without a second to think, she was on top of him, and he was ripping the condom open with his teeth and then quickly slipping it on. Before she could say a word, he lifted her up and slowly positioned her above his dick. His upper body strength amazed her, and she made a mental note to start working out in the gym he'd set up in the basement.

"I fucking need to be inside you," he gritted.

Savannah guided him, moaning as he pushed in.

"You feel amazing, woman," he grunted. Ryder stilled, remaining buried deep inside her as he kissed her lips.

She relaxed and melted into the kiss, and then he pushed up with his hips, almost knocking her over. Before she could catch her breath, he gripped her tightly, pulling her off his cock before slamming her back down. Up and down. In and out. Over and over he jackhammered into her, and she clawed at his chest as sweat trickled down her back. There was something animalistic about the two of them together. It was like their bodies were compatible on an instinctual level. It was raw. It was sexy. It was a downright wild connection.

The tension kept building inside her until it broke. "Ryder," she croaked, holding back her screams. Shuddering and gasping, her entire body spasmed as wave after wave of sensation hit her, each cresting higher than the last.

A rumbling groan burst from him, and she felt the pulsing of his dick against her quivering walls. She rested her head on his shoulder to quiet her trembling, the nerves and muscles in her body still tingling.

Ryder ran his fingers up and down her back as he panted. Tears stung the corners of her eyes, and her body relaxed, melding into his as they held each other tightly, basking in the afterglow of their spent desire.

Several minutes later, Savannah lifted her head up and locked her lips on his. His tongue slipped into her mouth and they kissed long and passionately for a while, and then she pulled away and smiled at him.

His dark eyes penetrated deeply into hers, and he stroked the side of her face. "You turn me on more than any other woman ever has, darlin'," he said in a low voice.

"You do the same to me," she whispered as she rolled off. He took off the used condom, she brought the trash can over, and then she switched off the lamp. Ryder yanked her back down next to him and slipped his arm around her, pressing her close. Savannah nestled into him, resting her head under his chin and cupping her hand over his sated dick.

"We're good together," she whispered.

"We are." He kissed the top of her head. "I haven't been this alive for a long time."

"Me neither," she said. "I want you to know that the way I feel isn't all just about sex. It's so much more."

"Yeah."

She didn't want to tell him that nothing she'd ever had with Bret even compared to what they'd just shared. With Bret it was wild and fun, but he never tried to know *her*. She'd kidded herself that they had this great relationship because they were fucking all the time, but after Timmy was born, the truth had shattered her heart: all they had between them was good sex. The truth had left her empty and lonely, but since Ryder had welcomed her and Timmy into his home, happiness twirled around inside her all the time.

How amazing is that?

Ryder's breathing was steady and peaceful, and she smiled. *I can't believe I'm falling in love with him. It's too soon, or maybe I've just been so lonely for too long.* But her heart told her that wasn't it. What she felt for Ryder was real, and because it came so quickly, it scared the hell out of her.

Scooting down a tad, she pillowed her head against his chest and closed her eyes as his heartbeats lulled her to sleep.

CHAPTER NINETEEN

RYDER AWOKE TO Savannah's warm body pressed against him as monochrome tones of gray filtered in through the shutters. He pushed up and leaned against the headboard and glanced over at her; she looked peaceful and beautiful. It had been over six years since he'd spent the night with a woman, and here he was, spending his second night with her.

Ryder slid his hand through her silky blonde hair and brought several long strands to his nose. As he inhaled the sweet fragrance, the need to wake up every day like this overwhelmed him. *Damn! I'm falling so fucking hard for her.*

When he'd first exposed himself to her, he'd been convinced that Savannah would mumble some platitudes and feign acceptance, but she didn't. She still saw *him* and not his disability, and it had blown him away, breaking down the hardened walls he'd built around his emotions.

"Savannah," he whispered as he watched her sleep.

A small whine at the closed door drew his attention from her, and he pulled the crutches toward him and stood up. As Ryder gimped to the back door, Brutus sat there patiently and waited to be let out. Since the ensuite in Savannah's room wasn't handicapped equipped, he crutched over to his master bathroom to relieve himself and wash up.

Brutus's barks signaled that he was ready to come in, so Ryder made his way to the back door and opened it. The German shepherd rushed over to his bowl and chomped down on his food. Ryder turned around and slowly headed back to Savannah's room.

She was still sleeping, although she'd turned on her side, facing the window. He rested the crutches against the space between the nightstand

and the bed, got back in and pulled the sheet over him, lying down on his good leg. Savannah stirred.

"Are you okay?" she asked drowsily.

"Yeah. Just had to let Brutus out. Go back to sleep—it's early."

"What time is it?"

Ryder glanced at his phone. "Almost six."

A small groan escaped from her. "That is early." She snuggled deeper under the covers.

He moved closer to her until her ass spooned up against him, then he ran his hand down the side of her body and smiled when her skin pebbled under his finger pads. Ryder couldn't help but keep his hands on her anywhere—*as* long as he touched her, he was good.

"Feels good," she mumbled.

Bringing his hand back up, he snaked it around her waist, resting it on the small pooch he loved so dearly.

"You smell good, baby," he said and brought his lips to her shoulder.

Savannah craned her neck, and he pressed his lips on hers as his hand inched up to the most incredible tits he'd ever seen.

"Oh," she moaned as his fingers flicked her nipples.

One of the many things he loved about touching Savannah was the way her nipples grew stiff under his ministrations. Wriggling her ass against him made his already hard cock needy as hell. *I bet she's wet as fuck.* The thought seared through him as his hand glided down her body and covered her pussy. As he massaged it, her juices coated his palm, and her whimpers fueled his lust.

"The sounds you make, darlin', drive me fucking crazy," he rasped, grinding against her as arousal flashed hot through his system.

A grunt rumbled from his chest when Savannah reached behind her and grabbed his ass cheek, sinking her nails into his flesh. He ran a hand up the side of her rib cage and cupping her tit, his fingers pinching her taut bud until she gasped and opened her legs.

Ryder smelled her sweet arousal and reached between her legs. "So wet," he murmured against her ear. Dipping two fingers between her folds, he coated them with her juices then brought them to her beautifully shaped rosy lips and fed them to her. Desire blazed deep inside him while he watched his fingers disappear in her mouth as she sucked them and curled her tongue around them—her eyes never leaving his.

"Do you like the way you taste," he asked.

Nodding, she grasped his hand and placed it on her pussy. "I love the way you touch me," she said.

Ryder propped up on his elbow and guided her upper leg back, hooking it back around his butt.

"Can you grab the condom on the nightstand?" he asked, his voice thick.

Once he was ready, he tangled his hand in her hair and yanked her head back, crushing his mouth on hers while he played with her nipples, and then her clit.

"Ryder," she whispered.

Breaking their kiss, he ran his tongue down to the sensitive spot where her shoulder met her neck and sucked on the skin. Savannah tilted her head more, giving him better access, and as he marked her, his fingers slid between her wet folds. With the lightest touch, he stroked the side of her nub. Her hips bucked and her gasp faded out to a guttural moan.

"You like that, darlin'?" he asked.

Nodding, she thrust her hips against his hand.

Taking her hand, he placed it against the headboard then kissed her deeply as he pushed inside. Pulling out, he shoved back in, then began pummeling her rough and fast, each bounce of her tits fueling his desire even more. His finger rubbed her sweet knot as he fucked her deep and hard, the tension building to where he was barely able to hold back any longer.

Savannah balled the sheets in her fist and stuffed them in her mouth as a muffled cry escaped from her throat. She tightened around him like he was caught in a vise, her pussy gripping him as it clenched and spasmed with her climax.

It was too much.

"Fuck, Savannah," he groaned, clutching her shivering and shaking body.

When Ryder regained his senses, he gently slid her leg off him then reached for the tangled covers at the foot of the bed. Savannah turned on her side, facing him, and burrowed into him as he draped the blanket over them. A small contented sigh came from her parted lips as her lids fluttered shut. Kissing the top of her head, he held her close, wanting nothing more than to stay like that forever. Savannah had sneaked into his life on a cold, snowy day and stirred emotions and desires he'd thought were lost to him.

Ryder dipped his head down and kissed her hair. "You're the part of me that makes me whole, baby."

And he had no intention of letting her slip out of his life.

"MOMMY'S STILL SLEEPING," Timmy said as he climbed up on the chair.

Ryder walked over and pushed the chair in for the young boy then ruffled his hair. "She's been so busy with decorating and shopping that she probably wore herself out." Pride coursed through him as he thought of the *real* reason Savannah was still sacked out at ten in the morning.

"I guess. Do you know what Mommy bought me for Christmas?"

Ryder held up his hands and laughed. "I'm no snitch. You'll find out in a few more days." He opened up the refrigerator and took out a carton of orange juice. "Are you ready for tonight?"

"Uh-huh. Braxton, Harley, and James are gonna be there." Timmy picked up the glass of juice Ryder had given him.

"It's a good party. There'll be a lot of other kids there too." Placing his hands on the island, he leaned forward, his gaze on the young boy. "Eggs and bacon good?"

Wiping his mouth with his pajama sleeve, he nodded.

"Don't let your mom catch you doing that. I used to do that when I was your age, and it drove my mom nuts." He bent down and pulled out the cast-iron skillet.

"You have a mommy?"

"Everyone has a mom, buddy." The coffeemaker beeped and he reached over and shut it off.

"Where's yours?"

"Right here in Pinewood Springs with my dad."

"How come she never comes here?"

A pain of regret streaked through him. "I-uh ... haven't wanted anyone over for a long time." With whisk in hand, he whipped the eggs in the bowl.

"Oh. Does your daddy come over?"

"Not so much. Are you missing your dad?" Ryder watched a small frown skate across Timmy's face.

"I dunno."

"It must be hard being away from him," Ryder said.

Timmy shrugged. "I never see him—only Mommy."

"Are you talking about me?" Savannah asked as she bent over and kissed her son.

"He's giving me the scoop on you," Ryder said, winking at her. A slight blush colored her cheeks, and he never thought she looked more beautiful than at that moment. *That's what I thought three hours ago, and then last night, and then the day before ... Damn.*

"You slept late," Timmy said.

"I was worn out."

Savannah's sly smile and wink hit him right in his dick. *Fuck.* This woman was like no other woman he'd ever known. Her taste, her scent, her eyes, her *everything* intoxicated him. He craved her like an alcoholic coveted his next drink; she was his straight shot of whiskey—smooth and potent with a burn. He doubted if he could ever get enough of her.

Brushing past him, she squeezed his ass as she made her way over to the pot of coffee. Her fresh scent wrapped around him, the clean smell of soap and body lotion. He wanted to pull her into his arms and kiss and nibble his way down to—

"You're burning the bacon again," she said as she rushed to the stove.

Fuck! This woman's killing me. He stood and rubbed against her from behind.

"See how you distract me," he whispered in her ear. When she shivered, he smiled.

"Mommy never burns the bacon," Timmy said.

Ryder looked over his shoulder. "I bet she doesn't." He patted her ass, then sliced more pieces from the slab and placed them in the sizzling pan.

After they'd eaten, Timmy trotted off to his room to play a video game, and Ryder sat at the table watching Savannah fill the dishwasher.

"Do you wanna tell me the real reason you were freaked out last night."

A millisecond of a pause.

"Brutus went ballistic. It scared the crap out of me."

"He's gone ballistic before and you seemed fine."

"But you were there to protect us." She smiled sweetly at him, but he wasn't buying the act for one fucking minute.

"We gotta be honest with each other and not hide shit."

Folding the dish towel, she glanced at him. "Don't give advice if you don't take it yourself."

Ryder jerked his head back. "What the fuck does that mean?"

"You have a lot of secrets you keep inside yourself, and they act as barriers to people who try to get close to you."

"People?"

The dish towel unfolded in her hands, and she fixed her gaze on him. "Me."

Frowning, he rubbed his hand over his face. "You're changing the subject. I'm asking what you were afraid of last night."

Savannah put the folded towel on the counter and shoved her hands in the pockets of her robe. "Someone followed me and Timmy when we were in town. It was the same guy who was staring at me a few nights ago."

"The fucker at the tree lighting?"

Nodding, she pursed her lips.

"Why the hell didn't you tell me that when I asked you? I could've gone out and tried to find him. That's why Brutus went crazy."

"I wanted to enjoy the night with you. I don't think he's going to hurt me" She kept twirling her hair around her fingers.

"How can you be so sure?"

"I'm not really. I'm pretty freaked out about the whole damn thing. What if he's here to steal Timmy? I wouldn't put it past Corinne to be behind all this. I can't let him take my baby. Why don't they just leave me the hell alone?" Savannah's voice hitched.

Ryder stood up and walked over to her and drew her into his arms. Her body trembled against him and he ran his hands over her back, his heart squeezing when he heard her soft sobs against his shirt. "Shh … don't cry, darlin'. No one's gonna take Timmy, I'll make sure of that. I'll make sure I never leave you two alone. I'll find out who this fucker is and take care of it."

"I'd die if Timmy were taken from me. I love him so much." More soft sobs. Sniffles.

"I know you do, and you're a damn good mom. I won't let anything happen." He placed his two fingers under her chin and tilted her head back and her eyes met his. "I'll make sure it's all good, okay?" Savannah nodded slightly and he wiped the wet streaks from her face then pressed his lips gently to hers.

"One of the things that kills me is that Bret doesn't even want Timmy in his life. The other is that my mom's the one who told him where we are. I spoke to her before coming to breakfast this morning and she confessed."

"Why the fuck would she do that?"

Savannah wiped her nose with a tissue. "Because she loves me and Timmy. She wants me to have the fairytale Disney marriage. And she wanted us home for Christmas." Once again, she twirled tendrils of blonde around her finger. "In all fairness, my mom doesn't know the whole story … only you do."

As Savannah spoke, anger burned inside Ryder, and he tucked her hands in his and gently squeezed them. "Baby, I'm telling you that I'll make sure you and Timmy are safe. No one's gonna bully you to do something you don't want to do. I swear that if the fucker comes back on my property, I'll take care of him."

A tiny smile tugged at the corners of her kissable lips. "I'll admit I feel better knowing I have you on my side. I'm just not sure what I'm going to do."

Ryder's stomach clenched. "Are you thinking of going back to him?"

Savannah shook her head. "Absolutely not. I'm not going back to Boston either. I'm better off without the Carltons, and Timmy doesn't deserve a father like Bret."

A long pause yawned between them until Ryder let out a long breath. "Stay with me."

Her eyes locked with his and he saw tenderness, compassion, and relief, but there was also fear in them.

"We've only known each other a short time," she said.

"I know, and it's fucking strange that I'm even asking, but I've been wanting a woman like you in my life since I can remember. I just didn't know it, and it's taken a lot of shit and pain to realize it."

Savannah slipped her hands away from his and cast her eyes downward. "What about Brandi? I mean she's so young—I know men prefer younger women."

Ryder stared at her slouched shoulders; she looked so petite and vulnerable at that moment. *The fucker really did a number on her.* "You're the woman I want. Brandi's a nice girl who helped me out when I got tired of my hand doing all the work. It wasn't like we had a romantic relationship or anything. It was just sex, and it wasn't all the time. Maybe a handful of times in a year. Brandi's age had nothing to do with us having sex—she was the only one who didn't mind that I didn't have a leg." He picked up his coffee mug and took a sip. "I'm not a cheater—never have been and never will be. I'm loyal to a fault." After a few seconds of silence, Ryder reached over and lifted her chin so her gaze met his. "I'm not Bret. The way he treated you and Timmy was fucking cruel, and he needs a good ass kicking for sure."

Tears filled Savannah's eyes. "I felt the goodness of your heart from the first day you came blustering into the trailer. I'm just afraid."

"Of what?"

"My feelings for you."

"I know what you mean. We're still getting to know each other, but my gut tells me this is right. What's yours telling you?"

"The same," she whispered.

Silence stretched between them until the chair scraping on the floor broke it and Ryder stood up. "I'll be right back." He walked out of the kitchen and straight to the workroom where he took out the cigar box, and then headed back to Savannah.

The box made a small thud when he put it on the table in front of her.

"This is my past." He sat back down on the chair.

For a second, her eyes just shifted between him and the worn-out box, then she placed her delicate fingers on it and opened the lid. She glanced up.

"Take the things out." He balled his hands into fists and inhaled and exhaled a couple of times. "You can ask me anything you want."

"Are you sure about this?" Savannah's eyes stayed on his fists. "I don't want to dredge up painful memories for you."

"It's about time I face the shit that's been holding me prisoner, and I want to do it with you."

After a slight nod, she picked up the photographs and browsed through them. Snippets of his past raced through his mind, and it seemed right that the woman who'd brought light into his life should be rifling through them—through all the darkness of his past.

Savannah cleared her throat and looked up from the last picture Dana, Colt, and Ryder had taken. It was before he went back over on what had become his last tour of duty in Afghanistan. *I had no idea that was going to be the last time I saw you, Colt. I'd have told you I loved you more and held you tighter if I would've known.* Ryder's body grew more rigid.

"We can stop," Savannah said, putting the photograph on the table and taking one of his fists into both her hands.

He just shook his head and stared at her.

"Okay … why did you break it off with your fiancée?"

"Dana broke it off with me after I lost my leg. She said she couldn't handle it."

Her eyes widened but she just nodded. "How long were you together?"

"Eight years."

"Oh, Ryder," she whispered, reaching over to stroke his face.

He jerked back. "Don't pity me, Savannah. I'm not doing this for that reason."

"It's not pity, it's compassion. I can't believe that after all those years, she left you because of a physical disability."

"She couldn't handle it. I was livid and hated her for years, but through therapy, I got to the point where I could acknowledge that the challenge of being with an amputee may have scared the hell out of her."

"Is that the reason she gave you?"

The inclination was to tell her yes, but he'd wanted her to know everything, even the shit that bruised his pride and made him feel less of a man for the past five years. "No. She told me it disgusted her, creeped her out, and she could never be sexually attracted to me again."

"Fuck," she murmured. "That's horrible."

"It's the way it was. She took Colt and bolted. Never even gave me a chance to see my boy again—that's what hurts the most."

"Does she have any family?"

"Dana's from Pinewood Springs like I am. We met at a party when I was twenty-one and she was twenty. Her mom, Maggie, was the only relative I knew of, and she disappeared along with Dana and Colt. I figured they changed their names."

"Did you hire a private eye to try and find them?"

"Yep. Hawk's been helping too, but so far nothing. I won't give up though. I figure when Colt gets his first job, he'll have to use his social security number. So far, Dana hasn't used any public programs, unless she got fake numbers for them. Maggie wouldn't do it because she'd be giving up her benefits when she turns sixty-five. I'm keeping track of all that."

"What an awful thing to do. Her not being able to handle it is one thing, but to take your son away from you? What a bitch." Savannah's hand flew to her mouth and covered. "I'm sorry." Her voice was muffled. "I shouldn't have said that."

Ryder shrugged. "Why not? She is a bitch. Dana punished me for getting my fucking leg blown off just like your fucker punished you for getting pregnant. They're both fucked up."

For a few seconds, they held each other's gaze, and Ryder's fists slowly unfurled.

"Was Dana the love of your life?" she asked in a hesitant tone.

"I thought she was, but now I'd have to say no."

Savannah picked up the Purple Heart and pressed it against her chest. "You fought for us. You're a hero."

Ryder snorted. "Fuck that ... I'm no goddamn hero."

"Yes, you are. My dad fought in Vietnam. I know how hard war can be on a person. He still goes to his VA group twice a month."

Surprised at her revelation, he leaned back in the chair and stared at her.

"The camaraderie has stayed with my dad—he still has a few buddies from the Army—as well as the atrocities. My dad was lucky though. He came back without any injuries, but some of his friends and members of his unit came back in body bags. It still haunts him today."

Chills ran up his spine as he shifted in his chair. *She fucking gets it. Her old man's a vet.* Memories of her calm, reassuring voice bringing him back to reality when he'd had his nightmare raced through his mind.

Can I do this?

"Do you want to talk about it?" Her calm voice touched him deeply.

Taking a big breath, he exhaled it slowly through his nose. "It was my third tour of duty, and my unit and I were engaged in combat against militants, driving them farther back into the province. After we succeeded, several guys in my unit, including myself, moved in to clear the compound—a cluster of old Afghani houses. We had to be sure there were no Taliban or mines there." Ryder tilted his head back as distant voices echoed in his head.

The feel of Savannah's hand tapping his arm pulled him away from the noise. "Stay with me. We're in the kitchen in your cabin. Don't leave me," she said.

He nodded and took a gulp of coffee; it was lukewarm and had a metallic taste like blood. *Get a grip. You can do this.* "Right before I reached the compound, I saw a movement out of the corner of my eye. I turned quickly and started shooting, which triggered the other guys to shoot as well. My best buddy, Jeremy, started running toward me. I told him to stay back, but he thought I was in danger so he kept coming." Another gulp of coffee. "I looked at who I was shooting at and … I saw a group of kids running and falling. For a second, it looked like I was playing a fucking video game."

Savannah kept tapping his arm.

"Then I saw who I'd shot—it was a boy around Colt's age. I ran toward him, forgetting about the war, forgetting about the mines, and all I saw was Colt on the ground bleeding with his guts spilling out. I just wanted to save him. When I was about twenty yards away, I heard Jeremy calling to me, and I turned around. That's when I heard the bang. Jeremy was up in the air and chunks of him started to break away."

"Stay with me, Ryder."

For a second he didn't recognize the woman's voice, but then her scent enveloped him as she came behind him and draped her arms around his neck. He rested his head against Savannah, inhaling her familiar fragrance.

"That's when I stepped on the landmine. There wasn't a boom, and my ears didn't even fucking pop. I closed my eyes and when I opened them again, I was upside-down and falling backwards toward the ground. I went to sit up and saw my knee coming off, and with the whole shinbone sticking out with no foot at the end of my left leg, I knew I was fucked. I looked over to find Jeremy, but I couldn't see further than my weapon because there was this fucking massive dust cloud. The pain was horrendous and there was flesh everywhere. In that second, everything hit me, and I knew my life would be forever changed."

"You were so brave," she muttered.

"I lived. Jeremy's the one who gave up his life. He's the hero, not me."

"You both were. Two young guys fighting under extreme conditions just trying to do the right thing. You were fighting for us. You wanted to save the young boy."

"I'm the one who fucking killed him."

"But it wasn't under normal conditions. You know you would've never done that if it hadn't been during wartime. You lost your leg by trying to save him."

The ends of her hair brushed against his hands that were on top of hers. "I told Jeremy to stay back. If I hadn't shot that kid, Jeremy would still be alive."

"You don't know that, and as hard as it is to accept, *Jeremy* made the choice to follow you, you didn't make him. You have to forgive yourself … Jeremy would want you to."

Ryder pursed his lips together and blinked rapidly. There was no way he wanted Savannah to see the tears threatening to stream down his face. As the seconds turned to minutes, a sense of lightness descended on him, and for the first time since that fateful day, the burden of what had happened didn't weigh so much on his soul. It was as if some of the chains fettering him had broken away.

He reached behind him and slipped his hand under Savannah's soft hair and cupped her neck, bringing her face down to his. He locked his lips on hers then swung her around as he pushed the chair back. Securing Savannah on his lap, he kissed her again as his heart hammered against his chest.

"I love you more than any other woman I've loved in my life. I want you and Timmy to stay and be a part of my life." The rush of emotion surprised him, but he'd never met a woman like Savannah before.

"Oh, Ryder. For so long I'd longed for this, and now I can't bear to lose it. Your affection, your love, your everything makes me feel so complete, but I'm scared to death that we're rushing into this too fast. I keep thinking that maybe we're just replacing the ones who hurt us with each other to make a patchwork quilt of a life together."

"Do you love me?" Ryder held his breath.

"I do, very much."

"Then we'll sort the rest out, woman. I'm not asking to get hitched right away—we gotta grow together a little more before that—and I know that I'm not replacing Dana and Colt with you and Timmy. I'm fucked up, but not *that* much. I just feel this is right, and I know my love for you is real. I've never fell so hard and so fast with any other woman before, and the depth of the love and admiration and respect I feel for you is more than I'd ever felt for Dana. You're the woman I've been looking for my whole life ... Dana was just the detour."

Savannah peppered his face with kisses then rested her head against his shoulder. "I do believe in wishes coming true and the magic of Christmas. You're my wish come true, not just for me, but for Timmy too—he's crazy about you. There was a reason we were stranded on your property." She poked him in the ribs. "I know you're rolling your eyes at me."

He chuckled. "Damn, you're good, woman." The truth was he didn't really believe in coincidences, but he had to agree with Savannah that it seemed like their stars must have aligned to bring her and Timmy to him. *Christmas magic? Who the fuck knows?* He turned his head and kissed her again.

"I'm still married to Bret—at least on paper. We've really been separated since Timmy was born, but I have a huge battle in front of me."

"I'll be there for you—even go to Boston with you." He ran his hand up and down her back.

"I know. I'm meeting with that attorney Cara recommended to me on Monday morning. Cara looked up the statute, and in Massachusetts, grandparents don't have a right to their grandkids. They may ask the court to order some visitation, but that's only if I don't let Timmy see his paternal grandparents, which I wouldn't do. But I do want sole custody of Timmy."

"And you're going to get it."

"I hope so. Corinne has a lot of money to fight me, and so does Bret."

"You gotta believe in yourself, darlin'. Don't worry about the money, I've got you covered. I get a share of the money the Insurgents bring in." He ran his finger over her frowning face and chuckled. "It's all legal."

"Do you want to play with me, Ryder?" Timmy asked as he stood in the doorway.

"Come over here, honey," Savannah said.

When Timmy was next to them, Ryder scooped him up and placed him on top of Savannah's lap.

"Ryder's asked us to stay. Would you like that?"

Timmy bobbed his head and wrapped his arm around Ryder's neck. "Would we live here?"

"If that's okay with you."

"I like it here. I like my friends. Can I go to the same school as they do?"

"Sure," Savannah said. She kissed her son and pressed against him. "I love you."

"Is Daddy going to be mad that we're not coming home?"

"Yes, but Mommy and Daddy haven't been happy for a long time."

"Daddy doesn't like me."

"Oh, baby," Savannah said as she rocked Timmy on Ryder's lap. "It's not *you*. Daddy doesn't like anyone but himself."

"I like you very much, kiddo," Ryder said.

Timmy smiled widely. "I like you too. Do you wanna play a video game with me?"

"Yeah. You're gonna need to show me what to do."

"I will," Timmy said as he scrambled down and dashed into the other room.

Ryder kissed Savannah again then helped her off his lap.

"I know I'm gonna regret doing this 'cause I know he's gonna kick my ass." He chuckled and patted Savannah's butt as he made his way into the family room.

CHAPTER TWENTY

HOLIDAY MUSIC CURLED around her as Savannah wove through the crowds. She pushed open the doors at the French Bistro and the aroma of freshly baked baguettes tantalized her as she entered the eatery. A quick scan around the small restaurant told her Cara hadn't arrived yet. Deciding to secure a table, Savannah rushed over to one in the corner that had just become available.

On one of the chairs, she stacked her packages then sat down with a contented sigh to finally be off her feet. The café had a warm feel to it, and amid the brightly decorated trees and dangling strings of lights, oil paintings depicting street scenes of Parisian life decorated the yellow walls.

"Would you like anything to drink?" a young waitress asked as she handed Savannah a menu.

"A friend of mine will be coming," she said and the waitress put down another menu. "I'll have a hot chocolate and a glass of water with extra lemon, please."

"I'll be right back with your drinks." The young girl rushed away.

The restaurant filled up, and soon there were no tables available for the line of people crowding the reception area. Savannah looked out the window, watching the shoppers as they clutched shopping bags and hurried down the bustling street. She saw Cara rushing across the road and she smiled. Cara had turned out to be a great friend to Savannah, and the family law attorney she'd recommended really knew her stuff. Savannah had met with Francine Roberts that morning then she'd dashed around buying last minute items and specialty foods for the dinner she planned to make that evening.

"Sorry I'm late," Cara said as she slipped into the chair across from Savannah. "The probation revocation hearing went on longer than I thought."

"That's okay—I just got here about fifteen minutes ago. I finally finished up all my Christmas shopping. Are you done with yours?"

"Pretty much. You're all coming tomorrow for our Christmas Eve party, right?" Cara asked.

"Yes. Ryder surprised me and said he'd changed his mind." Savannah smiled at the waitress as she placed the hot chocolate in front of her.

"Would you like anything to drink?" the young lady asked Cara.

"What're you having?" Cara said to Savannah.

"Hot chocolate—I'm obsessed with it. This one's to die for—so chocolatey and decadent."

"Sounds good, but I think I'll stick to my usual café au lait with a dusting of nutmeg. We might as well order."

After the waitress walked away, Cara propped her elbows on the table. "How'd you like Francine?"

"She's awesome," Savannah replied.

"I knew you'd like her. She's a real fighter. What did she say?"

Savannah put her mug down. "I have to file for divorce in Boston since I'm not a resident of Colorado."

"Yeah, you have to live in the state for six months to establish residency. Did she recommend an attorney in Boston?"

"She did. I already went to see one before I left, but I wasn't too excited about him. I'm going to check out the one Francine gave me. I wish she could practice law in Massachusetts."

"Yeah—she's one of the best in the whole county. She does a lot of divorce work in Aspen, even Denver sometimes. Does she think you have a good chance of getting sole custody of Timmy?" Cara picked up her coffee and brought it to her lips.

"Yes. When she heard the recordings, she clapped her hands and said I've got more than a ninety-five percent chance of getting sole custody in spite of Bret's money."

"Ham and brie baguette?" the waitress asked.

"Uh … that's me. That was fast," Savannah said.

The young woman set the plate in front of her then placed a Croque Madame in front of Cara.

"Do you need anything else?"

"I'm good," Savannah said.

"Me too," Cara added.

"Enjoy your lunch." The fresh-faced woman smiled then hurried away.

"This sandwich is to die for. It's as good as the ones I had in Paris. Good choice." Savannah savored the smokiness of the ham coupled with the tangy creaminess of the brie. "And the bread is awesome. Do they sell baguettes here?"

Cara, cutting into her sandwich, nodded. "They have a full service bakery in the front. The owner chef is from Aix en Provence. I love this place. It opened a few years ago, and they do a real steady business. People stand in long lines for the croissants and baguettes in the morning."

"I'm going to buy a loaf for dinner tonight. I'm making Irish stew."

"Sounds good. What recordings were you talking about before our food came?"

Savannah wiped the corners of her mouth with the napkin. "The ones I've been taping ever since I decided to leave Bret. I'd been doing it for the past several months, but I didn't know if it would mean anything considering the clout the Carlton family name carries. Francine said they're a gold mine."

Cara burst out laughing. "I love it!"

"I just knew in my gut that no one would believe me about the way Bret talked about Timmy, so that's why I started recording him and keeping a journal. Every awful thing he said about our precious son is on tape, and every memory of what he did to me and Timmy is written down." Savannah shook her head. "When I married him, I never thought I'd be gearing up for such a nasty battle. I still can't believe he doesn't love his son. How could a parent not love their child?"

"I know ... it's so hard to believe, but in the line of work I'm in, I see horrible things people to do their kids and others all the time. Timmy's just very lucky that he has you in his life."

"I'm the one who's lucky." Savannah's voice quivered and she dabbed the corner of her eyes. "Let's change the subject." She sat up straighter in the chair. "Do you want me to bring anything to the party tomorrow night?"

Shaking her head no, Cara patted Savannah's hand. "You know I'm always available if you need moral support. You'll get through this, and with Ryder having your back, you'll be even stronger." Cara placed her knife and fork down on her plate. "Hawk told me that he's never seen Ryder happier, and for him or any Insurgent to comment on something like that means it's really surprising. I'm guessing you're the reason for that."

A flush of heat reddened Savannah's cheeks. "We're going to see how things work between us."

"I'm so happy. You guys fit together so well, and Ryder is a great guy even if he is a bit hard to get to know."

"Yeah—he's so brooding and gruff, but underneath all that, he's got the biggest heart. I'm crazy about him, and I feel like I'm doing the right thing in staying. Timmy adores him, and Ryder's so good with him. Sometimes I think things are going too fast and that I must be out of my mind, but then when we're watching a Disney film in front of the fire, and he tugs on my hair, I know this is right for me—for Timmy and me."

"It is. One thing I learned from dating and marrying Hawk, is that you have to go by what you feel. My mom and so many of my relatives were against us, but I went by how I felt, and I've never regretted my decision for one second. Hawk's the love of my life and I couldn't be happier."

"Will there be anything else?" the waitress asked interrupting the women's conversation.

"I'd like another cup of hot chocolate," Savannah replied.

The waitress nodded as she picked up their empty plates.

Cara glanced at her phone. "Nothing for me, thanks." The woman walked away. "I have to go. I have an evidentiary hearing and Judge Rollins doesn't tolerate the attorneys to be one minute late. I'm so glad we got together and you liked Francine." Cara pushed her chair back and stood up then placed a twenty dollar bill on the tray. "I'll see you tomorrow night."

"See you." Savannah watched her friend weave through the patrons before exiting out the door and disappearing into the throng of shoppers. Savannah smiled: she liked Cara a lot. She was looking forward to meeting more of the women who loved the Insurgent men. Ryder told her that all the old ladies would be at Hawk and Cara's party the following night, and if they were anything like Cara, Belle, and Clotille, she suspected that she'd get along well with them. *My life is falling into place and I've never been happier. Finally… after all this time.* She picked up her new cup of cocoa and licked the whipped cream before taking a sip.

"Savannah?"

She averted her eyes from the bustling street to the person standing by her table. *Bret! I can't believe he actually came here.* She'd just assumed that the creep who'd been following her would try and threaten her into coming back to Boston, or maybe he would serve divorce papers on her, but she never figured Bret would trek over to Pinewood Springs.

"What're you doing here?" she said.

"Is that any way to greet your husband?" Bret smirked. Without asking, he pulled out the chair and sat down, his gaze scanning over her. "You look good. The high altitude seems to agree with you. It looks like you lost weight."

"What do you want?" All of a sudden the whip cream and rich chocolate were making her stomach queasy; she put down the cup and stared at him.

"I've come to take you and Timmy back. You've had your tantrum and now it's time to come home."

"Come home to what? A selfish bastard who's a pathetic excuse for a husband?" She took out her wallet and placed the money on the tray; she wanted to grab all her packages and run away as fast as she could from this man whom she no longer recognized.

"I didn't come over two thousand miles to be insulted. Your fucking antics have caused me a lot of problems. You're going to get your ass back to Boston and that's final. I'm done with this shit."

"I don't need to listen to you anymore. My attorney will get in touch with you. I'm finished with you."

"I'll be the one to decide when it's over," Bret said, gripping her wrist tightly.

Savannah tried to pull away. "Let go of me." She leaned toward him. "Do you think I'd ever go back to you? You insulted me then raped me," she whispered.

"I fucked you. You should be thanking me for that." He moved in real close. "A husband can't rape his wife—she's supposed to put out for him. Why the fuck do you think men get married?"

"I've nothing more to say to you. It's over. You don't care about me ... or Timmy. You haven't even asked about him since you sat down. He deserves a better father."

Bret pushed her hand away so strongly that it hit the corner of the table sending jolts of pain up her arm. "Like that cripple you're shacking up with?" Bret laughed dryly. "Don't look so shocked—I know all about your fucking blue collar love nest. I don't think a judge is going to take too kindly to what you're exposing our son to."

"Just shut the hell up. You know nothing about Ryder. He's more of a man than you'll ever be."

"He's a fucking outlaw biker, he's fucked up in the head, he's lives like a goddamn hermit, and he's missing a leg. Oh ... and that's just for starters. The judge won't like any of that."

"I *will* fight you all the way, Bret. I'm not afraid of you, your mom, your family's name, or your money. I won't allow you to use Timmy as a pawn in your warped game." Savannah rose to her feet and collected her packages. "We're through—I'm done talking to you. Leave me the fuck alone." She brushed past him, but he grabbed her hand and squeezed it so hard she thought it was going to break.

"This isn't finished, bitch," he hissed.

With all the strength she possessed, Savannah jerked away and a few packages dropped on the floor.

A young waiter ran over. "Let me help you with those, Miss," he said, picking them off the floor.

"Thank you." Without a glance backward, she stalked out of the restaurant, her heart slamming against her ribcage.

By the time Savannah arrived at the cabin, she was a bundle of nerves. The whole ride back, her gaze kept shifting to the rear view mirror expecting to see a car trailing her. *He doesn't even get what he did to me. What a fucking asshole. I can't believe he's in Pinewood Springs. We're never going back to him. Never!*

The first thing she noticed when she walked into the family room was the additional wrapped presents. For several minutes she looked at the twinkling tree, with its tiers of lights and the glittering packages under it. Her stomach fluttered and heat radiated through her chest melting the anger inside her.

"How did the meeting with the attorney go?" Ryder's deep voice washed over her. Strong arms curled around her waist, and the familiar scent of the man she loved enveloped her. He nuzzled her neck and the shopping bags she held in her hands fell to the floor as she spun around and planted a passionate kiss on his delectable mouth.

Breaking away slightly, she smiled at him. "It went great." She kissed him again. "I missed you so much."

Ryder chuckled then jerked her closer to him, his hands cupping her ass. "I missed you too, darlin'."

After smooching for a while, Savannah picked up the bags from the floor and put them in her room. When she came back into the family room, Ryder sat on the couch, and she noticed a steaming mug of cocoa on the coffee table. A rush of emotion flooded her, and she inhaled deeply then walked over to the couch.

"Did you make this for me?" She picked up the cup and took a sip; it was weak and watery and filled with love. "It's the best cup of hot chocolate I've ever had."

Ryder beamed and gestured her to come sit beside him. Snuggled in the crook of his arm, she ran her hand up and down his denim-clad thigh.

"Bret's in town," she said.

Ryder twitched. "What the fuck?"

"After Cara left to go to court, he came into the restaurant. The thug he hired must've been following me."

"What the hell did the pussy want?"

"To take us back."

Savannah felt his arm stiffen. "What did you say?" he asked in a low voice.

"Basically to fuck off."

A booming laugh resounded through the room and he tilted her head back and crushed his mouth to hers. The muffled sound of crunching snow drew them apart, and Ryder hoisted himself up and walked to the front door and peered out. Brutus jumped up and barked.

"We got company." There was a steely edge in his voice.

"Who is it?" Savannah rose to her feet and sauntered over to him.

"I think it's your pussy and the fucker he's hired." Ryder turned around. "I'll be right back. Don't open the door." Brutus kept growling and barking.

A shiver tiptoed up her spine as she watched Bret and the hired goon get out of the brown SUV and begin to approach the cabin.

"Move aside, darlin', I'll take care of this."

Savannah stepped back and noticed the shotgun in Ryder's hand and a handgun in his waistband. Her stomach pitched.

"What're you going to do?"

"The fuckers are on my property. They gotta leave one way or the other." He opened the door and stepped out on the large wrap-around porch. Brutus bolted out and stood in front of the two men, snarling and barking ferociously.

Savanna stepped into the doorway, arms folded, lips pressed together, heart pounding.

"You're fucking trespassing," Ryder bellowed as he leveled the shotgun at the two startled men.

Bret held up his hands and shook his head. "We don't want any trouble. I've just come here to talk to my wife."

"Call your dog off," the other man said.

"She's got nothing to say to you, asswipe." Jerking his head at the private eye, Ryder bared his teeth. "And you don't tell me what the fuck to do on my property. Now take your goddamn cell phone out and throw it on the ground." He glared at Bret. "You too, fucker." Both men complied. "Brutus, stay." The dog froze, but his eyes remained fixed on the men. "Slowly open your jackets and show me what you got inside."

"I don't have a gun, if that's what you're asking," Bret said.

"I'm not *asking* shit, I'm *telling*. Fucking do it. Now."

Bret glanced at Savannah, but she stood resolute in the doorway, although inside she was dying, praying that the situation didn't get out of hand. It was true that she despised Bret, but she didn't want Ryder to kill him. *He wouldn't do that, would he?*

"Toss your piece real slow toward me, and if you do something stupid I'll blow your fucking brains out," Ryder said to the private investigator. The man complied.

"I don't go in for guns. I'd never have one," Bret said as he held his jacket open widely.

Brutus growled, his bright eyes fixed on her shaking soon-to-be ex-husband.

"Why the fuck do you keep talking? I don't give a damn what your fucking thoughts are on guns." Ryder went over to the handgun that was on the ground and picked it up, his gaze never wavering from the two men. He tossed it behind him and it landed with a thud on the wooden porch. Savannah jumped—her frazzled nerves were sparking.

"Savannah said she already talked to you and told you to fuck off. You being on my property tells me you didn't take her seriously." Still holding the gun on them, Ryder took a couple of steps backward. "Darlin', do you wanna talk with this fucker?"

She cleared her throat. "No. Bret, I told you everything I wanted to say at the restaurant. We're finished. Please leave me alone."

"You can't be serious about wanting this uncouth barbarian. The guy has a gun on me. Is that how low you've fallen?"

"You're on his property. You're bothering me. He's protecting me—something you never did."

"What the hell does that mean?"

"You never stood up for me once when your mother was so horrible to me. You tried to make me feel like white trash all the time. You threw your mistresses in my face, telling me how much better they were than me. You're were an awful husband … and father."

"Can't we talk about this without having a damn shotgun pointed at me?" Bret said.

"There's nothing more to talk about," Savannah said. "I don't love you anymore. I want a divorce."

"My mother was right to say I shouldn't have gone over to the other side of the tracks for a wife. You never fit in—you were always an embarrassment to the family."

Savannah gripped the wood bannister. "I fit in just fine with the rich world, but you're right about not fitting in with your family, and I'm glad I don't. If I did that would mean I'm cruel, cold, and manipulative. I pity you, Bret."

Bret's nostrils flared. "You ungrateful bitch!"

In less than two heartbeats, Ryder was on him, punching and kicking him. The goon started to run over, but Brutus rushed toward him and he stopped dead in his tracks then the dog grabbed his pant leg with his teeth.

"Get him off me!" he yelled.

"Brutus!" Savannah yelled. The dog backed away a bit, but he stood erect with eyes fixed on the trespasser, ready to pounce at the slightest provocation. She bent down and picked up the handgun then pointed it at the man who'd scared the hell out of her for the past week. "Stay where you are. It's their fight, not yours."

Savannah watched as Ryder kicked Bret's ass good, happy that her man stopped when it was obvious that Bret was defeated. Ryder picked up the cell phones and it seemed like he was checking them out, and then he lifted the shotgun and waved it at the hired hand.

"Pick that piece of shit up and get the fuck off my land. If you come back, I won't be talking, just shooting." Ryder tossed the phones at him.

The man glared at him and then at her before he bent down and helped Bret to his feet then to the car. Bret didn't even glance at her, and a thread of relief wove through her. *It's finally over.* She and Ryder stood on the porch until long after the SUV disappeared from sight.

"I don't think they'll be coming back," Savannah said.

"They better not. Are you okay?" He draped his arm around her shoulder and kissed her.

"More than better—it's finally over." She rested her head on his shoulder. "Why were you so interested in their cell phones?"

"I wanted to make sure they weren't filming anything to use against you in the divorce." He whistled for Brutus and the dog came bounding up the road.

"I love you," she said. "Thank you for being my rock."

"I love you too, baby." He spun her around and kissed her deeply.

Then she saw the redness forming under his right eye. "You're hurt," she said, running her fingers over the place where Bret landed a punch.

Ryder chuckled. "A lucky shot. Damn, that pussy couldn't fight for shit."

"I don't think he's ever been in a fight. Thanks for not overdoing it."

They walked into the house and the warmth from the fire surrounded them.

"I've gotta admit it was hard to stop. I kept thinking of what he did to you, and I wanted to kill him. But then I thought of Timmy and how the fuck's still his dad, and that's what made me stop."

Savannah hugged him and his arms folded around her, and she never wanted to let go. "You're the best," she whispered.

They walked into the kitchen, and Savannah took out two dog treats and Brutus went wild with excitement. "You did a good job watching over us," she said as Brutus took the treats from her palm and crunched them while looking at her.

"I want to show you something," Ryder said as he handed her an envelope.

She opened it up and took out a piece of paper then looked up at him. "What's this?"

"I got tested. I'm clean. I just wanted to share that with you because I'd like to really feel you, baby."

She giggled then poked him playfully. "That's good to know. I started on the pill. Clotille told me about this clinic in town, and I went to it last week."

A frown creased his brows. "You weren't on it before?"

"No. There wasn't any reason to be." When his eyes widened, she patted his forearm. "I know ... I was scared about STDs and getting pregnant when Bret forced himself on me. I got tested as soon as I could while Timmy and I were on the road, and I'm good. The week after we left, I got my period—I was never so happy to get it in my life."

He chuckled and pivoted her into his arms. "You're really something special, darlin'." He pressed his lips on hers. "I want to be inside you and fill you up," he said.

"I want to really feel you," she replied as she looped her arms around his neck and tugged him closer to her.

Ryder kissed her again—hard and hungry, then pulled her sweater above her head, and tossed it on the floor. He stepped back and his gaze lingered on her ivory sheer bra. "Fuck, you look beautiful. I'll never get enough of your tits, baby." He grabbed her hand and led her over to the table then reached behind her and undid the hooks. The straps slipped down and he pushed them off and flung the bra off then bent down and swiped his tongue over her nipples.

Arousal flashed hot through her system and she sank her fingers into his hair and pulled it hard. The way he played with her breasts drove her crazy with wanton desire, and she threw her head back, pushing her breasts into his face.

"Oh, darlin'," he rasped.

Then Ryder slowly turned her around so that she was facing the table, and his hands slid over her back, around her waist, to her belly, and into the waistband of her leggings. She held her breath, her body trembling, as he pushed aside the crotch of her panties and buried one finger between her folds.

"So damn wet," he murmured.

Savannah leaned across the table, her hands gripping the edges of it to steady herself. She heard the familiar sound of Ryder unbuckling his belt and unzipping his jeans and heat pulsed between her legs. She felt his weight as he bent over her then the warmth of his hand as he swept her hair to one side. His mouth was on her ear, her neck. "You drive me fucking crazy, woman," he rasped.

"Ryder," she moaned.

He pulled her leggings and panties down, spread her legs wide, and slid his finger between her folds. She knew she was sopping wet; she could feel it, hear it as his finger moved back and forth slowly. Then he pressed another finger into her, and his low, hungry grunt drove her arousal higher.

Ryder reached down between her open thighs and cupped his hand over her sex. "This is mine. Only mine," he said, as his other hand smoothed over her butt.

There was something incredibly sexy about the way that sounded. "Only yours," she breathed as she parted her legs wider and ground into his hand. "Please...Please take me," she said in a thick voice.

"Fuck, woman," he growled. His fingers dug into her fleshy behind as he thrust into her.

Savannah let out a long, breathy sigh, and then groaned, grasping at the table as he began to move in her, his dick pushing in and out, his finger stroking her clit.

It was rough, deep, and quick—Ryder was soon thrusting harder, smacking her ass, rubbing her sweet spot—and she bucked against him, urging him, barely able to contain herself.

"You feel amazing, woman," he grunted.

A tidal wave of pleasure overtook her as she spasmed her release. She felt him bucking into her and heard him grunt as he found his pleasure, the warm rush filling her.

They stayed bent over the kitchen table for a moment, spent and gasping. Savannah turned her head to smile at him. "What the hell did you just do to me?"

Ryder pressed his face in her hair then trailed his lips to her mouth and kissed her softly. "I could ask you the same thing." His hands were warm and tight around her until he patted her ass and moved away, letting her get up.

When she stood up, he handed her clothing to her and she gave him a quick kiss and dashed off to her room to wash up and get dressed before Rock brought Timmy back; she'd dropped him off earlier that morning at Rock and Clotille's house to play with James.

Savannah walked backed into the family room and sat down next to Ryder on the couch. "I hope you like lamb stew—that's what I'm making for dinner."

He kissed the side of her head. "I love it. You'll find I'm not a picky eater." He pulled away and took her hands in his. "I want to make sure you understand what you're getting into."

Savannah cocked her head to the side. "What do you mean?"

"My disability is an added responsibility I have to consider every day, and I'll never be as carefree as if I was able-bodied. Sometimes I'm gonna be pissed as hell and my patience is gonna be shit because my muscles burn or I got sores on my stump from wearing the prosthesis too damn long." He scrubbed his face. "All I'm saying is that it can be fucking challenging to live with an amputee. I just want to make sure you get that."

She tucked his hand in hers and rubbed it gently. "Thank you for sharing that with me. I'm sure there will be challenges for both of us. I'm not always on the upswing, and can be a downright crazy bitch sometimes during my period. If I don't understand for whatever reason, remind me what you're feeling, okay? The best thing is for us to be open and communicate so if you're in pain or feeling shitty because you hate not having your leg, tell me. I promise not to analyze you. I'll give you your space—I know you like alone time. We're both starting on level ground and there will be some adjustment period, but we have to be open about what we're feeling and what we want and need."

"I agree." He leaned over and kissed her.

A car door slammed and Savannah ran her hand down his rugged face and smiled. "I think Timmy's home." She stood up and ambled to the window and saw Timmy running up the porch steps and swung open the door.

"Mommy!" Timmy hugged her legs then rushed into the house, the sound of his laughter wrapping around her heart.

Rock lifted his chin at her as he walked inside, the chains hanging down from his pockets jingling. He bumped fists with Ryder then sat on the chair across from him. Savannah scampered into the kitchen and took out two tumblers and the bottle of Jack and brought them into the room, setting them on the table. Ryder tilted his head at her as he brushed his fingers across hers, and then he reached over and picked up the bottle.

"Timmy, come into the kitchen and tell me all about your day while I make dinner," she said.

And as her son knelt next to Brutus, excitedly telling her all the things he did, she heard Ryder's deep, steady voice as he visited with Rock and she knew that she'd finally found the man she was supposed to be with and the home in which she was supposed to be.

CHAPTER TWENTY-ONE

Christmas Day

R YDER WATCHED TIMMY'S face scrunched in concentration as his nimble fingers ripped off the red shiny wrapping paper. The boy stared at the big box, his eyes wide then he turned to Savannah.

"Go ahead and take the lid off," she urged.

Timmy giggled and placed his small hand over his mouth for a second then gripped the sides of the top and lifted it up. For a few seconds he just stared without moving then he took out the painted train cars. "It's a train set!" He turned his head to Ryder. "You made it for me. You really fooled me!"

Ryder smiled and leaned back in the chair and enjoyed watching Timmy take out the forty pieces he'd crafted. Savannah gazed at him, her blue eyes brimming with love and tears as she knelt by her son and helped him put the tracks together.

"Ryder told me it was for the other kids, but it was for me." He kept turning the locomotive's lights on and off then he pushed the button and it whistled. "It really works, Mommy."

"It's a beautiful train set. Did you thank Ryder?"

The boy put the wooden piece down and leaped up and dashed over to him. He climbed up on Ryder's lap and flung his arms around his neck. "Thank you. It's what I really, really wanted," Timmy said hugging him tightly.

He paused for a moment, a flood of emotion whirling though him then he wrapped his arms around Timmy and held him tight. "I knew that, little buddy." He darted his eyes to Savannah and she leaned back on her haunches a big-ass smile plastered over her face.

Timmy squirmed and Ryder let go and plopped him on the floor, and the boy crawled back over to the gift.

"Are you finished with it yet, Mommy?"

"Almost," she said, ruffling her hand through his hair.

Ryder watched the two of them as they set up the track and village, and he let the good feelings of the moment wash over him. *How in the fuck did I make it without them in my life?* He'd lived in darkness for so long, that he'd forgotten what brightness felt like; life's deceit had broken him, and from the pain that bore it, came an honest, bright love which consumed him. And that was the way he'd fallen in love with Savannah—all at once, as if struck by a gun shot.

Savannah stood up and walked over to him and he tugged her down on his lap then nuzzled her neck. "You're my passion, my love, and my life," he whispered.

"I didn't know it was possible to love someone as much as I do you," she whispered back.

"The lights go on in the houses ... and the church ... and the buildings!" Timmy clapped his hands and laughed, and Ryder and Savannah joined in the laughter with him.

Ryder held her tight as they watched Timmy and listened to the crackling fire and Brutus gnawing on the bone he'd received for Christmas.

The minutes turned into hours, and soon they were seated around the table at Ryder's parents' house—Savannah in the middle between him and Timmy. Ryder inched his fingers up her leg, underneath her skirt, and let them rest on her thigh—he loved the softness of her skin.

Ryder's mother patted his other hand and then leaned over and kissed him on the cheek. "You gave me the best Christmas present—the light back in your eyes," she said softly.

"Savannah and Timmy are the ones who gave you that gift, Ma," he replied.

"She's a beautiful woman and the little boy is adorable. I'm happy for you, *tesoro*."

All through dinner, Savannah kept pressing her leg into his, brushing his arm with her fingers, squeezing his biceps, and a whole bunch of other things that made him feel like he was the most important man in her life, and he loved her for it.

Ryder glanced down at the skull bracelet she'd given him, and tenderness wove through him again just like it had when he'd first opened the gift. What had surprised him was how well she knew him, and even though she'd downplayed it, he knew that she took a lot of time in finding such a unique gift, especially in Pinewood Springs.

During dessert, Savannah kept fingering the necklace hanging about her neck, the diamond pendant shimmering in the chandelier's light. It was his gift to her, and for the past several Christmases, he'd never contemplated buying anyone a gift, or putting up a tree, or drinking hot chocolate, but here he was, embracing the whole damn thing like a reformed man. *Life can be too fucking strange sometimes, but also wonderful.*

After several hours of eating and talking, Ryder noticed the glazed look in Timmy's eyes and the yawns Savannah tried to stifle. He rose to his feet, taking her with him, and walked over to his mom and kissed her on the cheek.

"We gotta go, Ma. It's been a long day and Timmy's tired as hell."

"Thank you for having us," Savannah said as she hugged his mom briefly.

"I'm very happy to meet you and your little one. You've made me so happy, and I can see how happy you make my son."

Savannah blushed, and Ryder thought he was going to lose it. There was something about the way her cheeks flushed pinkish red that turned him the hell on. It was probably some kinky thing with him, but he loved the flush of color on her cheeks, neck, tits, and ass. Those streak marks did it for him every time. He chuckled and Savannah looked up at him, her forehead creased in puzzlement.

"What's so funny?" she asked.

"You ... but not funny—just fucking adorable," he whispered in her ear. "I gotta get you home now, woman."

Timmy fell asleep on the drive back and Savannah rested her head on his shoulder while they listened to Twisted Sister's rendition of Christmas carols on the radio. Ryder craned his neck and brushed his lips across her forehead.

"Did you have a good time?" he asked.

"Yes, it was wonderful. I'm glad I came from a big family, otherwise I never would've been able to keep up with all of you." She laughed.

"Yeah, we're a pretty rowdy bunch. It probably also helped that you worked in an Italian restaurant."

"It definitely did with the food. I'd forgotten about how much of it there is at Italian get-togethers."

"My mom loves it. My sisters come over along with my aunts and cousins and they bring out the Chianti, gossip, and bake or peel peppers or do whatever they do. By the end of the afternoon, they're drunker than fuck." Ryder laughed as an endearing memory from his childhood played through his mind: his grandma, mother, and aunts elbow high in flour, kneading pasta dough and filling the pizzelle iron.

"My mom's the same. My aunts come over and we all spend all afternoon baking, although our drink of choice is Bailey's." She chortled.

"You must miss your family like hell, especially today." He pressed his lips on her forehead again.

"I do. It was good that Timmy got to talk to them this morning. I have to admit that it feels a little weird not being with my family on Christmas. Do you know this is the first one I haven't been with them?"

"We'll go to Boston next year for the holiday," he said.

Savannah tilted her head up and tugged his face toward her. With his eyes fixed on the road, he met her lips. "Thank you," she said after breaking away.

The garage door opened, and Brutus's steady barking welcomed them home. Savannah slipped out of the car, and Ryder unbuckled Timmy and scooped him up in his arms and took the tired boy straight to his bedroom.

A half hour later, Savannah came into the room wearing that clingy, fuzzy robe that drove him fucking crazy with lust the second day she and Timmy were with him—it now seemed like that was a lifetime ago.

"Come to me, darlin'," he said, and she pressed next to him, her legs tucked under her ass.

He'd changed into a pair of flannel pajama bottoms—a gift from Timmy—and a long-sleeved T-shirt. He'd taken off his prosthesis and Savannah's hand rested on his limb. *I never thought I'd allow a woman to touch me the way Savannah does, or to see me with all my faults and fucking demons.* But he had, and she'd let him in too. They both had suffered in their lives before becoming each other's comfort from the storm of life. Ryder loved Savannah with all his heart and he knew she loved him. They came together on a dark, snowy night: a meeting of two souls who fully accepted the dark and the light within each other. They were bound by the commitment and courage to grow and support one another through struggle into bliss.

Ryder squeezed her hard and she yelped. "Sorry, baby, I just can't help myself." He chuckled.

Savannah lightly swatted his hand. "I'm breakable you know."

"I'm here to pick up the pieces."

She sighed. "It's going to be quite the fight."

"It'll be worth it, and you won't be fighting the battle alone—I've got your back … always."

"There's no way Bret's giving up this easily, and his mother will pull out all the stops to make sure he gets sole custody of Timmy. I'm pretty sure Bret's headed back to Boston because he knows he can't fight on your turf, but there's no doubt in my mind that he's already called his parents and they've retained a top-notch divorce attorney." She sighed. "I just want Timmy to be happy, but they're going to make sure to drag him in the middle of all this shit. I have to be strong for him. What a fucking mess."

"He's got both of us fighting for him. And you've got me to lean on," Ryder said.

"I know." She brought his hand to her mouth and kissed it. "Timmy had a great day."

"Yeah, and he's happy he's staying here."

"He loves it here. He has a group of friends, and after the first of the year, he'll be starting at the same school Braxton is in, and he adores you and, of course, Brutus. My first trip back to Boston to meet up with the attorney, I plan to take Timmy so he can see my parents and Bret's parents. I don't want to shut Corinne and Wayne out of his life, I hope they understand that. I'd like it if you could come with us to Boston."

"I'll be with you every step of the way, darlin'." He played with her hair, letting the silky strands fall through his fingers like golden sand. "Have you ever wanted any more kids?"

Savannah looked up at him. "Yeah. What about you?"

"Definitely."

She rubbed her hand up and down his arm. "Let's see how things work for us, but if they go the way I think they will, we can start thinking about having a child together. I'm not getting any younger, you know."

"That's right, you're older than me," he joked.

She punched him lightly. "Only by one year. Anyway, I'd love to have your child."

"If that happens, we're gonna have to get hitched, but we can deal with all that when we get to it."

"Any news about Colt?"

"No, but I'll never stop trying."

"It's all going to be okay," Savannah said.

Ryder nuzzled the top of her head. "I know." *She's going to help me heal and find a way to cope with the demons from my past that still lurk deep inside me.* "I'm looking forward to our life together."

"Me too. I love you," she said drowsily.

"Love you too, darlin'." He nestled her head against his shoulder and smiled when her breathing deepened.

He watched the flames curl and sway as the dry wood crackled in the fireplace.

She was his everything, and they were both in it for the long haul.

And he wouldn't have it any other way.

Make sure you sign up for my newsletter so you can keep up with my new releases, special sales, free short stories, and other treats only available to newsletter readers. When you sign up, you will receive a FREE hot and steamy novella. Sign up at: http://eepurl.com/bACCL1.

Notes from Chiah

As always, I have a team behind me making sure I shine and continue on my writing journey. It is their support, encouragement, and dedication that pushes me further in my writing journey. And then, it is my wonderful readers who have supported me, laughed, cried, and understood how these outlaw men live and love in their dark and gritty world. Without you—the readers—an author's words are just letters on a page. The emotions you take away from the words breathe life into the story.

Thank you to my amazing Personal Assistant Natalie Weston. I don't know what I'd do without you. Your patience, calmness, and insights are always appreciated. Thank you for stepping in when I'm holed up tapping away on the computer, oblivious to the world. You make my writing journey that much smoother. Thank you for ALWAYS being there for me! I'm so lucky on my team!

Thank you to my editor Lisa Cullian, for all your insightful edits and making my story a better one. You definitely made this book shine. As always, a HUGE thank you for your patience and flexibility with accepting my book in pieces. I never could have hit the Publish button without you. You're the best!

Thank you to my wonderful beta readers Natalie Weston and Jeni Clancy. You rock! Your enthusiasm and suggestions for Christmas Wish: Insurgents MC were spot on and helped me to put out a stronger, cleaner novel.

Thank you to the bloggers for your support in reading my book, sharing it, reviewing it, and getting my name out there. I so appreciate all your efforts. You all are so invaluable. I hope you know that. Without you, the indie author would be lost.

Thank you ARC readers you have helped make all my books so much stronger. I appreciate the effort and time you put in to reading, reviewing, and getting the word out about the books. I don't know what I'd do without you. I feel so lucky to have you behind me.

Thank you to my Street Team. Thanks for your input, your support, and your hard work. I appreciate you more than you know. A HUGE hug to all of you!

Thank you to Carrie from Cheeky Covers. You are amazing! I can always count on you. You are the calm to my storm. You totally rock, and I love your artistic vision.

Thank you to my proofers who worked hard to get my novel back to me so I could hit the publish button on time. There are no words to describe how touched and grateful I am for your dedication and support. Also much thanks for your insight re: plot and characterization. I definitely took heed, and it made my story flow that much better.

Thank you to Ena and Amanda with Enticing Journeys Promotions who have helped garner attention for and visibility to the Insurgents MC series. Couldn't do it without you!

Thank you to my awesome formatter, Paul Salvette at Beebee Books. You make my books look stellar. I appreciate how professional you are and how quickly you return my books to me. A huge thank you for doing rush orders and always returning a formatted book of which I am proud. Kudos!

Thank you to the readers who continue to support me and read my books. Without you, none of this would be possible. I appreciate your comments and reviews on my books, and I'm dedicated to giving you the best story that I can. I'm always thrilled when you enjoy a book as much as I have in writing it. You definitely make the hours of typing on the computer and the frustrations that come with the territory of writing books so worth it.

And a special thanks to every reader who has been with me since "Hawk's Property." Your support, loyalty, and dedication to my stories touch me in so many ways. You enable me to tell my stories, and I am forever grateful to you.

You all make it possible for writers to write because without you reading the books, we wouldn't exist. Thank you, thank you! ♥

Christmas Wish: Insurgents Motorcycle Club (Book 12)

Dear Readers,

Thank you for reading my book. This book started out as a standalone without being attached to any series, but the Insurgent MC men wouldn't hear of it—they wanted a bigger part, so it's turned out to be the twelfth book in the Insurgents MC series. I hope you enjoyed it as much as I enjoyed writing Ryder and Savannah's story. This gritty and rough motorcycle club has a lot more to say, so I hope you will look for the upcoming books in the series. Romance makes life so much more colorful, and a rough, sexy bad boy makes life a whole lot more interesting.

If you enjoyed the book, please consider leaving a review on Amazon. I read all of them and appreciate the time taken out of busy schedules to do that.

I love hearing from my fans, so if you have any comments or questions, please email me at chiahwilder@gmail.com or visit my facebook page.

To receive a **free copy of my novella**, *Summer Heat*, and to hear of **new releases**, **special sales**, **free short stories**, and **ARC opportunities**, please sign up for my **Newsletter** at http://eepurl.com/bACCL1.

Happy Reading,

Chiah

Animal's Reformation: Insurgents MC
Coming January 2019

A member of the Insurgents MC, Animal is a rough, free-loving biker. Hanging with his brothers, riding his customized Harley, and partying with the ladies are his idea of the ideal life.

Years ago, he made a stupid mistake with a woman he barely knew, but he pays the child support every month and sends cards and presents to his out-of-state daughter on her birthday and on holidays.

He doesn't want a steady woman, and he certainly isn't ready to settle down and have a family. Life is just too good now, and there are always so many women who want to come and play with this rugged biker.

Then one afternoon, the mother of his child struts into the clubhouse with his daughter in tow and tells him she's done. She walks away, leaving Animal and Lucy staring at each other.

What's he supposed to do? He knows about bikes and hard partying, not seven-year-old girls.

He has to change his ways, and his new hot next-door neighbor isn't helping to keep his libido in check. The way her long dark hair swings just above her sweet behind has him thinking all kinds of nasty thoughts, but she doesn't give him the time of day.

What's up with that?

Olivia Mooney is very aware of her neighbor's good looks and his finely chiseled body, but she doesn't want to get involved. He doesn't realize it, but she's his daughter's tutor at school, and she can't get involved. She spends her nights thinking about him and chatting with an intriguing man on an after dark dating site.

Then a series of murders occur in the surrounding counties, and it looks like they are creeping closer to Pinewood Springs. At first the cops are stumped, but over time a pattern begins to emerge: the women all used an after dark dating site.

As fear and danger slink closer, Olivia is thrown into the arms of the sexy biker, forever changing their lives.

The Night Rebels MC series are standalone romance novels. This is Army's. This book contains violence, abuse, strong language, and steamy/graphic sexual scenes. It describes the life and actions of an outlaw motorcycle club. HEA. No cliffhangers. The book is intended for readers over the age of 18.

Other Books by Chiah Wilder

Insurgent MC Series:

Hawk's Property
Jax's Dilemma
Chas's Fervor
Axe's Fall
Banger's Ride
Jerry's Passion
Throttle's Seduction
Rock's Redemption
An Insurgent's Wedding
Outlaw Xmas
Wheelie's Challenge
Insurgents MC Romance Series: Insurgents Motorcycle Club Box Set
(Books 1 – 4)
Insurgents MC Romance Series: Insurgents Motorcycle Club Box Set
(Books 5 – 8)

Night Rebels MC Series:

STEEL
MUERTO
DIABLO
GOLDIE
PACO
SANGRE
ARMY

Steamy Contemporary Romance:

My Sexy Boss

Find all my books at: amazon.com/author/chiahwilder

I love hearing from my readers. You can email me at chiahwilder@gmail.com.

Sign up for my newsletter to receive a FREE Novella, updates on new books, special sales, free short stories, and ARC opportunities at http://eepurl.com/bACCL1.

Visit me on facebook at facebook.com/AuthorChiahWilder